LAND OF SWEETHEART DEALS

Wajdi Al-Ahdal

Land of Sweetheart Deals (Novel)

Originally published as *'Ard al-Mu'amarat al-Sa'ida'*

Translated by: William M. Hutchins
© 2024 Dar Arab For Publishing and Translation LTD.

United Kingdom
60 Blakes Quay
Gas Works Road
RG1 3EN
Reading
United Kingdom
info@dararab.co.uk
www.dararab.co.uk

First Edition 2024
ISBN 978-1-78871-101-2

Copyrights © dararab 2024

dararab
دار عرب للنشر والترجمة
DAR ARAB FOR PUBLISHING & TRANSLATION

All rights reserved. No part of this publication may be reproduced, stored in a retrieval system or transmitted in any form or by any means, electronic, mechanical, photocopying, recording or otherwise without the prior permission of the publisher, except in the case of brief quotations embodied in reviews and other non-commercial uses permitted by copyright law.

This is a work of fiction. Unless otherwise indicated, all the names, characters, businesses, places, events and incidents in this book are either the product of the author's imagination or used in a fictitious manner. Any resemblance to actual persons, living or dead, or actual events is purely coincidental.

The views and opinions expressed in this book are those of the author(s) and do not reflect or represent the opinions of the publisher.

Text Design: Nasser Al Badri
Cover Design: Hassan Almohtasib (Cover art: Helmi Fahmi)

WAJDI AL-AHDAL

Land *of* sweet heart Deals

A NOVEL

TRANSLATED BY BY WILLIAM M. HUTCHINS

daab

Dedication

To a man of a type rare in our times:
Ahmad Naji Ahmad al-Nabahani

Yemen tempers

Those not tempered by time.

Hammoud Shanta

Tuesday

Chapter 64

I clearly remember those crazy moments that bisected my life when I wasn't paying attention; they altered my familiar, settled world in sweeping ways that proved more than a person could bear.

At noon one hot summer Tuesday, when people had their heads lowered to avoid the dust, executive editor Riyad al-Kayyad summoned me to his office and asked me to cover a story in the coastal governorate of Hodeida. My mission was to investigate an incident that had allegedly occurred the previous day in the remote valleys of the Tihama. The executive editor, whose eyes were obscured by the thick prescription lenses of his glasses, spoke briefly about my assignment. Then he handed me five wads of money, each worth five hundred rials, and asked me to prepare to leave at dawn the next day.

What concerned me at that unforgettable moment wasn't the assignment but my fear of being able to withstand the infernal heat of those coastal valleys and the chance that I might contract malaria if I had to stay there long. I went home feeling assured and confident, though, that nothing—no matter how powerful—could disrupt the course of my life or destabilize it.

When I opened the door, my three children ran to meet me. I embraced them, one by one, and headed to the kitchen, drawn by a delicious aroma and the sound of oil sizzling in a pan—a sound lovelier than the warbling of any nightingales. I found that my wife was busy fixing lunch, and our eyes met amorously. In a moment, we were clasping and kissing.

I changed clothes in the bedroom and dropped the wads of cash at the foot of the wardrobe near my dirty socks. I mocked myself for never having learned to love banknotes or to treat them with respect.

While washing up in the bathroom, I noticed a little pimple on the bridge of my nose. Small and red, it seemed to stare idiotically at my naked body's topography. I tested it with my middle finger and guessed what it had in store for me. Once I descended the mountains to the coast, it would swell and fill with pus and putrefaction, exploiting the insalubrious climate. The temperature there soars above forty degrees centigrade, and the region's extremely high humidity opens the skin's pores. Examining the pimple in the bathroom mirror, I warned it that, should it expand, I would prick it with a needle and disinfect it with antiseptic. Suddenly realizing the paradox, I mocked myself. Since my name is Mutahhar, which means "Purified" or "Disinfected," once this lady pimple is pierced and disinfected, she will become Mutahhara. What a brilliant couple we will make: Mutahhar and Mutahhara! While combing my hair, I wondered why my family had chosen this puzzling name: Mutahhar—who had purified me? When? Or, would this only occur later? No way—I didn't want to be treated like a pimple and have someone prick me with a needle! I left the bathroom feeling jittery about the possibilities my name raised.

For lunch, my wife set out ten different dishes; a large fish, a *derak*[1], was the main course. I immediately realized that my wife had been to the market that morning and as usual spent vast sums on meat, fish, vegetables, and fruit—far more than we needed—and that most of this would end up in the garbage. I'm not stingy, but extravagant

---

1. *Derak* is narrow-barred Spanish mackerel.

expenditures just to pile food on our table make me uncomfortable and give me a guilty conscience.

I married Houriya five years ago after a love story that echoed throughout our faculty at the University. During the first year of our marriage, she ran up a lot of debt, because of a penchant to spend lavishly on dresses, outings, and meals in fancy restaurants. I tried hard to reform her, but she changed me instead.

While we ate, I noticed that my first-born child, Habel, who is four, was whispering to his sister Najat and laughing. Annoyed, I frowned and asked, "What's the matter?" He pointed at my nose and said, "You've got a boo-boo. An ant bit your nose." Then he shook with gales of laughter. I was perturbed and wondered how I would fare with other people, since this child, who is a bit of an ass, had noticed my pimple so quickly. Would they notice it too? If they did, would it make them laugh? *Damn! All I need to increase my suffering is a ludicrous boil disfiguring my face.*

After lunch I selected a German novel—*Buddenbrooks* by Thomas Mann—and stretched out on the bed, feeling that nothing would ensure a sound nap so definitively as a genuine German author.

While hovering between sleep and wakefulness, I felt someone press my groin. At first, I suspected the German writer's hand; perhaps he wished to encourage me to continue reading his novel. When I felt this hand move to an adjoining region, I told myself I had better rise and open my eyes before the impudent German novelist grabbed my balls.

Sloughing off a light slumber, I found that my wife, who was sharing my bed just as God intended, was to blame. *Oh—that fish wasn't merely an idle gesture!* Like any other stud descended by a direct lineage from an authentic Arab tribe, I did everything expected of me and more.

I stayed up late that night to watch Germany play in the World Cup. Houriya, who, at least in my presence, pretended to root for the German team—for fear I would divorce her—dared to ask me why I supported the Germans as devotedly as if my aunt had married their Chancellor? So, I told her, during halftime, that the Germans are Europe's masters and that we descendants of the Arab tribal chiefs also consider ourselves the masters of our land; therefore, our superior status links us. Her cheeks flushing red, she asked me about the Brazilians, for whom she seemed to be rooting privately. I replied haughtily that the Brazilians are uncivilized street urchins and that I would not root for rabble.

When Germany was defeated and exited from the World Cup, I went to bed, pretending not to be troubled by the defeat of the masters of the universe. Collapsing on the bed, I pulled the blanket over my head. Sleep eluded me for an hour or two as I wept brokenheartedly, my tears flowing nonstop.

Wednesday

Chapter 63

After a troubled sleep swarming with nightmares, I awoke at dawn and hastily packed my bag. I turned on my laptop and checked my email, although I did not open any messages. I spent some time in the mental hospital called Facebook and registered likes as if raising a hand in greeting while charging past. I looked at the clock on the bedside table and cursed the minute hand, which was racing around the dial as if someone were chasing it with a knife. I closed my laptop, put it inside its black case, and then thrust that into the suitcase with my clothes.

My wife had fixed a hot breakfast, but I told her I would not eat breakfast at home. Habel and Najat were sleeping. Only our youngest child, beautiful Karama, who was two, had opened her eyes to come looking for me.

I've never traveled before on a Wednesday, because it's an unlucky day. Tribes avoid fighting on hump day, for fear of defeat. After embracing my wife and little Karama, I said goodbye and set off. Sorrow's sword slashed my heart, but I convinced myself that I was feeling forlorn because Germany had been eliminated from the World Cup, not on account of my trip.

With each step I took down the stairway, a weird feeling became more entrenched in me; I felt I had lived this moment at some point in the past. *Where and when?* I didn't know. Frightened and depressed, I shivered, felt weak, and released a long gasp.

Once out on the street, I hailed a taxi. As we drove off, a mysterious, heavy, alarming, grim, subterranean pain overwhelmed me. This angst reminded me of nothing so much as the pain our forefather Adam felt when he left his home in paradise.

We paused at a kiosk so I could buy the day's newspapers. I felt too anxious, though, to flip through them. Even so, the driver, whose eyes shone with curiosity, asked, "What do they say in the papers?" I felt like tossing them out the window but calmed my nerves and replied loftily, "They say that Adam should return the apple he stole." I could tell from the gleam in his eyes and the way he pursed his lips that the driver was fascinated by my response.

He retorted, in a way I hadn't anticipated: "I get it! You mean that if he had, the Yemeni people would be more conciliatory and forbearing." I paid him, praising God that the driver wasn't educated. Otherwise, he would have patronized opposition casinos.

I hate buses, because they reek of vomit, even from a distance. Anyone who considers traveling by bus will be obliged—as part of the journey's schedule—to throw up. Since I hadn't eaten breakfast, my stomach was empty and had nothing to contribute, they wouldn't let me ride their anti-digestive buses, which were especially outfitted for communal vomiting.

Instead, I booked a place in a small Peugeot van and paid extra to have the entire two-person front seat to myself. That would allow me to relax and stretch my limbs as much as I wanted, because I can't bear crowding or being pressed against other people's bodies. Once the Peugeot filled with passengers, it began to creep slowly toward the pavement. Compared to my traveling companions, who were packed into the rear seat like a drove of livestock, I seemed an elite passenger. Yes, wealth is the guarantor of a man's humanity. Despite my heroic attempts to overcome my formative years and upbringing, though, I still felt embarrassed if one of my father's leftist comrades saw me enjoying a royalist seat and comporting myself like a lifelong member of the bourgeoisie.

I sighed deeply when the bald driver pressed on the gas and flew out of the station. We stopped halfway down the mountains in Manakhah, where passengers scattered in every direction. Some went to answer the call of nature, and others left to purchase items from the small shops.

I headed to a restaurant known for serving fresh liver carved directly from animals slaughtered that morning. When the steaming hot dish was served, I was surprised to find I had lost my sense of smell. I gained control of myself and didn't let my agitation show. I polished off the liver the way any hungry person would, and why not, since the taste in my mouth was extremely delicious. Apparently losing my sense of smell would not deny me gastronomic pleasures. The same thing had happened when I was young. Back then I frequented the neighborhood's trash site and rummaged through rubbish drums for edible food. My nose colluded with me then and kept me from smelling the nasty stench of the garbage and losing my appetite. I paid no attention to whether the food I consumed was fit to eat or spoiled. My father was frequently imprisoned and, if released, would soon be returned to prison, because he refused to work clandestinely. He also ignored any path that we, his family, found to feed ourselves while he was incarcerated. What mattered to him was making a name for himself in history writ large and playing the hero for his party comrades. My self-centered father achieved his goal, but at my expense and that of my six brothers. He achieved a glory that cost us dearly and left us impoverished, ill-clothed, and subjected to the vagaries of life. I swear he caused my mother's death; she died of unspoken sorrow.

I rose, paid the tab, and looked for the low-roofed qat shops, which are as cramped as coffins. I purchased a cluster of qat branches with fiery red leaves and raised them to my nostrils to inhale their fragrance, but my nose failed me. I told myself sarcastically that my nose, which dated back to the Soviet era, was now critically expressing its frank opposition to my lifestyle.

I stood looking down the western slopes we would soon descend. The gray clouds were nourished by the water vapor that rose from below scaling the heights. Clouds raced up past me, competing to reach the sky. I felt so light and joyful I could have floated away with them. The passengers assembled once more, and we left Manakhah, which resembled an eagle's egg in the bosom of lofty, trackless mountains.

As we descended to narrow, winding valleys where the ribbon of asphalt appeared to follow a spiral course, an elderly woman vomited. I was astonished to find that my nose—may God not bless it—had started functioning again and conveyed this revolting odor to me. I was reminded of the pimple, which had appeared on my nose the previous day, and wondered whether there was any relationship between it and my troubled sense of smell. I looked in the side mirror and peered intently, only to find that the pimple had vanished without a trace.

I continued to survey my features. From my mother, who grew up on a farm, I had inherited a complexion the color of field dirt and a luminous glow suggestive of tranquility and spirituality. From my father I inherited the lineaments of a noble face: a wide, smooth forehead, a protruding chin, a broad lower jaw, delicate, coal-black eyebrows and mustache, and the ebony eyes that women find fascinating and that mark men as courageous.

We crashed on a curve where the road was blocked by two buses that had been racing each other. To avoid hitting them, our driver had to graze the metal railing, and we barely escaped tumbling off the cliff, down into the ravine's abyss, where we would have met certain death. Some of us were slightly bruised, and blood trickled from the driver's head. My right index finger was twisted and began to send pain signals—as if it had just been amputated—to the rest of my body.

Since I had no time to lose, I pulled my bag from the vehicle and moved somewhere the driver and the other passengers could not see me hail a different vehicle. I regretted never purchasing a car of my own. It certainly would have helped me perform assignments in less time. Foolish and fantastical considerations had prevented me from buying an elegant automobile, one of the latest models. I feared people would say—censoriously—that I was changing my spots. My excessive sensitivity about conspicuous consumption was pointless, because my stern, Communist father had died, and opinions in our society had changed a lot. No one cared now whether I sided with the opposition or the government. In the past, anyone who wanted to play the hero joined the opposition. Then society would wink at him and treat him like a rock star. Today, people have tired of this nasty game. There is a consensus everyone summarizes this way: "Sign up and find a foothold for yourself in the regime." Society has matured, and notions of heroism evolve from one age to the next. That's why I count as a hero in this age.

A small mosque down the hillside caught my eye. It was the smallest mosque I had ever seen and looked scarcely big enough to hold the imam and a single row of worshipers behind him. I admired its unpretentious dome and minaret, its walls washed by the white light, the green banana plants surrounding it, and the stream that glittered like diamonds in the valley below. I don't know why, but I felt a sudden urge to scramble down there, even though I'm secular and never pray. I mocked myself for feeling such a desire and mused that I had been charmed by the mosque's vintage appearance.

I signaled to a four-door, Toyota Hilux pickup truck, which stopped. All the seats were occupied, and I was forced to sit in the cargo bed, surrounded by crates of chickens and gunny sacks of qat, with seven individuals of varying ages, all of whom were feeling nauseous. They had been silenced by the stifling heat and the blazing sun's dominion over their brains. We watched our descent with stony glares as each person sank into a reverie of self-examination. We could easily have been a band of sinners bound for hell.

When we passed through Bab al-Naqa—Camel Pass—we finally caught sight of the Tihama coastal plain, which spread as far as the eye could see—all the way to the horizon. We were also greeted by the distinctive fragrance of the sesbania shrubs that carpet wide swathes of the area. The air was hazy with dust and so hot it felt fiery and viscous. Everything seemed ready to melt.

We stopped in the city of Bajil, where I bought an antimalarial drug and a splint for my finger at a pharmacy. Nearby I spotted a restaurant packed with patrons. Therefore I conjectured that it served good food. I entered and ordered fried chicken, which I consumed quickly, while nearly drowning in a sea of sweat as my eyes smarted from the salty perspiration dripping into them from my forehead. Then I realized why God grants some people bushy eyebrows! I used my left hand to eat, because the index finger of my right hand had swollen, and the lightest movement hurt. I wondered how I was going to write my article with a crippled hand. A prolonged "Uffff!" escaped from my lips, and I felt downhearted about this whole assignment.

With help from the restaurant's manager, I located an air-conditioned taxi. As I set off, I began chewing qat. We arrived in Hodeida at 1:30, and I telephoned my wife to reassure her. I transferred then to a different vehicle and started off to the village of Bab al-Minjal—Scythe (or Ibis) Gate. The driver claimed he could get me there in four hours, and I was keen to reach my destination before sunset to learn the lay of the land and discover the village's landmarks. Perhaps, if I had time, I could snap some pictures. But the trip did not proceed according to plan.

Once the asphalt ended, we were on a dirt road, and, eventually, the car's wheels sank into muddy sand. We tried to push it out but failed. The plump, brown driver apologized for this mishap. Unfortunately, I had paid him in advance, but he promised that he would deal with the matter. I sat on my suitcase, brooding about this setback. The driver changed the tape for yet another one by the same singer, Faisal Alawi, and started dancing to while away the time.

To my chagrin, two hours elapsed without a single vehicle appearing. Many motorbikes passed, but I refused to ride on them; I wasn't foolhardy enough to risk another accident. By sunset, I was so desperate that I accepted the last form of transport available when the pot-bellied driver paid a boy with a donkey a sum of money—I wasn't able to see how much. I mounted the ass, and the boy carried my suitcase on his head. So, we set off, after I bade adieu to the driver, who said he would sleep in his car. We left him there, still listening rapturously to the songs of Faisal Alawi, so intoxicated by the music that he seemed separated from the physical world.

After an hour or more, yellow and white lights appeared in the distance, and the donkey quickened his pace, recognizing the way home and no longer needing any guidance. Behind us, the fourteen-year-old boy did his best to keep up. When I gazed at the sky, I was astonished: millions of stars ravished my eyes and elicited from me a gasp of surprise. This was the first time in my life that I had witnessed this awe-inspiring, celestial spectacle. I felt overwhelmed and regretted that we city-dwellers are destined to live beneath skies with a severely limited number of visible stars. Meanwhile, like an inspired musical ensemble, the night's crickets released a firm, robust chirping, repeating a single sound endlessly: Susususususususu.

When we finally reached the village of Bab al-Minjal, aggressive dogs rushed to greet us with deafening barks, but my intrepid donkey, which I reckoned had earned the rank of colonel by this time, continued on his way steadfastly, ignoring them. I asked the boy to take me to the home of the president of the local council, and he asked, "Jabir Shanini?"

"He's the one," I replied.

When we knocked on the door, a short, jovial, middle-aged man appeared. He was solidly built, his complexion was dark, and his white hair resembled carded cotton. He welcomed me and invited me to step inside. When I dismounted, I felt atrocious pains in my posterior. I tipped the boy and sent him on his way.

My host's seven or eight kids wrestled for my suitcase, each wanting the privilege of carrying it. While all of them were pushing and pulling, it fell open and its contents spilled onto the ground. They immediately stopped their tumult, fell silent, and stood frozen in place for a moment. Then they fled, butting each other, as they dashed into the house like so many young goats, chortling with enviable delight. Jabir Shanini collected my effects, after liberally cursing his children, and handed the bag to his pregnant wife, who had been peeking at us cautiously from behind the door.

I made a point of taking charge of the camera, my recorder, and the chocolate bar, which I quickly thrust into my pocket. I asked Jabir Shanini if we could go at once to the home of Jalila, the girl whose grandfather claimed she had been sexually assaulted. He excused himself briefly and returned wearing a bamboo *kofia*.[2] In one hand he grasped a thick walking stick and in the other a flashlight.

On our way, I asked, "What's the latest on this affair?"

Gasping, he replied, "It's an affair . . . ah . . . the girl Jalila was examined by a Rushan woman doctor the shame day ash the incident. Yeshterday, the Rushan woman shubmitted her report to the police."

I asked, "What did it conclude?"

He said, "We don't know, because Dr. Tatiana wrote her report in Rushan, and the polishe shent it to a reliable transhlation bureau in Hodeida."

I noticed he had difficulty pronouncing the "s" sound and consistently substituted "sh" for it. I feared his embarrassing slur might prove contagious. Trying to keep my tongue from slipping, I asked, "When will the Arabic translation of this report arrive?"

He replied, "Tomorrow—Thurshday. Then it will be read aloud in the preshensh of all partiesh." We fell silent, and I congratulated myself on my timing.

Jabir Shanini started laughing, and I asked him why. He replied, "The problem ish that our Shaykh, Bakri Hashan, hash been afflicted by God . . . with a loooong one!" To demonstrate the length of that

---

2. Kofia: "a short, circular hat woven from bamboo," cf. "Dholas and other Straw Hats come into Season," Kawkab al-Thaibani, April 10, 2007, *Yemen Observer*

penis, he stretched out an arm and grasped its elbow. Then he began laughing and coughing. His laughs and coughs mixed together till I no longer knew which would prevail. Then he stuck a finger in his mouth, extracted a wad of something, and tossed it far away. I realized then that his slur had been caused by chewing tobacco stuffed inside his lower lip.

Furrowing my brow, I cautioned him: "Watch what you say, Jabir. Shaykh Bakri has denied the accusation. He claims someone else assaulted the girl and that his enemies are exploiting the incident to blackmail him."

He replied, "I say this only to you, because you're a journalist who is trusted by the state." I blushed and felt that this villager had already sized me up and stripped me naked. We made our way in a tense silence down narrow, twisting alleys.

We reached a modest house that reeked of antiquity. The door to the courtyard was ajar, and a pale, yellow light and the racket of children playing ball flowed from it. With his stick, Jabir Shanini shoved open the wooden door's shaky panels and shouted, "Hajj Hadi!" We stopped in the courtyard, and the children abandoned their game to train their eyes on me—perhaps because in this village, people rarely saw a visitor clad in a shirt and trousers.

A gray-haired man of sixty-five appeared at the door of the parlor. He wore a white sarong that reached halfway down his legs, a white T-shirt, and a bamboo *kofia*, tilted slightly back. A traditional leather belt, a *kamar*, was fastened around his waist, and he held a walking stick. His complexion was brown, and his beard and mustache were a salt-and-pepper mix. Beneath his broad forehead, which resembled a bull's brow, small eyes lurked in their cavities. I introduced myself and explained the nature of my assignment. Then he vowed without hesitation to cooperate with me.

We entered the parlor, which contained three seats. Its central feature was a water-pipe—a *mada'a*—with its stem stretching to the daybed[3] reserved for the head of the family. In another corner, five young girls were playing house. They had lined up many empty tins, bottles, and plastic spoons to use as kitchen utensils. The girls were so absorbed in their play that they didn't notice us until the grandfather called his granddaughter: "Jalila... Jalila."

The girls stopped playing and turned toward us. One of them—a girl I thought was about eight—stood up. When she saw me, her smile vanished, her color changed, and her eyes sank into a sea of fear.

The grandfather sent the other girls away and motioned for Jalila to step closer. Then she limped toward me and sat down.

I asked her grandfather and my companion, Jabir Shanini, to leave us. Jabir sped out, and after some hesitation the grandfather complied with my request and departed, closing the door behind him.

Once we were alone, I explained who I was and the nature of my assignment. I asked her to speak truthfully, faithfully, and frankly about what had happened to her, promising to print her statement in the newspaper just as she uttered it, without any additions or deletions. Bringing out my recorder, I asked, "Do you agree?"

She raised her open hand and gasped.

This was the strangest "yes" I had ever heard.

---

3. Author's note: *al-qa'ada* is a bed with a wooden frame and rope matting. It is higher off the ground than other rope beds.

Thursday

Chapter 62

When I woke, I asked myself: *Where am I?* Roused by the heat and my thirst, I found I had been sleeping on a sofa in the large chamber Jabir Shanini used as a parlor and guest room. A shelf on the wall above me held a decorative display of plates and glasses, and on the opposite side of the room a huge lizard lay motionless on the floor. It might have been watching me since yesterday, asking itself: *Who is this stranger?*

I removed the splint from my index finger to inspect it. I found that it was no longer swollen and that I could use it, but cautiously, because it still hurt. Checking my hands and feet, I discovered that five mosquito bites had left small red pustules on my skin. I entered the bathroom with my towel over my shoulder, carrying my razor and toothbrush. I bathed after shaving but had forgotten to bring soap with me from Sanaa, and my host hadn't thought to provide any. The bathroom did not have a mirror either. I can shave without one but wished I had a mirror to inspect my plebeian nose, where I feared that a new pimple might appear to diminish any pretense I had of being a powerful person. As water sprayed over me, Jalila's words spilled out and roamed over my body, after tormenting me all night long:

Aunt Ni'mat woke me early, because it was my turn to herd our flock. I slipped on a black tunic with yellow flowers and then found my grandfather waiting to eat breakfast with me. He rises every day for the dawn prayer. Then he finds his breakfast waiting for him when he returns from the mosque, except on days when I herd the flock. On these days, he asks to eat breakfast later, so he can feed me by hand. Yes, my grandfather loves me very much. Shortly after sunrise, placing a broad-brimmed hat on my head, I set off with our flock—we have thirty-three animals—and headed to the valley to water them. Our dog, Mirbat, accompanied me. When we reached Wadi al-Dud, I found boys from Dayr Bani Musaʿid swimming naked. On catching sight of me, they told me to take my clothes off and swim with them. Some of them spoke rudely. An older boy with a mustache was with them. He sat bare-chested on a boulder and wore a brown sarong around his waist. He had spread his sky-blue shirt on the side of the rock to dry. When he saw that I felt uncomfortable and was upset by what they were saying, he yelled at them, threatening to pummel the head of any boy who said another word to me and then grind it like peppercorns. His voice cowed them, and none of them dared to look at me. After I watered the flock till they were satisfied, I headed to the pastures of al-Qurma. On the way there, my dog, Mirbat, stopped, would not move, and began barking for some unknown reason. I hit him with a stick and forced him to catch up with the flock. Once we reached al-Qurma, I let the flock graze and sat down to eat a bean-flour pancake, a *jabiz*, that I had brought. I suddenly choked on a morsel that stuck in my gullet and started to cough, trying to breathe. . . . I know that stuff like this happens either when someone says something bad about you or a person with bad intentions is watching you. The area was deserted scrubland, and, when I looked around, I didn't see anyone. But when I checked behind me, I found Shaykh Bakri Hasan standing like a jinni in the distance, his gaze fixed on me.

The water gave out in the shower, and the child Jalila's words stopped flowing from my memory. Why was my spirit tormenting me by replaying her quavering, nasal voice? Wasn't it enough that I had recorded her words on my machine?

I donned fresh clothes and inspected my black equipment bag. The clock showed it was 8:30 in the morning, and, without asking permission, Jabir Shanini barged in with a skillet and some bread. We ate white beans with eggs. The executive editor called and told me that: "al-Ayyam," an independent, opposition newspaper published in Aden, had printed a detailed interview with young Jalila about the rape and that public opinion had swung toward her. I told him I had conducted an interview with her just as soon as I arrived from Sana'a the previous night. He asked me pointblank to edit the interview to make it seem that her attacker was unknown and then send the edited version to the newspaper as quickly as possible. He emphasized that the interview we published had to shift the balance of popular opinion in favor of the shaykh, because our mission, which was dictated by the national interest, was to portray this shaykh as wrongfully accused. I promised to work on the interview that afternoon and email it to him before sunset.

When I hung up, I had a lump in my throat and found I had lost my appetite. I needed to take a malaria pill, to protect me against this disease for the next twenty-four hours. I picked up a bottle of mineral water but found it empty and was forced to swallow the pill without water.

The assault had occurred at noon the previous Monday, and that afternoon Hajj Hadi had presented to the police a report in which he accused Shaykh Bakri Hasan of raping Hadi's granddaughter Jalila. Accompanied by a representative of the public prosecutor's office, they had taken the girl to the clinic in the town of al-Jurum, where a female Russian physician and half a dozen female nurses from India examined her. She was bleeding and needed stitches in the places where she had been violated. Shaykh Bakri Hasan was arrested that night and jailed. It was the shaykh's bad luck that a correspondent for

Aden's newspaper *al-Ayyam* was visiting his relatives then and wrote about the incident. On Tuesday morning, this newspaper published the report on the front page with a banner headline. In a matter of hours, all of Yemen knew the story.

The government in Sana'a, sensing that a conspiracy was being launched against a loyal party member, sprang into action. The authorities pointed to the speed with which the opposition had seized on the incident as proof of a conspiracy to pump up publicity for them and to bring the ruling party's name into disrepute.

The day after the assault, on Tuesday, the Russian physician submitted her report to the police—in Russian. Then it was sent to an approved translation bureau in the city of Hodeida. By noon that day I had been in the office of the executive editor, who assigned me to cover this thorny case.

Wednesday night I arrived in the village of Bab al-Minjal. The Arabic translation of the medical examiner's report was delayed by bureaucratic procedures. An influential figure was making urgent efforts to free Shaykh Bakri Hasan and trying to obstruct the course of the investigation, but the police chief of Bab al-Minjal refused his mediation and insisted on keeping the shaykh locked up until the medical report arrived.

The case was advancing extremely quickly, and I was charged with intervening as forcefully as I could to change the general mood and switch popular opinion to our side. I admit that the responsibility thrust on my shoulders was so huge that it could have crushed the hump of a camel.

We reached the police station at 9:10. The courtyard was so crowded with men, women, and children of all ages it seemed that the weekly market had moved there. The inner corridor was swarming with government soldiers and armed men from Shaykh Bakri Hasan's tribe. There was a tense standoff between the two sides, and fingers caressed triggers.

Someone's gaze pricked me. When I glanced around, I saw a girl as brown as chocolate staring at me with wide eyes from which an amorous gleam flared like blazing torches that scorched everything in their path. That one glance, which I did not repeat, left my heart feeling singed as its temperature reached a boiling point. I thought she must be some foolish young girl whose heart might be swayed by any visitor from the capital—an ingénue or tender damsel who had not seen more than fifteen springs.

A fearsome looking, giant, black soldier from the low-caste Akhdam community prevented me from entering the police chief's office. I showed him my journalist's card, which he examined while wiping sweat from his brow. Then he let me in. He tried to keep Jabir Shanini from accompanying me, but Jabir flashed his canine teeth, opened his eyes till they bulged out, and told the soldier coarsely, "I am Jabir Shanini, Preshident of the Local Council—or don't you know me?" Thrusting the soldier's arm away rudely, he followed me.

The police chief's chair was empty, but young Jalila and her grandfather Hadi were present. I would have liked to approach and greet them but couldn't. Some psychological barrier separated us and made it impossible for me to take this simple step. Near them stood a woman who was around thirty-five. She had a sweet expression, and her scarf had slipped to her shoulders, revealing her black, shingle-cut hair.

Jabir Shanini supplied her name—mispronouncing it as: "Shalam Mahdi"—and explained she was an activist with a human rights organization. Next, Jabir pointed out a young, brown-complexioned man, as thin as a reed and with clearly defined features and curly hair. He said "thish bashtard" was the journalist who had published news of the case in the Adeni newspaper "al-Ayyam". I couldn't keep myself from laughing when, with his characteristic lisp, he told me that the chap's name was, "Shami Qashim." My giggle annoyed Jabir, and he scratched his crotch as his mouth tilted to the right and black saliva dripped from it.

At this time, a balding middle-aged man, wearing a coffee-colored suit and a rose-colored necktie, which were both inappropriate for the stifling weather, appeared unexpectedly. The pockets of his coat bulged in a ridiculous way. Glancing nervously at the splint on my right hand, he said, "Good morning, Mr. Mutahhar. I am Mr. Hammoud Shanta, the Shaykh's attorney."

My belly contracted as if someone had tickled me. Showing little concern for his feelings, I replied sarcastically, "The honor's mine... but where is your *shanta*, your attorney's briefcase?"

This attorney, Hammoud, rocked back and forth uneasily and frowned. Prodding my chest with his finger, he told me bitterly, "I hate bags and men who carry them. I detest effeminate men who dangle packs from their shoulders. From life experience, I've learned that guys with shoulder bags are effeminate sissies."

My black bag was slung over my shoulder, and the correspondent for the Adeni paper "al-Ayyam" also had a shoulder bag. With a mocking smile I asked, "In this case, why not change your surname to something more manly? How about Abu Hamil al-Athqal, for example—a name fit for a champion weightlifter."

The giant, black, Akhdami soldier, who had been watching us out of the corner of his eye, now made a sound like a cow lowing. Then he burst out laughing so loudly that his reverberating guffaws shook the walls. Everyone joined in. Even young Jalila forgot her fears long enough to giggle. Attorney Hammoud's face turned as red as the flesh of a watermelon, and—placing a hand near his face—he shouted: "F. . . your mother!" After cursing me, he turned the other way to control his anger while we attempted to restrain our naughty giggles.

The journalist Sami Qasim approached and shook my hand warmly. I experienced atrocious pain in my index finger and agonizing jolts down the vertebrae of my back. All the same I manned up and did not withdraw my hand.

"Mr. Mutahhar Fadl?"

"Yes."

"May God grant you a long life! I'm a fan of your columns and like your writing style."

"Thanks, but I consider myself a rookie journalist."

"You are young, a member of my generation, but you have burst off like a rocket and achieved a massive popularity among readers."

"That may be on account of my father's prestige and because I began writing a weekly column when I was in secondary school."

"I remember your column! 'The Scythe's Harvest: *Qitaf al-Minjal.*' Isn't that right? May your father rest in peace. He was a daring militant. You must be here on assignment for the paper *The Red Star: al-Najma al-Hamra*, aren't you?"

I was nonplussed. He assumed I still wrote for the Communist

Party paper. Stuttering, I replied in a low voice, "No... I work now for *al-Sha'b*."

He pulled his hand away from mine as if a thorn had just pricked it. His smile vanished, and his expression suddenly soured. "You're with *them*!"

Summoning all my resolve, I retorted: "I'm not 'with' anyone.... I side with the truth."

He nodded and commented: "I hope so, Pal.... People trust you and your pen. They respect the legacy of your militant father."

I smiled and sighed with relief. When I glanced at his almond-shaped eyes, I noticed that they were wet with tears and resembled roses flecked with dew. He left me and returned to his group. Unconsciously, we had separated into two, socially distanced pods.

Jalila asked me, "Have you published my statement in the newspaper?"

I bowed my head, trying to fake a smile, and told her, "Not yet... probably in two or three days."

As her imagination transported her far away, she rested her cheek in her hand.

I gazed at her now in the daylight. She truly was a very beautiful girl. I had never seen beauty to match hers anywhere. Her complexion was the light gold color of a Sa'di apple. Her round face resembled the full moon. Her eyes were as flat as a sole's, and their honey-colored pupils radiated sweetness and charm. Her eyelashes were long and black, her evenly matched cheeks were separated by a thin nose, her pert, rose-colored mouth suggested sincerity and high-mindedness, her crescent-shaped eyebrows were dark black, and her wide eyelids lent her a noble allure. . . . Her thick, black hair wasn't stringy or curly; instead, it looked silky to the touch, and its strands twisted around each other. They weren't braided; instead, she had allowed them to grow spontaneously till they intertwined like the tendrils of wild shrubs.

A man with a tawny complexion and a colonel's insignia on his shoulder entered, and I surmised he was the police chief. He was nearly sixty and clean-shaven. The crown of his head was sparsely covered with hair. A dignified man, he was short and sturdy. His glances suggested a keen intelligence. He carried some documents and seated himself on the chair behind the metal desk. Several armed soldiers flanked him. He glanced at us and then asked for the shaykh to be brought from his cell. We all felt nervous, and, in the heavy silence that followed, we could hear, with lethal clarity, the buzzing of flies and mosquitos.

Shaykh Bakri Hasan entered without any shackles, and no soldier dared to even grasp his arm. He looked to be around fifty-five and was brown skinned. He had dark freckles at the top of his cheeks. Of medium height, he was powerfully built. His chin was clean-shaven, and he had a skinny mustache. His black eyes sparkled, and their whites were so red they almost looked bloody. His thin eyebrows curved down at both ends. An open wound at the center of his forehead was shaped like the trunk of an elephant. His black hair was salted with white and, from neglect, had turned as coarse as a sheep's wool. Anyone sticking a finger in it would have had trouble pulling it out, because his hair was twisted and knotted like a fishing net that had been hastily folded and nailed in place. He wore a white sarong with a black vest. The red shawl on his shoulders was embroidered with gold thread. He sported a curved dagger, a *khanjar*, at his waist. He stood there self-importantly and glanced around scornfully. I noticed that he was still packing his own pistol, which hung from his belt. Six bullets were attached to its holster.

The police chief looked the Shaykh straight in the eye, threateningly. His lips parting with anger he did not bother to conceal, he announced: "The medical examiner's report confirms rape."

Furrowing his brow, the Shaykh turned toward young Jalila and subjected her to a terrifying, menacing glare. She fidgeted in her seat and evaded the shaykh's gaze, which resembled molten lead glowing in the dark. Hadi, her grandfather, placed his arm on her shoulder and hugged her to show that he would protect her.

Attorney Hammoud Shanta leapt toward the police chief waving his forefinger in the air. "Mr. Ahmad, this medical report is fabricated! Dr. Tatiana is in cahoots with *them*."

The police chief gestured angrily and shouted to his face, "Shut up!" Attorney Hammoud Shanta wilted and retreated to a distant corner.

The police chief continued in the same stern tone as he scanned the crowd like a hawk: "The day after tomorrow—Saturday—the case file will be transferred to the public prosecutor, and Shaykh Bakri Hasan will be transported to the prosecutor in the town of al-Jurum."

The Shaykh placed his hands on the rusty metal desk and leaned forward to address the police chief: "I'm not involved in this case. How am I linked to the sex games of young children?"

He flexed his torso and placed a hand on the hilt of his dagger. "I'm out of here and heading home. If you try to prevent me, I swear I'll use your head for a ball on my farm."

He turned and walked away. The police chief chased after him, yelling: "Shaykh! Shaykh!" They exited together, and we all followed. As he dashed out, the police chief quickly did something that few people noticed; he gripped the Akhdami soldier's upper arm as if to push him back. Then this soldier disappeared back inside instead of trailing after us.

The Shaykh shouted to his armed companions, "Let's go, men!"

His supporters surrounded him, and they all moved into the courtyard. The police chief barked orders over their heads for the gate to be closed. Brandishing their weapons, the Shaykh and his men rushed to force their way out. Then the soldiers loaded their rifles and prepared to fire. Women screamed and people shoved each other as they tried to flee. The police chief snarled loudly enough to be heard over the commotion, ordering the shaykh to back down. My group had rushed after the police chief and stood behind him, but when everyone began pointing their weapons at each other and a massacre seemed imminent, we separated. Attorney Hammoud lay flat on his belly on the ground, oblivious to any potential damage to his elegant suit. Hajj Hadi embraced his granddaughter and crouched by the wall, turning his back to the combatants. The journalist, Sami, and his companion, Salam, the human rights activist, fled back inside the corridor, and I raced to my left to perch on a masonry bench from which I could observe how this confrontation, which reeked of death, played out. Meanwhile the villagers pushed each other aside as they retreated. I sat down and began to hunt quickly in my bag for my camera.

An unidentified man in the crowd threw a rock at the head of Shaykh Bakri Hasan, who staggered and howled like a beaten dog. He drew his revolver, loaded it, and turned to his left, toward me, because that was the direction from which the rock had flown. He pointed his gun indiscriminately at the villagers, who were already agitated and upset, and demanded threateningly: "Who threw that stone at me? Tell me who did it, or I'll kill all of you." People fled from his revolver like flies from a can of insecticide. Many bumped into each other and fell to the ground. One person trod on another while attempting to evade this would-be terminator who stood a few feet away.

My hand froze, and I did not dare take my camera out of the bag. The shaykh's frightening mien dissuaded me. If he saw me taking photographs when his emotions were wounded by the humiliation he had suffered, he might stop seeking his attacker and vent his anger by filling me with bullets.

The police chief charged the shaykh head on, using his body to shield the civilians from any stray shots. He grabbed the revolver with both hands and forced its muzzle into the air. The two men wrestled for control of the gun and slammed into each other, employing his full weight against his opponent.

Without meaning to, I leapt in the air, and my bag fell to the ground, when, for a split second, a fleeting glint overhead caught my eye. Then a terrifying sound louder than thunder made me tremble and shattered my nerves.

The huge Akhdami soldier was on the roof with a heavy anti-aircraft gun, a DShKM, and had fired once into the air. That made everyone freeze where they stood, and a sudden silence settled on the area. We might as well have been in a desolate wilderness.

The Akhdami soldier aimed this heavy machine gun at the chests of the Shaykh's armed supporters and bellowed at them in a reverberating voice that made their bodies tremble: "Throw down your weapons! Obey this order! Quickly!"

Their mouths gaping open, they dropped their rifles on the ground. Fear had sapped their willpower. Then the police chief easily wrested the revolver from the Shaykh, whose energy had evaporated as had his will to resist. The soldiers opened the small door, and the Shaykh's followers filed out, one behind the other, each scratching his butt, his head bowed. Once they were gone, the door was locked, and a short soldier began to collect the rifles, which he rested on his shoulder. Stretching out an arm, the police chief ordered the Shaykh back to confinement, and the defendant moved downcast in that direction, panting and exhaling hot air from his mouth. Before disappearing, he glanced around at the villagers, challenging them to look him straight in his red, predatory eyes, which resembled those of a tiger ready to attack. Then he vanished inside, escorted by the police chief and a group of soldiers. His departure was met with cries of disbelief that exploded in a crescendo from the throats of the crowd: "*Wayyyyyyh, wayyyyyyyyyh . . . wayyyyyyyyyyyyyyyh!*"

Then the gate's panels were opened wide, and the people poured out. They left happy and uplifted. Smiles of victory glistened on their lips, as they held their heads high, bodies erect, and chests proudly raised. They were all talking at the same time in loud and resonant voices, as if rendering the national anthem in a unique manner.

When I reached al-Qurma, I let the flock graze while I sat down to eat a bean pancake, a *jabiz*. I was really hungry and ate quickly. Then I choked on a morsel that got stuck in my gullet. I began coughing and had difficulty breathing. Suddenly an unknown person struck my back from behind. The morsel popped out of my mouth, and I fell on my face. That unidentified person pressed my head into the earth. Dirt got in my eyes and entered my nostrils and mouth too, making it impossible for me to scream or move my head. He bound my hands behind my back with rope. Then he shoved my tunic up to my waist and stripped off my panties. I managed to turn with difficulty but couldn't tell who he was because he was veiled: his face was covered with a dotted, white shawl. He wore black trousers and a red shirt. Next, he flipped me onto my back and placed a black plastic bag over my head. There was a small hole at my nose so I could breathe. After that I couldn't see anything. He spread my legs apart. Then I felt his thing hurt me. I don't know when he left or where he went. I never heard his voice. He vanished as suddenly as he had appeared.

I finished revising my final draft of Jalila's statement that afternoon and loaded photos of her onto my laptop. Then I wrote my coverage of the events that had transpired that morning at the Bab al-Minjal police station. After sunset, I spat the twist of qat from my mouth and drank a glass of milk fresh from the cow, with Jabir Shanini. Afterwards we set off in his Toyota Hilux for the town of al-Jurum.

He dropped me off at an internet shop and went to check on some of his diverse business ventures. I emailed the interview, photos, and my journalistic coverage to my newspaper. I was in no hurry to contact the executive editor to tell him I had completed my assignment. I knew his routines well enough to understand that I should not. By this hour, he would have reached his office, hung his topcoat on the hanger, and begun to enjoy executive time with his beautiful secretary, who was thirty years younger. After that, he would be busy writing the lead editorial for the next day's edition. He was an orderly man who knew how to organize everything.

I quickly checked four or five political sites. Then I opened my Facebook account but was not able to concentrate on anything. So I paid and left the internet store. I could barely breathe inside there, because of the heat, the cigarette smoke, and the stench of the customers' sweat.

I started walking down the town's main street in search of a promising restaurant. I didn't have any specific type of food in mind; I just felt hungry. Numerous beggars—men, women, and children—accosted me. They weren't aggressive, and their faces reflected the abject poverty they suffered. I also encountered naked madmen whose private parts were covered only by layers of grime. Women cast me inquisitive looks and did not avert their gaze from mine. They were so daring that not one looked away! Motorbikes sped past haphazardly, like so many flies, and I was almost hit more than once. Trash was everywhere, and plastic bags covered the ground like a malignant organism. They are a modern replacement for the noxious thorn bushes that used to grow in fields.

Someone called me from behind, and I turned to find Sami Qasim, the correspondent from "al-Ayyam," quickening his pace to catch up with me. We shook hands, and when he asked where I was heading, I told him I was looking for a great restaurant. He said he knew one and, grasping my hand, hurried me away with him as if I were an old friend. We continued in that same direction for a short distance and then turned down a side street, which was wide at first but gradually narrowed and split into twisting alleyways that led to the old city. The street was lined with shops that sold gold, electronics, ready-to-wear clothes, fabrics, and perfumes. I also saw money changers and photo studios. Eventually we reached a traditional restaurant that was reputed to be very famous. Groups of patrons sitting outside were eating ravenously. Smelling the meat fried in oil, salad, and many spices, I began to salivate, and my stomach reminded me how hungry I was. Inside we found all the tables taken. Moreover, the heat defied description, and we seemed to have walked into a clay oven. I felt frustrated and thought we should look for another restaurant, but Sami Qasim drew me by my shirt sleeve to an inner corridor that led to a staircase, where I saw a placard reading: "Family Section." We climbed to the second floor as my nostrils inhaled an array of appetizing aromas. There were numerous rooms on this floor, and gauzy blue curtains served as their doors. The din of voices faded into the distance, and the oppressive heat diminished. The entire atmosphere was transformed; we seemed to have entered a small, clean paradise with a temperate climate provided by air conditioners.

We headed to a cubicle where the blue curtain was raised, and I was surprised to find the human rights activist Salam Mahdi inside with a guy I didn't recognize. We sat down without any introductions and were immediately swept into a heated discussion.

The man I didn't know said, "I'm telling you that this girl was my pupil and that I know her story very well."

Salam replied, "Fine. Is she prepared to accompany us to the police station to file a report on him?"

"No."

"Fine." Then pointing to Sami, "Would she at least share what happened to her with the press?"

"Impossible. What girl, anywhere in the world, would voluntarily shame herself and her family?"

"What's the point, then, Husayn?"

Sami intervened at this point: "What girl are you talking about?"

Salam replied, "Husayn claims that other young girls have been assaulted by Shaykh Bakri; he wants me to meet with them."

"Why not? Do it and record their allegations. That might help us apply pressure on the Shaykh," Sami told her.

I wanted to comment, to object to endangering these young girls and forcing them in a foul manner into the fiery furnace of a political battle, but the waiter arrived then and placed an earthenware platter of meat and bread on the table. That caused me to delay my objection till after I ate!

The diced meat was extremely tasty. I had never tasted anything like it before and started eating like a lion. The waiter soon returned to place a carbonated soft drink before each of us.

They kept repeating their disgusting gossip and adding new details about young girls Shaykh Bakri Hasan had assaulted, including some incredible claims. Anyone hearing them would have thought the shaykh had a member seventy cubits long!

I listened intently when Husayn volunteered that, next Saturday, pupils from the school where he taught would demonstrate in front of the public prosecutor's office. Gradually my three companions noticed my silence and discomfort and started to be more cautious about what they said. Then I realized that they were mentally distancing themselves from me and starting to look at me hostilely.

Once the tension between us had become unbearable, we rose. I don't know who paid the bill and didn't bother to ask. I quickly said goodbye, pretending to yawn. Then I hailed the first motorcycle that passed and left town, heading back to the village of Bab al-Minjal. I felt upset and disturbed by the entire evening.

Before retiring to bed, I washed, to clean off the smell of my sweat, and slipped on clean underpants. Because it was so hot, I didn't wear anything else. I opened the window and immediately stretched out beneath it. Although I was virtually naked and had no cover over me, I had great difficulty falling asleep. I would close my eyes and order my brain to stop brooding; but it was too hot for that to happen.

After what may have been two or three hours of me alternating between wakefulness and sleep, I felt thirsty, raised my torso a bit, grasped the bottle of water, and drank straight from its mouth till I emptied it. Then I rolled it toward the door and lay back down. At this moment I sensed that a face was looking down at me through the window, which was wide open. I stared outside but could not discern anyone there because it was so dark. Feeling drowsy, I didn't bother to investigate.

Friday

Chapter 61

The next morning I remembered seeing a face look down at me through the window but could not decide whether that had really happened or was the part of a dream.

Shortly before time for the Friday communal prayer, executive editor Riyad al-Kayyad phoned and addressed me hostilely. He said he had run my story but not the interview I had conducted with the girl Jalila, because in it she seemed to be a victim with whom people should sympathize. I asked him what exactly he wanted. He said bluntly: "I want you to rewrite the interview in a way that discredits the girl a little." I promised to revise the interview and have it ready to publish that evening. He then asked me to interview Shaykh Bakri Hasan and present his point of view to our readers and public opinion.

That afternoon, when I was in the parlor masticating qat, working over the dialogue, the executive editor contacted me again to complain that the picture I had sent of the girl Jalila did not help our cause: "If we print this photo, people will sympathize with her and fall in love with her because she looks beautiful. People should never notice her beauty. Photograph her again from an oblique angle. Even a fuzzy picture will be better." As usual, he hung up without saying goodbye.

By the end of that hour, I had finished a new version of the interview. The main change I made was to have Jalila declare that when she went to the wadi and saw the boys skinny-dipping, she had taken off her clothes too and swum with them but that they had harassed her. When she went to the pastures of al-Qurma, a boy with a mustache followed her. He was wearing a brown-striped sarong and a sky-blue shirt. He was the one who had inserted that powerful thing into her, with her consent. When I had asked her why she had accused Shaykh Bakri Hasan and not told the truth, she told me she wanted to protect the boy, because he was her friend and that she feared her family would attack him. This rephrasing paralleled the facts, and the cantankerous executive editor would feel relieved. I spat out the qat leaves I had masticated and rinsed my mouth. Then I left my host's house and went to look for Jalila, whom I found playing on see-saws made from tree trunks with her peers on a sandy plain. I asked her to return to her house with me and don a long veil so she would be properly attired. I then took a photo of her, which was widely distributed by the media, from the side, in a shadow. That long veil covered her head and chest, making her look several years older than she was. I departed quickly, hoping privately that I would never see her again.

While walking toward the police station I felt nervous about the children playing with marbles, competing with one another to knock them into shallow holes in the ground. I felt like scolding them and telling them to stop playing this game, even as something inside me was whispering that I had tripped and fallen into a hole myself: one of those inevitable pits we confront on life's path and can't escape.

After completing my interview with the shaykh, I planned to travel that same night to Sana'a and sleep in my own bed. I was determined to climb out of the "Jalila pit" as quickly as possible.

By the time I reached the police station, the sun had fled, leaving behind one small, pitiful cloud swimming in a sea of blood. A policeman opened the cell for me, I entered it, and he locked the door behind me. Shaykh Bakri Hasan was performing the sunset prayer with enviable piety. I snapped a picture of him, thinking that publication of it would give readers a good impression of him. Once he concluded his prayers, I approached him and explained what I proposed to do. He listened to me without interruption and then said calmly: "Pose your questions and answer them yourself. That's your job, not mine." His cutting reply struck me like the blade of a sword. All I could do was swallow and nod my consent.

As I left, I encountered the correspondent from the Aden newspaper *Al-Ayyam*: Sami Qasim. When I asked him why he was there, he said he wanted to interview the shaykh. I told him the shaykh had refused to offer any statements or interviews to the media. He spat to one side—a gesture that startled me—and said he was charged by his newspaper to request an interview. If the shaykh refused, he would have performed his task.

I telephoned my host Jabir Shanini and asked him to come and bring my suitcase. Moments later Sami Qasim emerged with a visibly paler face. I asked him, "What happened?"

He replied in a faint voice: "The shaykh refused to let me interview him." I noticed that his hands were trembling and that the circle of sweat beneath each of his armpits was enlarging. He continued as his gaze wandered, "The shaykh threatened me.... He swore three times by God that he will kill me."

I felt his fear spread to me and sensed that my heart rate had increased. Trying to calm him, I said, "Don't worry. That's just an outburst from a man who has lost control of his nerves." Our eyes met, and I realized, as he did, that I was gazing into a dead man's eyes. I asked him where he was heading, and he said he was going to al-Jurum. I told him I was heading there too and proposed we travel together. He consented thankfully.

Sami Qasim was living in his father's house in that town and had, in addition to his position as a newspaper correspondent, a small telecommunications shop with a fax and photocopy machine. One of his brothers worked there. When Jabir Shanini arrived in his Toyota Hilux pickup truck, I found myself in an awkward position, because Jabir refused adamantly to have my fellow journalist with the pale face ride with us, despite my attempts to persuade him. I deduced from his wink that he wanted to be alone with me. I apologized to Sami Qasim and climbed in with Jabir against my wishes, but this was not the moment to be a hero or for Jabir to think me a scoundrel. At that moment, my top priority was to leave the village of Bab al-Minjal and the entire coast as quickly as possible.

As if sensing my unspoken desire to sail far away, Jabir Shanini pressed on the gas pedal and shot off at a reckless speed. I looked around for my suitcase but did not find it. Then I asked him where it was.

He told me frostily, with his lower lip protruding like a dais: "Shorry. I didn't bring it. There have been shome developmentsh."

I felt dizzy—as if I were rolled up in a carpet someone was pushing down a hill. Jabir continued speaking as remnants of chewing tobacco flew into the air with the drizzle from his mouth: "The opposhition will organize a demonshtration tomorrow with Jalila in front of the public proshecutor's office in al-Jurum."

"What does that have to do with me? I've completed my assignment."

"Don't be in a hurry. There are ordersh from on high to organishze a counterdemonshtration in shupport of the shaykh, and you are ashked to provide newshpaper coverage for the demonshtration."

Feeling steamy anger rise from my overheated brain, I replied sharply: "I don't take orders from you, Jabir! Do you understand?"

He spat out his black saliva as he exited. Then he faked a laugh that sounded like a donkey's bray. Plastering a triumphal smile across his countenance, he said, "I told you, Shir: don't be in too big a hurry. When we reach al-Jurum, I'll drop you off at the internet shtore, sho you can finish your work while I attend an emergenshy party meeting. Do you know who will chair thish meeting?"

Naturally, I didn't know, but I surmised from the gleam in his eyes that it was someone important. When he whispered the name, I did not believe my ears. He dropped me off at the store and drove away.

I emailed Jalila's doctored dialogue and photo to the executive editor and then surfed newspaper and news sites with a muddled mind. I was wondering how such a figure, in flesh and blood, would attend a trivial party meeting in a distant, hard-to-find, insignificant community on the coast and what had caused this particular case to assume such importance. I no longer felt capable of surfing the web and challenged the computer to a game of chess to calm my nerves.

Jabir Shanini returned at ten-thirty to retrieve me. By then I was burning with a desire to learn the news. Once I pressed him, Jabir spoke—for the first time since I had met him without his mouth filled with a wad of chewing tobacco: "His Excellency attended the meeting and gave us some pointers on organizing two demonstrations. The first in support of Shaykh Bakri Hasan will head to the police station in our village and demand his release. The second—against the Shaykh—will head to the public prosecutor's office in al-Jurum and demand his surrender."

Jabir fell silent as his thoughts wandered. His silence enraged me, and I goaded him to continue: "Was that all?"

"No... each of us was given specific orders. I'm not clever enough to comprehend the goal of all this. Fortunately, I don't hold a major office."

I sensed that Jabir was conversing with himself more than with me. Buried somewhere in his words was the revelation of some conspiracy or corrupt scheme to depose one or more major figures.

"Who knows?" I told him. "You may become governor of this coastal province one day!"

Jabir's eyes widened, and the bridge of his nose quivered. He had detected the cunning revealed in my comment, and its hot brand had stung his skin. Speaking slowly and carefully, giving weight to each consonant, he said, "His Excellency mentioned you by name and assigned you tasks I'll tell you about shortly."

Saturday

Chapter 60

I crawled into bed around midnight but could not fall asleep for the next four hours. I slept a scant two hours before dawn when Jabir Shanini came to wake me up. I shaved, washed, and left the bathroom attached to the guestroom naked, except for the red towel wrapped around my loins. Then I was startled to find a brown-complexioned, fifteen-year-old girl standing at the window and staring at me audaciously. The round gold ring in her nose resembled the petals of a flower. She was tall and slender, and her slim chest had not blossomed with its fruit yet. I approached her, enchanted and dazzled. She seemed too beautiful for my heart to bear. I thought I should kneel before her so she would allow me to touch her. She had ravished me entirely, and I could not take my eyes off her. The stars would be jealous of such natural beauty, which wasn't touched by cosmetics or marred by other human intervention. Her complexion was as dark as night, and her teeth as white as milk. The formation of her face was exquisite—like a pure sky with azure rays. The splendid features of her forehead, eyes, and mouth caused me to float beyond time and space. She turned; a young boy was out there with her, speaking and trying to pull himself up to peek inside. I drew even closer to her until only the wall separated us. Around her curly hair she wore a black scarf. Her blue blouse was embroidered with orange flowers. I gazed deep into the pupils of her eyes and felt love percolate through my veins like a tree's sap rising from its roots via its bark and through its branches—gushing till it reached each leaf. She, from her side of the wall, gazed at my face fondly, not blinking even once. She seemed to wish to memorize my features so she would never forget them.

The wooden door of the room opened, causing its rusty hinges to squeak like the gate of an ancient castle. My dark gazelle was startled. She took the boy's hand and moved away. The person who entered was Jabir's oldest son bringing my breakfast.

As I devoured Marie brand cookies with tea—people here typically start their day with a light snack like this—I realized that she was the same girl who had caught my eye at the police station. Strange ideas crossed my mind as I longed, for example, for slavery to return and allow me to imitate my ancestors, who had been tribal leaders. When they admired a girl, they kidnaped her and held her in bondage. I don't know how this primal phantom sprang from my unconscious and drugged me to think this way. The girl's beauty had disoriented me and aroused in me an intense lust. No female had ever inflamed me this way. I am thirty-three, and this is the first time I experienced such unbridled sexual arousal. I wanted to cling to her like a hyacinth bean vine mounting a tree till I could climb no higher. Then I would die content, having achieved the ultimate ecstasy that the physical world can provide.

After checking that my camera, recorder, and laptop were in my bag, I prepared to depart. Jabir's eldest son returned with a bean sandwich and another cup of tea. I downed the tea quickly and thrust the sandwich in my bag to consume on the road.

At eight a.m. we were outside the gate of the police station. Supporters of the ruling party had been able to muster approximately a hundred people, a third of whom were women. These protesters formed a human barrier that prevented anyone from entering or exiting the police station's gate. The demonstrators were demanding the shaykh's release. Their human shield created a reality, and they were able to prevent the shaykh from being handed over to the public prosecutor. I started to take photos from many different angles and recorded statements from both male and female demonstrators. I was nervous and did not know how this standoff would end. I was certain that the police chief, Colonel Ahmad Fatini, would be subjected to a torrent of messages and threats and fail to deliver the shaykh to the public prosecutor. Then he would be forced to release him on bail. As the demonstrators became increasingly partisan, it seemed probable that the Colonel had refused to reconsider his decision and would continue to pose a threat to the Shaykh and his supporters.

Colonel Ahmad Fatini's vehicle arrived at approximately nine a.m., and he brought armed guards with him. The demonstrators refused to let him enter the police station. An exchange of insults ensued between one of the guards and Attorney Hammoud Shanta as the situation quickly escalated. Jabir Shanini threw the first stone at the vehicle's windshield, and dozens of others followed. The Colonel was forced to retreat after most of the windows of his vehicle were smashed. I took multiple photographs of the fleeing vehicle, but dust kicked up by its tires prevented me from clearly depicting its getaway. The demonstrators celebrated their victory by pelting the station's locked gate with rocks, creating a terrible din. I assume that this terrified the policemen sheltering inside the station.

A youth with bushy hair scaled the wall and threw down the metal placard that had hung over the gate. Then everyone took a turn trampling it under foot. Another young man, carrying a cudgel, also climbed the wall and approached the post with the only light fixture that lit the station's entrance at night. He broke its watermelon-shaped bulb, and shards of glass rained down like grains of salt. Others cut the electric line. They were growing frenzied and irrational—like children who smash their own toys for the fun of it. It was a strange situation. These people, who nourished a secret resentment against the government, had been provided with an opportunity—ordered by the government itself—to express their repressed anger at their lengthy humiliation, targeting a symbol of the state and the organization that represented it in their district.

I told myself: "How lucky they are!" I documented everything that happened with my camera and began to identify emotionally with the protestors, who seemed to be preparing to attack the police station. The escalating series of events suggested that this was likely.

Suddenly a vehicle with no tags appeared, and an individual stepped out. One look at him sufficed for me to know that he was from the intelligence services. He asked me to climb into his car. I glanced at my watch and found that it was precisely ten a.m. I did as he said, feeling somewhat surprised by his punctuality, since we Yemenis—as individuals or a nation—struggle to do anything in a timely fashion. Our intelligence services seem to be the exception that proves the rule.

I got out in front of the public prosecutor's office in the town of al-Jurum. Thousands of individuals were demonstrating there in the fiery noon sunshine. I noticed the vehicle of the police chief of Bab al-Minjal parked near the prosecutor's office. Most of the demonstrators were primary and middle-school students—boys and girls, who had walked out of their classrooms in their school uniforms.

I squeezed between them with enormous difficulty. Their mounting anger and resentment had made them pack together and left them oblivious to everything else. I had to use force to shove them out of my way, one after the other. They seemed to have suddenly shed their juvenile weakness and become insolent boors who ignored any prior training or discipline. They had screamed themselves hoarse, demanding justice and equity for Jalila. I admit I felt moved by this solidarity, which left a permanent scar in my soul. These boys and girls in the bloom of their youth had come out to defend one of their schoolmates. Even if I had been a stone, the sight of these children would have moved me.

I entered the prosecutor's office after showing my journalist's card to the soldiers. The portico was crowded. Husayn al-Battah, the demonstration's organizer, approached me, holding a copy of the newspaper *Al-Sha'b*. He used totally inappropriate words to refer to me and was in an insane state of agitation. Sparks flew from his eyes as he attempted to assault me, but the soldiers grabbed him and pushed him away. I noticed that the eyes focused on me were almost shredding me alive. The executive editor had published the interview I conducted with Jalila, and as a result I had been unmasked. Newspapers from the capital arrive here after noon, but unfortunately for me, they had arrived early today. Was this a mistake or deliberate? Was it in someone's interest to expose my life to danger at the hands of a raging mob? From the man we work for, we must expect anything.

Escorted by two policemen, Jalila left the office of the public prosecutor, trailed by her grandfather and the rights activist Salam Mahdi. When they saw me, they stopped. They seemed incredulous that I could be the same person they knew. With an angry look of disgust on her face, Salam asked me: "How dare you show your face here?"

Playing dumb, I asked her, "What's happened?"

Her reply summoned the fires of hell: "Because of the silly, fabricated dialogue you published, the public prosecutor has issued a memo to detain Jalila and arrest the innocent boy you falsely accused!"

I wanted to defend myself, but a damn stutter stopped me. Jalila asked me in a hurt voice: "Why? Why? You have raped me too." Tears ran down her cheeks and she started sobbing. The soldier pulled her away forcefully to detention. As her grandfather rushed after her, his malicious, hate-filled prayer rained down on me. The rights-activist Salam merely spat in my face. Then she went outside to incite the crowd against me.

My knees trembled and my face turned white when I heard the crowd chanting the slogan that the naughty rights-activist Salam had taught them: "Mutahhar Fadl, damn you! Your conscience died, Idiot!" The situation had very quickly grown tense. I saw troops fire warning shots to prevent the crowds from entering and reaching me. People I did not know approached and asked me to leave by the back entrance. They told me that they had secured a way for me to escape. I jumped out of a window, and a man with sloping shoulders led me down narrow alleyways. Then I found a blue Mercedes with reflective glass windows waiting for me. I climbed into the front passenger seat and closed the door abruptly, forgetting in my terror to thank the man with sloping shoulders. The vehicle sped away, and I did not try to look back, even though I imagined that a mob clamoring to shed my blood was pursuing me.

In a few minutes we left the town of al-Jurum, and I started to relax in the refreshing chill emitted by the air conditioning to classical music coming from the MP3 player. It was to my taste: an exquisite piece by Johann Sebastian Bach. From the storage compartment between our seats, the driver, whose cologne was clearly expensive and whose awesome mustache suggested that he was an officer, drew out two cold bottles of beer and handed me one. We appreciatively sipped its heavenly taste. I exchanged a few words with him about the excellence of the beer and various brands of beer. Then each of us retreated into a delicious silence.

I must have dozed off from my enormous fatigue, because the next thing I noticed was us stopping for a traffic light on a street in the city of Hodeida. I wiped away the spittle drooling from my mouth, and the man, who was scented with cologne, smiled and handed me a tissue. Through some clouds I heard him say, "For a morning, this is a good night." I felt nauseous and deprived of a sense of time. I had difficulty opening my left eye. When I looked in the mirror, I discovered a yellow deposit on its lashes and that the white of this eye was red as blood. The fragrant man remarked, "You seem to have encountered an infected person who passed the infection on to you. We'll buy you some eyedrops."

We stopped in front of a pharmacy, and he got out. He did not ask me for money. He soon returned and handed me a bottle of eyedrops. I thanked him and started to put a hand in my pocket, but he gave me a stern glance that caused me to stop in embarrassment. Ten minutes later we reached a fine hotel—a five-star hotel. I received the key to the room reserved in my name, thanked the fragrant man for looking after me, and ascended to my room.

It was a magnificent room with a view of the sea. I dropped my bag on a chair and stretched out on the bed, incredulous that I had actually escaped. I put some eyedrops in my eye and then telephoned my wife. I'm not the type of person who is comfortable calling home frequently, but many suspicions were besetting me this day, and I longed to reassure myself. Houriya informed me that my cell phone had not stopped ringing since that morning, after its number was made public. I was silent and did not comment, conscious that my hand was sweaty and my ear burning. In a low quavering voice, she told me that many of her friends had rung her to condemn the content of my article in *Al-Sha'b*. I told her I would explain everything when I returned home. She fell silent, and I sensed that she was hiding something. At that moment I was not prepared to hear any more abuse. I wanted to ask whether she had read the interview but preferred to stop this psychological torment and wished her a good night. Then I hung up.

My eyes absorbed the eyedrops and dried out. I felt an immediate improvement in my left eye. I headed to the bathroom, and bathed for an entire hour, enjoying the cool water, which calmed my nerves and reenergized my circulation. I dressed again, feeling very hungry. Opening my bag, I was disappointed to find I had eaten all my chocolate bars. I went out on the balcony where relief flowed over my spirit as I gazed at the glittering sea. The sun was directly opposite me, posed on the horizon, looking me straight in the eye. It looked like a person challenging and provoking me with its direct, horizontal, dismissive glare. I retreated inside, closed the heavy, purple drapes, and turned on the air conditioner.

The executive editor called and asked me what had happened. I related everything to him in detail. He asked me to write expansive journalistic coverage of the events and send that to him pronto. I applied myself to my laptop and wrote more than three thousand words in one spurt without stopping for an hour and immediately emailed that report to him without any revision. Only ten minutes later, the executive editor called me again and asked me to open Facebook and go to the page of activist Salam. From his tone, I sensed I would find something unpleasant—as if a military commander had ordered me to ward off an enemy attack.

Salam Mahdi

Post

Man with Warped Perspective

He looks banal, but the journalist Mutahhar Fadl, who does not deserve to bear the name of his father, a champion of the great, historic struggle, is a handsome young man with a gift for writing essays and investigations--one that is possibly unparalleled in this entire country. Unfortunately, God... occasionally grants a blessing to someone who does not merit it. We have all read the concocted interview he published as that of the girl Jalila in the semi-official newspaper *al-Sha'b*, thus displaying his violation of journalistic integrity. I, however, will describe my personal encounter with him, and that will disclose how little he deserves the reputation he has earned as a respected journalist. We met last night at a dinner party in a restaurant. While I was talking with two colleagues, Sami Qasim and Husayn al-Battah, about Shaykh B., who assaulted young Jalila in the village of Bab al-Minjal, I mentioned that the system as a whole supported the rapist and focused my eyes on our brother Mutahhar, who was listening to us with the hostile neutrality of someone who wanted to teach us a lesson. His hands were in his pants pockets and his arms were spread to express his desire to challenge and oppose us. Meanwhile his head was tilted to one side while he regarded us with half an eye, dismissively, pompously, as if he was saying to himself: "Who are you, Scum, to talk about your masters this way?" His eyebrows were contracted in a threatening way that revealed his evil intentions. I noticed on numerous occasions during our dinner, which lasted approximately an hour, that whenever we referred hostilely to the regime, he displayed this same hostile neutrality and the same mocking grimace distorted his face, indicating a covert threat to report us to the security services and to stop us riffraff in our tracks. Equally cheeky and sleazy was his lack of sympathy for young Jalila, who is now falsely accused of sexual assault; he seemed to side with the shaykh who raped her. He appeared ready to defend him and protect him from our tongues. I felt he would have liked to muzzle us and prevent us from tarnishing the shaykh's reputation!

Comments:

(R.A.) This journalist is an accomplice in the crime and needs to be judged.

(S.Q.) Mutahhar Fadl was a leftwing opposition figure but sold himself to the regime. Now he shines his masters' shoes and cleans the dirt off them.

(H.B.) He isn't a "Purifier." He's a "Defiler."

(A.A.) Everyone should know that the regime's thugs filmed him engaging in perverse acts and are blackmailing him. That's why he obeys all their commands.

(T.M.) The column he writes for the newspaper *al-Sha'b* is as thin as the string of a rebec and as worthless as a fly.

(M.S.) This creature has defiled the honor of our tribe.

(J.D.) God will take vengeance on him; you will see.

(M.A.) If you don't stop cursing and trashing him, the regime will reward him with a top post!

(N.H.) I don't believe Mutahhar Fadl would commit such a brazen mistake. We need to check this out first. Perhaps the newspaper *al-Sha'b* staged this interview, not Mutahhar Fadl.

Post

Mutahhar Fadl

The rights-activist Salam Mahdi makes a living off the sexual exploitation of underage girls. She has amassed a fortune in indecent dollars and purchased a fancy palace in a very ritzy neighborhood. She is nothing but a mouthpiece for foreign nations that want to shove their noses into our internal affairs. This lady takes an interest in girls' cases because she is jealous of them. She envies them the pleasure they enjoy. Believe me: this woman is sexually repressed. She takes a voyeuristic pleasure in searching young girls' panties and demanding to perform a medical examination. By concatenation of circumstances, we did dine together in a popular restaurant. Unfortunately for her, when she opened her large handbag I noticed inside it a large dildo. Here, as a pious Muslim, I offer a bit of advice to her respectable husband: inspect her handbag once she returns safely to their conjugal nest. From sources at the hotel where she is staying, I have heard she is a very liberated woman; they assert that she practices oral sex with members of the Akhdam caste.

Comments:

(Qasim al-Tahhan, executive editor of the newspaper *al-Masabih*) How are you, Darling? Tomorrow we will publish a special section on male and female activists—handbag fetishists who betray the nation and collaborate with suspect foreign organizations. We ask your permission to publish your testimony about the activist Salam Mahdi in this supplement. Best wishes.

(GH.N.) God damn this lascivious woman! The police should raid her room in the hotel, catch her in the act, and impose the Shariah penalty on her. I will throw the first stone at her, God willing.

(S.KH.) It's too bad she uses that plastic dildo when handsome young men (like me) are available.

(Z. K.) My thanks to the dear fellow for his reference to us. Women's handbags contain only God knows what misfortunes. I request the establishment of disciplinary corps to patrol the streets and markets and examine women's bags.

(D.M) Whooore!

(F.T.) Brethren, don't you know the name of the hotel where this activist (may God disfigure her) is staying? The writer of the post unfortunately forgot to mention the establishment's name.

(A.KH.) To Brother (...): Why are you asking for the name of the hotel? Do you also want to become kindling for God's fire?

(F.T.) God forbid, Shaykh (. . .)! My intention was to avoid booking a room in that hotel, because I travel frequently to the Hodeida Governorate.

(A.KH.) Blessings on you, Brother (...)—we have a duty to warn people away from obscenity and forbidden pursuits, to uncover any of our people who engage in indecent behavior and to prosecute them.

(H.W.) The Organization for the Defense of Girls' Rights, which is headed by Salam Mahdi, and other such "charities" pawn our country to foreigners.

(J.A.) Al-Na'im Hotel!

I ate dinner in the hotel restaurant and rushed back to my room to follow Facebook, which had become a blazing battleground. Hundreds of people were exchanging sword blows, and slashing taunts opened wounds and shed the blood of our stalwarts and theirs.

The executive editor contacted me at nine, which is a time

when he is in a good humor after imbibing three glasses of whisky.

"How do you like the hotel?"

"It's beautiful, but there are almost no other guests. It seems deserted."

"Great. You can enjoy the swimming pool all by yourself. . . . Listen: I have transferred a hundred thousand rials to your account."

"I appreciate it, but I'm returning tomorrow morning to Sana'a."

"No. You are not to leave Hodeida till informed otherwise."

"But. . . ."

"I will transfer a hundred thousand more."

"What's with this sudden generosity?"

"If you only knew who had called me not long ago, you would swallow your tongue and stop raising objections."

"Who was it?"

"Listen. I asked the hotel management to provide you with a bunch of qat and box of cigarettes to keep you company tonight."

"Cigarettes? But, I don't smoke."

"In that case, the time has come for you to begin."

"What am I to do?"

"I want you to write two columns about the police chief of Bab al-Minjal. The first will be a moderate attack on him, and we will publish it in our paper. The second should a filthy smear—as filthy as your unrestrained imagination can make it. We will publish that second one under an assumed name in the newspaper *al-Masabih*."

"Has he done something?"

"Yes, an hour ago he surrendered Shaykh Bakri to the public prosecutor."

"I don't know. In my opinion, we're done with him and there's no point pinching his ear."

"Who is talking about pinching his ear? After the Minister of the Interior ordered this man to set the shaykh free, he dared to defy that order."

"Why doesn't the Ministry of the Interior refer him to a committee of inquiry?"

"At this time, we cannot touch him. We can't arrest or even transfer him."

"Understood. I'll do what you've asked."

"We have been very patient with Colonel Ahmad Fatini for years as he turned a deaf ear to orders—a rotten, deaf ear. By the way, your friend Salma Mahdi committed a lethal error in what she wrote about you."

"How so?"

"Didn't you notice?"

"No."

"She was guilty of blasphemy—of being disrespectful to God."

"Oh. Now I remember."

"An opportunity like this is not to be missed. I'll call Shaykh Kafrut to declare her an infidel."

"Great."

"She'll become chewing gum in the mouths of preachers on Friday sermons."

The executive editor Riyad al-Kayyad started talking to someone else and hung up on me.

I wasn't offended, because I have grown accustomed to his supercilious way of terminating conversations. It makes clear to me that he considers the people he works with his servants and inferiors—boors on whom good manners should not be wasted. To cleanse myself of the troubling psychological impact of conversing with my boss, I pulled up a porn site and masturbated. After I had released my tension and ill humor, I began writing and imagining.

My wife called me several times, but I avoided answering her. I had an increasingly guilty conscience because this was the first time I had masturbated since we wed. But I won't deny that it felt great. I imagined myself enjoying sex with that fascinating, dark-complexioned girl.

I heard someone knock on the door, stopped writing, and rose to open it. A valet handed me a fine bunch of Shami qat and a carton filled with packs of cigarettes. I noticed that he was eyeing the carton of cigarettes and told him to wait. I removed the cellophane wrapper and gave him a pack. So, he left happy. I washed the qat leaves three times and estimated that they had cost ten thousand rials.

I granted myself a half-hour break and started to pluck the little, green, qat leaves, which were as tender as virgins' breasts. I rolled them together in my mouth. I had decided to distribute the packs of cigarettes to my acquaintances who smoked, but the sight of the whole carton of packs of cigarettes lying on the bed was extremely seductive. I decided that the time had in fact come for me to enjoy life and savor the small pleasures it affords us. I rang down to the hotel desk and requested a lighter. They provided it to me in a minute. Then I stretched my hand out to the carton, drew out a pack, and smoked the first cigarette of my life.

I finished work at one a.m. and dispatched my two requested columns. As I expected, the executive editor Riyad al-Kayyad called to greet me and shake my hand. I asked him, "Please stop shaking my hand," because my forefinger still hurt. Then he laughed till he choked. He informed me that Colonel Ahmad Fatini had affirmed his hostility to the state and disclosed his reckless deeds by receiving from the public prosecutor a warrant for the arrest of the boy Ata, who had committed a lewd act with Jalila, but–instead of sending his soldiers to arrest the boy—had sent a warning to Bani Musaʿid and asked them to hide their child. I told him that the colonel was a traitor to the country and deserved to have the insignia perching on his shoulders removed.

I returned to Facebook, where I wrote posts and received hundreds of comments. I was obliged to respond to these comments but was also waiting to see what Salam Mahdi would post so I could quickly traverse her shit. Around six the next morning, slumber benevolently overwhelmed me.

Sunday

Chapter 59

I had scarcely slept five hours when disturbances erupted. My mobile phone was ringing nonstop. The hotel phone started practicing its ringtone as well. Then I heard a light knocking on the door. It quickly grew louder and more insistent. I rose drowsily, opened the door, but then found I could not see, because my eyelids were stuck together by glue-like conjunctivitis. The valet informed me that a car sent by Shaykh Bakri Hasan was waiting for me outside. I asked him why the shaykh had sent it, but he did not know. I dismissed him and felt astonished by my own stupidity. After washing my eyes with hot water and soap and applying some drops, I regained my ability to see to an acceptable degree. I turned on my cell phone and tapped the messages icon. I found a text from the shaykh's attorney, Hammoud Shanta, celebrating the shaykh's release on bail and a message from the shaykh's number. The stilted tone of the shaykh's text made me think that someone else had drafted it. He was inviting me to a luncheon in his home in Bab al-Minjal to celebrate his release.

I felt uneasy, because I had promised myself never to set foot again in the village of Bab al-Minjal. While I was thinking of an acceptable excuse for skipping his banquet, my phone rang, and it was the shaykh's number. I attempted to weasel out of the invitation, but he made it clear that there was no way I could refuse. This seemed a deep-rooted conviction. He ordered me in a decisive tone to fly to him.

I shaved, bathed, put on a clean suit, and placed my dirty clothes in the laundry hamper. I felt a burning urge to open Facebook but knew that if I did, I would remain stuck to the screen for hours, dead to the physical world around me. Instead, I organized my bag, checked to see that I had all my gadgets, and departed.

I asked the driver, whose face resembled a ram's, to stop on our way at a stationery shop that sold newspapers. I sat in the rear seat so I could open my laptop when I wished and wade through Facebook. The vehicle was the latest model red, Mitsubishi Pajero SUV, and its seats were still covered with plastic. A strong smell of chemicals wafted from every part of this vehicle, and the blend was stifling and enough to poison the lungs. With a wrinkled nose, I asked the driver when the shaykh had bought this vehicle. Turning back toward me and releasing a drizzle of chewing tobacco toward my face, he replied that he had just picked it up from the ship. Astonishment sealed my lips, and I convinced myself that this was the scent of wealth and similar to the smell of billionaires. I imagined the fancy mansions they lived in and their new vehicles, which always smelled like this. But my nose, which has Marxist tendencies, did not relax and wasn't convinced by my ideas.

We passed by a newsstand, where I purchased all the newspapers released that day, and then continued. The driver, who looked like a ram, wanted to engage me in conversation, but I ignored him; I wasn't prepared to wipe my face every time he released a sentence. I began to flip through the paper *al-Sha'b*, and found my profile of Colonel Ahmad Fatini on the last page. I browsed through the inside pages, where I found articles that attacked rights organizations and mentioned Salam Mahdi. I opened the opposition paper *al-Ayyam* and searched for articles attacking me but did not find any. There was a small news item, which started on the front page and continued inside, about Shaykh Bakri Hasan being presented to the public prosecutor late the previous evening. I did not dare look through the newspaper *al-Masabih*. I could only hope with all my heart that they hadn't published my column. I left that newspaper folded up and read the other ones.

The next thing I knew I was in front of a massive gate behind which loomed a gleaming white villa. I must have dozed off en route. The driver honked the horn several times to get someone to open the gate. I put down the window, and hot air seared me, restoring the warmth to my bones, which had congealed from the vehicle's powerful air conditioning. I looked at the ground, which seemed green. Examined it more closely, I found that it wasn't covered with grass but star-thistle. Once the gate opened, we drove inside and could hardly find a place to park, because the expansive courtyard was packed with vehicles. When I climbed out, I looked down to find that star-thistle covered the ground here as well. I walked behind the driver, making sure the thistles did not cling to the bottoms of my trousers.

A powerful vehicle covered with jasmine garlands was parked by the entrance to the villa, and I surmised it was the shaykh's car. When I passed it, I saw written on the rear window: "Gazelle Hunter." The shaykh himself greeted me at the door of his villa. He welcomed me and escorted me to the dining room. He asked his staff to take good care of me and, after telling me that he hoped I enjoyed my meal, retired to the parlor. Most of the other guests had arrived earlier and had already eaten lunch. The staff presented me, the driver, and four other men who had arrived late like us meat and rice followed by shredded bread drenched with the finest quality Yemeni Sidr honey and yellow clarified butter. It was a meal worth the trip, and I filled my stomach till I was barely able to rise and stand on my two feet.

I made my way with tottering steps to the washrooms, where I encountered a surprise. I saw the brown-skinned girl who had looked at me through the window of Jabir Shanini's house. She stood waiting there to assist guests with a white towel and a bottle of cologne. I used the soap to wash my hands, rinsed out my mouth, and washed it. The moment I turned around, I saw her heading toward me with a smile as radiant as the rising sun. I accepted a towel from her and dried my hands and mouth. She started to claim the towel, but I grasped her hand and smiled. She looked at me and sighed. I asked what her name was, and she replied immediately: "Mona." Gazing at her hand, I saw she was wearing, on the ring finger of her right hand, a white plastic ring with a cheap glass diamond set in it. I raised her hand and printed a kiss on it. She gasped and looked very embarrassed. I gazed into her dazzling eyes and tried to kiss her hand once more, but she drew it back and said, "Oh! I'm the one who is supposed to kiss your hand." I realized that Mona considered herself of little value, and, with the speed of lightning, dark thoughts passed through my mind like a clip from a film: the shaykh, who was keen on young girls, had "seized her" in a humiliating fashion and cloaked her in a robe of ignominy. The way she conducted herself fit this scenario. Jealousy flared up in my heart, and the world turned dark before my eyes.

The driver with a ram's head cleared his throat as he headed to the washbasins and shot me a look that made me nervous. He quickly doused his head under the faucet and washed his kinky hair. Mona took the towel and sprayed perfume on my shirt and hands. Then she retreated with her head bowed.

When I entered the parlor, the shaykh welcomed me thunderously and made a place for me beside him. He handed me some qat leaves, and his servants brought me a flask of sparkling water, a bottle of mineral water, a spittoon, and paper napkins. Among those present were Jabir Shanini, president of the local council, and attorney Hammoud Shanta. The shaykh spoke gloatingly of Colonel Ahmad Fatini, who had been turned into a dust cloth and become a subject of conversation on every tongue up and down the land. The shaykh said that the paper *al-Masabih* had published a report under the banner headline: "Human Wolf Prowls Disguised as Colonel in the Police!" The article's author had discussed the types of torture Colonel Ahmad Fatini employed in the Bab al-Minjal police station. These included lashing detainees with military belts, prodding them with electric shocks, beating them with iron pipes, burning them with cigarettes, and pouring scalding water over their privates. The shaykh gave me an appreciative pat on my shoulder, although I did not appreciate it, and continued: "The writer referred to the deviant tastes of Colonel Ahmad Fatini and said he preyed on young men and arrested them on flimsy charges in order to torture them sexually." The shaykh stopped speaking suddenly and started to act out a theatrical scene. Grasping what rested between his thighs and bending his knees out a little, he sarcastically imitated Colonel Ahmad Fatini's husky voice: "If you don't confess, my son, I'll give you the ass's prick."

The parlor rocked with laughter, and some of the men grasped their bellies, pretending that they hurt, to express to the ultimate degree their loyalty to the shaykh, who sat in his place delightedly, nodding his head as if to congratulate himself. Uninhibited licentious comments splattered from mouths, and guffaws gushed from different spots and spilled onto the carpet like coffee bubbling in a pot over a fire. The shaykh ended this clamor by beating his bamboo cane on the brass spittoon. Looking at me admiringly, he began: "The real punishment for this silly queer were the photos. They are pictures so ugly even Satan would be repulsed by them. Frankly, the least that can be said is that the author of this article peed on him."

I was astonished when I heard the shaykh mention photographs. I wondered with bewilderment what photos he was praising. I had not sent them any pictures. Then the shaykh ordered that the newspaper be brought out. The driver with the ram's head brought in a stack of copies that he placed at the shaykh's feet. Then other servants handed a copy to each of the visitors, who numbered more than sixty. Some guests took more than one copy. The driver plucked a copy from the floor and held it out to me as if offering me alms, while gazing at me contemptuously and licking his lower lip. He made me feel uncomfortable, and his every gesture added to my unease. I had never experienced such churlishness. Perhaps there was some clash of sensibilities between us.

I looked at the front page, which had a banner headline that read: "Human Wolf Stalks in Police Colonel's Uniform." I turned to the page indicated and read the name attached to the end of the article. It was mine! Without meaning to, I jerked my head back, as if a bomb had just exploded in front of my face. I don't know whether anyone noticed the way I recoiled like a revolver that has released a shot, which can never be sucked back into the ammunition chamber. I was sweating profusely. I could not understand how the censors had allowed images as scandalous as these. They had published pictures of naked young men on whose bodies the traces of torture were clearly visible. There were also photos of boys, one of whom was ten, on whose buttocks the traces of beatings with military belts were apparent. I did not take a second look at the pictures and attempted to expunge them from my memory as I closed the newspaper. I blushed and felt humiliated. Everyone else was smiling, and their sparkling eyes gazed at me with admiration and approbation. A towering rage overwhelmed me; my deal with the newspaper had been to publish the article under an assumed name. Now I understood why the shaykh viewed me with such confidence. I grasped that I was the victim of a conspiracy to drag my reputation through the mud.

I wanted to call the executive editor Riyad al-Kayyad and dish out curses to relieve my heart. But the shaykh did not allow me an opportunity even to scratch my head. He subdued all of us by his powerful presence and tyrannical domination. He said he had purchased five hundred copies and was distributing them free of charge throughout al-Jurum. He also volunteered that he had phoned Qasim al-Tahhan, the editor of *al-Masabih*, and asked him to run a second printing at his expense. He said he would distribute the paper to all the coastal villages from Yemen's northern border with Saudi Arabia south to Bab al-Mandab.

Sorrow blinded and deafened me, and even the qat in my mouth acquired a bitter taste. For an hour or more I suffered in a fiery oven, consuming my anger and blaming myself. I tuned into my surroundings again when the clamor suddenly ceased, and everyone fell silent. Indeed, the men stopped fidgeting in their seats and listened intently. The shaykh was speaking, his voice quavering with emotion: "I told her: 'Your herd has entered my pasture.' She replied, 'Your pasture is surrounded by fencing, and my flock can't enter it.' She infuriated me. So, I seized a ewe and drew my dagger, threatening to slay it. Then she acted all pitiful and kissed my hand. My heart was touched, and I released the ewe. No sooner had I turned and taken three steps than I heard her muttering behind my back. Then I succumbed to an intense fury and this time I seized the girl herself and held my dagger to her neck. Her dog jumped me, and I felled it with a shot from my revolver. I dragged her to the car, tied her up with a rope, and showed her who Shaykh Bakri Hasan is!"

At eight that evening I asked permission to leave, and the shaykh gave me enough qat for ten men. He ordered his driver to take me back to Hodeida. When I climbed into the vehicle, I realized that I had lost my sense of smell. I told myself: "Fine. I no longer need that sense."

All the way back, I kept trying to contact my wife. But she ignored my calls and did not answer. I wanted to hear the voices of my children Habel, Najat, and Karama and reassure myself about them. I waited for the executive editor to contact me at his usual time, but he didn't. He realized that I would treat him to a raspberry for all his maternal ancestors from whose wombs he had emerged—extending back to his seventy-seventh great-grandmother. I did not try to call him. I was exhausted, and my nerves were shot. My anger had left me; it had evaporated when I heard Shaykh confess to his deed with my own ears. What's happened to me is that I am trying now to get angry and to excite my fervor; but I'm unable to rouse this power. A kind of paralysis has affected my central nervous system. I have become fluff, drifting in the wind, indifferent to the fluctuations of my destiny.

When we reached Hodeida, we stopped at a supermarket and got out. The driver bought a pack of power drinks, and I purchased an assortment of fancy chocolates, an electric kettle, coffee, sugar, and a dozen cans of tuna. When he saw me shopping for tuna, the driver laughed at me and said, "*Tanqah*! You buy canned tuna when you are in Hodeida—fish capital of the world?" I didn't know the meaning of "*Tanqah*," and so grudgingly swallowed this insult.

At the hotel I spat the ball of qat from my mouth and bathed. Then I heated water and prepared a cup of coffee. I wasn't hungry, because the rich food at lunch had left me feeling full. I brought out the bundle of qat I had received from the shaykh and began to chew a second round. I also summoned my courage and smoked my second cigarette, ever. I enjoyed its taste more this time.

I quickly drafted some journalistic coverage of the day's events, the most important of which was the shaykh's release from detention. I sent it off without any revision, because I couldn't stomach reading through it again. I hesitated momentarily about surfing Facebook, because I had a hunch that the locusts had devoured both the green and wilted parts of my reputation.

Post

Husayn al-Battah

Mutahhar Fadl is nothing but a miserable newshound whose assignment is to falsify the rape of the girl Jalila, to traduce the actual events, and to minimize the crime by saying that a boy had done it with her with her consent. He has been tasked by his masters with attacking those who sympathize with the cause of the raped girl, launching a campaign against them in the media to ruin their reputations and to force them to go under cover and withdraw, abandoning the child to confront the shaykh's tyranny alone.

Comments

(M.A.) The goal of Mutahhar Fadl's column in *al-Masabih* was to distract and divert public opinion away from the case of the girl Jalila.

(S.Q.) The journalist Mutahhar pretends to be independent and neutral but supports the authorities. That's how he has gained the trust of readers and garnered popularity in cultured circles. His true face was disclosed when he began to write biased journalistic coverups concerning the rape of the eight-year-old shepherdess by an influential shaykh.

(Y.A.) He knows what really happened but obeys directives from the security forces.

(Q.H.) Mutahhar Fadl was my close friend and, honestly, a very good man. When the ruling party recruited him, they initially asked him to remain true to himself and to criticize the government as much as he wished. On the surface, everything seemed agreeable to him and compatible with his desires, because joining the ruling powers did not cost him anything. His employment opportunities improved, and he gradually sank into honeyed wealth until the critical moment arrived. That was when they assigned to him the case file for the events in the village of Bab al-Minjal.

Post

Salam Mahdi—Rights Activist

Have you all entered the page of the person calling himself (M.F.)? Read carefully what he publishes on his page. He admires every dissident writer from the Left. His role model is the Russian novelist Mikhail Bulgakov, who split from the Soviet authorities and opposed them. Mutahhar Fadl imitates his role model and considers that he fashioned himself to be Bulgakov's comparable local example when he split with the Left and joined the ruling elite. But our stupid friend has not noticed the difference: when Mikhail Bulgakov split with the Soviet authorities and became an opposition figure, he paid an enormous price. (M.F.), on the other hand, left the opposition and joined the ruling elite, thus gaining a fine position and millions of rials in exchange for his treachery, abasement, and vice. Thus (M.F.) suffers from a chronic misunderstanding. His intellect is muddled by error. He explains cases of resistance ethics in a distorted, exploitative fashion. He imagines himself to be an exemplary hero who has split from the Left, whereas he is merely a pitiful, ruined rogue chasing money. His understanding of the truth is viciously elastic, and the moral example he sets is base and decadent.

I could not continue and read any more of the thirty-plus comments. I shut down the computer and spent an hour staring glumly at the wall. Without doubt, this has been the worst day of my life.

Monday

Chapter 58

I rented a Hyundai Santa Fe, which I charged to the newspaper, and drove to the town of al-Jurum. I reached the public prosecutor's building behind schedule; Jalila had already been released on bail. I learned that the Organization for the Defense of Girls' Rights had retained an attorney for her: a man named Shu'ayb al-'Ujayl. As for the boy, Ataa al-Musa'idi, who was accused of robbing Jalila of her virginity, they had not still been able to locate and arrest him.

The attorney Hammoud Shanta invited me to eat lunch with him at his house, but I begged off as graciously as I could. Then I gave thanks to God for sparing me that man's company. I walked out of the prosecutor's office, heading for my vehicle, but he caught up with me and asked me to drop him off on my way to the city of Hodeida. He claimed he had some sub-rosa deals he wished to conclude. En route we passed through the town of al-Mallah, where he told me there was a fine restaurant patronized by Saudis and Yemenis who had returned from working in Saudi Arabia. Since he left me no way to escape, I let him direct me to its location.

The square in front of the restaurant was crowded with powerful vehicles with Saudi plates. We entered and ordered a regional specialty: *kabsa*, a spicy rice and roast meat stew, with a soft drink. After I paid the bill, he suggested we pass by the qat market, where he led me to his friend who sells excellent qat. I shelled out the price of my qat and his.

As we proceeded on our way, he gave me a headache telling me about all the benevolent works the shaykh undertakes. From one of his bulging pockets, he extracted papers that he referred to as documentation and suggested I write an article in which I clarified to Yemenis the Shaykh's "true nature." I accepted these papers from him, without giving him any clear response. I said, "I'll see." He was smoking up a storm, but I didn't light up; I was still hesitant to smoke in the presence of other people.

We reached Hodeida in the afternoon, and I dropped him near a building that seemed to be a military barracks. Armed soldiers guarded its entrance, but I did not want to ask him whether my hunch was correct. The feeling I got from seeing that paint was peeling off its walls and its windows were darkened, but not very professionally, sufficed for me to curb my curiosity and drive off.

I saw a kiosk, stopped, and purchased all the newspaper published that day. The vendor proudly pointed out a newspaper that had just begun publishing in Hodeida, and I bought one. It was called *al-Nidal*—"The Struggle"—and this was number 0. I fled to my airconditioned vehicle and began to flip through the papers as I sat behind the steering wheel. I started with *al-Sha'b*. They had finally printed my interview with the Shaykh, which I had composed from A to Z. I noticed that all the columns I had written before I left Sana'a had been published. Today, I would need to force my mind to excrete some political shit to fill my column for the next day's paper. The newspaper's writers concerned with public affairs who constituted our heavy artillery had contributed five fiery columns denouncing foreign interference in interior affairs via rights organizations. With various degrees of shrillness, all these writers agreed that such organizations—no matter how their tendencies and titles differed—worked against the national interest. Other newspapers allied with us followed the same form of attack, at times even more acerbically. One writer demanded the closure of all rights organizations and that those who worked for them be charged with high treason. The opposition papers, led by *al-Ayyam*, condemned the release of the Shaykh and demanded the speedy conclusion of those investigations so the case could be adjudicated. There were stiff attacks on the Shaykh and calls for him to be executed.

I picked up *al-Nidal*, which had as its lead story a report on Hodeida's flooding sewers. At the bottom of the page I found a story about the girl Jalila with a color picture of her. I flipped through the pages and found more than ten articles taking Jalila's side. In three of them, I was slapped—in passing, as you might say—and as if all roads to the Shaykh necessarily led through me! These columns were by Salam Mahdi, Sami Qasim, and Husayn al-Battah—the instigator of the students' demonstration. The seven other articles were pedestrian and might well have been written by students from the school where Husayn al-Battah teaches. The editorial, which also referred to Jalila, was by the paper's executive editor, Ghalib Zubayta, whose name I was reading for the first time. I drove by a trash can and tossed all the papers in it.

I returned to the hotel exhausted. My leg muscles hurt as much as if I had walked all the way, instead of driving a comfortable SUV. I shaved, bathed, and then I smoked a cigarette. I felt an overwhelming desire to write poetry, a pressing need to vent my emotions, and a forceful drive to confess. I was a wreck and needed to collapse on paper.

The executive editor, Riyad al-Kayyad, called to urge me to complete my chores quickly. I wrote an essay for my daily column at warp speed, cursing the West which raises its girls so poorly that they feel free to do whatever they want, unrestrained by any standards, but then crowns itself a moral arbiter for Yemen and appoints itself the guardian for a young girl, who may have lost her virginity because of her own shameless conduct. Without a second thought, I emailed this column to the executive editor. Then I began writing follow-up coverage of the day's events. By sunset I had finished that as well and sent it off.

I felt lighter after I had relieved myself of these burdens. Then I remembered I was supposed to write a report about the Shaykh's eleemosynary activities. But the call of the sea proved stronger, and I decided to postpone writing that report till later in the night.

I descended quickly and crossed the street to the shore. Families and groups of young men were scattered along the Corniche. I was looking for a place where I could enjoy some solitude, and my eyes fell on a deserted spot. So, I quickened my pace and sat on a boulder near the crashing waves. I gulped in the moist sea air, filling my lungs, and experienced an enormous serenity. I could feel drizzle dampen me from my nose—which is frontal boundary of my body—to the bottom of my back and cleanse me from inside, washing away the filth that clung to my spirit.

I spent hours gazing at the horizon and thinking about my future and where my steps were leading me. I could no longer retreat. The best I could do was stand my ground, until I could buy a house and secure my children's future.

Feeling hunger's pangs, I looked at my watch and discovered it was 9:40. Then I proceeded very slowly back to the hotel, where I immediately entered its restaurant. I filled my first plate with salad and the second with tuna sandwiches, which had a distinctive flavor. I would have liked to ask where they sourced their tuna. Then like a genie emerging from his flask, the Shaykh's driver with the head of a ram, appeared and sat down opposite me. Helping himself to a sandwich from my plate, he asked, "Where have you been, Sir? We have turned the world upside down looking for you." He did not wait for me to answer before he devoured the sandwich in one gulp. When I did not reply, he replied somewhat indistinctly: "We kept phoning you, trying to contact you, but your phone was turned off."

"Eat your fill," I said, "and then we'll talk."

Rising, I went to fetch a second plate of tuna sandwiches and two glasses of orange juice. We ate voraciously and finished even the crumbs. It was already past 10 p.m., which was when the dining room closed, and the waiters were exchanging glances and looking at their watches. I gestured to Ali, and we left.

As I headed to the hotel's lobby to claim my key, I asked, "What does the Shaykh want?" I thought he might want to know whether I had written a report about his charitable activities.

Licking his mustache with his lip, Ali replied, "The Shaykh has sent you a present." I was gazing at his shirt's open buttons and the thick hair of his chest, feeling uncomfortably certain that I knew what sort of person he really was.

I held my hand out to him and said, "Okay." I expected the present was more money. He looked at my hand, which was stretched toward him, and burst out laughing. Feeling uncomfortable, I withdrew my extended hand and put it in my pocket.

Casting his gaze below my belly button, he replied, "The present is in your room." Then he exchanged a conspiratorial glance with the desk clerk, who handed me the key to my room with a broad smile.

I raised my index finger, which I waggled at him admonishingly. "It better not have been opened."

He bent over at the knees twice, making a rude gesture. "Tonight, there'll be some hanky-panky." Then he left, guffawing naughtily.

I climbed the stairs to my room, my mind at a loss while I wondered what kind of present this was. When I approached the door, I put my ear to its wooden panel. I heard the television, turned on at full volume. I listened for a minute. Whoever was inside was watching kid shows. I was overcome by anger and thought of going back down to the front desk to complain to the hotel's management about allowing strangers into my room in my absence. But I decided to enter the room first and find out who the Shaykh had sent me. I opened the door and went in, furrowing my brows and preparing to defend my privacy tooth and nail. But my eyes fell on a sight that caused my heart to leap from side to side and left me speechless.

It was Mona, my dream date in paradise—if I am ever allowed entry there. She was lying on her stomach on the bed with her head resting on a triangle composed by her hands. She looked at me once and smiled. Then she pretended to be preoccupied by her show. I approached her dizzily but stopped to admire her naked body. The pain I felt in my heart could not have been more acute had someone chopped it in two with a meat cleaver. I was terrified that her unparalleled beauty would drive me crazy.

Tuesday

Chapter 57

I dreamt I was touring a citadel and that when the tour ended, I was asked to leave. I searched for an exit, which I found, with some effort. The door was extremely narrow. In fact, it was a small window in a huge gate, which was firmly closed and guarded by two soldiers. I don't know how I managed it, but I decided to put a leg through the window while holding its frame with one hand. Then I thought I could put my entire body through. I was able to push my legs outside but became stuck around my waist and could not go farther or pull back inside.

Opening my eyes, I looked at the clock. It was two p.m. The room was chilly, Mona was asleep and so cold that her head was by her knees. I turned off the air conditioner and walked unsteadily to the bathroom. I shaved, brushed my teeth, and showered. I quickly lifted the receiver of the hotel phone and ordered a rich lunch brought to the room. I turned on my laptop and started to write my newspaper column for the next day.

While I wrote, I kept glancing at my brown-complexioned, paradise houri. This time I feared that the executive editor Riyad al-Kayyad would call and ask me to return to Sana'a! I was the happiest man on the face of the planet and did not wish to leave this blessed room! Mona woke when the waiter knocked. I wished her a good morning, and she whispered, "May your morning be luminous."

I opened the door, pulled the trolley inside, and thanked the waiter. The room now filled with the aromas of kebab and shish tawook. I congratulated myself that my nose was no longer on strike and fully operational again. Mona stretched, sat up, and emitted a sigh of delight. I held my hand out to her, and she jumped down gracefully and embraced me. I sensed the love in her heart and heard from her the sweetest words of passion—ones I was surprised she dared to utter. I sat her on my lap and began to feed her. She would bite off half a morsel and have me eat the other half moistened by her nectar. The bite of her teeth left a flavor like honey's aroma. I asked her in jest: "Are you a bee?"

She replied truthfully: "To tell the truth: I'm the queen bee!"

My eyes had never observed anyone more lovely. Her beauty was precisely what my taste desired. The lineaments of her face inspired in my soul feelings of the utmost bliss and roused all the pleasure receptors in my brain. For my entire life I had focused on light-complexioned, blonde women and ranked their beauty as my ultimate ideal. Mona, however, had forced me to recognize new truths about my true self and shown me that in my subconscious I preferred brown-complexioned women so dark no words could describe it and that this color fascinates me, enchants me, and causes my blood to boil, in a good way. How had I become infatuated with this color that I had shunned in my youth? I don't know. All my triggers for lust struck paydirt with Mona, and I explored with her actions I had never thought I might be able to perform.

Wednesday

Chapter 56

I sprang from bed feeling an enormous creative drive and wrote four essays for my daily column. I also drafted a tribute to the enormous charitable efforts undertaken by that generous and benevolent man, Shaykh Bakri Hasan, on the Tihama Littoral. I lifted him to a rank comparable to Gandhi's! After he received it, the executive editor Riyad al-Kayyad called and praised me for this report more than he ever had for anything I had written previously. He said he shook my hand. I replied that he could shake it all he wanted, because my index finger had healed now.

Mona returned from her excursion heavy laden with purchases but refused to allow me to embrace her. She protested that she was dripping with sweat. She took off her clothes and entered the bathroom to bathe. I allowed myself to examine her sacks. In one was an assortment of an old type of cookie that was no longer sold in groceries in Sana'a and other large cities. Cookies like that were widely sold when I was a child, between the ages of four and seven, as best I remember, and then gradually disappeared from shelves as they were replaced by other types. I was incredulous that plants somewhere were still churning them out. The taste of this cookie transported me to the past, and I began to rummage through memories of my miserable childhood. It had been at least ten years since I had tasted one of these cookies, which used to delight kids and were made expressly for them. But when I saw these old-fashioned confections, I salivated and craved them as if I were a child again. I tore open the first packet and devoured them delightedly—followed by the second and the third—experiencing the same feelings of contentment and pleasure I had when I was a kid.

Mona emerged from the bathroom with a towel around her waist. She gasped when she saw the empty packets of cookies: "Oh! What have you done, Mountaineer?"

I attacked the sack and proceeded to eat more. She also assaulted the cookies and began to eat them voraciously. In a matter of minutes, we devoured all the ones she had purchased.

The lover mounted the dais and prepared to deliver his sermon of love. I drew her towel from her and took her to listen to his extemporaneous, improvised sermon.

After lunch, Mona took a nap. Then I drove my car to Suq al-Mitraq and bought her an Italian ring. I chose platinum, because that precious metal wasn't common here and would not attract the attention of other Yemenis. I also purchased some qat and stopped at a bookstore that sold newspapers to purchase all the day's papers. Then I sat behind the steering wheel perusing them.

The Government-affiliated papers were continuing their attacks on civil society organizations. On an inside page I found my journalistic investigation of complaints by citizens of Bab al-Minjal about a breakdown of security and the mounting number of thieves. Everyone was complaining about the chief security officer, Colonel Ahmad Fatini.

In the opposition newspapers, attacks against the Shaykh were intensifying. Writers demanded that Parliament pass a law specifying eighteen as the legal age for marriage. Thank God, they had stopped attacking me; in fact they ignored me. Leafing through Hodeida's newspaper *al-Nidal*, I found a dangerous column by an unidentified eyewitness who said he had heard Shaykh Bakri Hasan confess to his crime in the reception room of his house to a crowd of more than seventy people. He named prominent citizens of the district and ended the column by mentioning my name. He said he was prepared to testify in court to what he had heard. I sensed that the sky had fallen on my head. This was the last thing I needed. This was an ill-omened case, and whenever we attempted to patch one side of it, another side we had neglected was ripped open.

I returned to the hotel feeling upset. Mona received me with an embrace. She did not ask anything, especially not why I looked worried. She sat me down on the side of the bed, removed my shoes and socks and began to massage my feet, gently, with light pressure. I lay back on the bed and stared at the ceiling. I sensed I was sinking down a deep well, from which there was no hope for escape. Something else I felt before I dozed off was Mona kissing the bottom of my foot.

I dreamt I was setting off for some war with a rifle in my hand. I exhausted my ammunition, left my post, and fled. I was leaping from one roof to another while my enemies pursued me. I encountered an artist, with whom I had only a passing acquaintance in the real world—we had barely said hello to each other—and asked him for a weapon. He took me to his car, where he pulled a bottle of perfume out of the glove compartment. After smelling its fragrance, my heart felt reassured, and my enemies disappeared.

I was awakened by the ring of my mobile phone. It was the executive editor Riyad al-Kayyad, who was beside himself with rage. He said the rabble on Facebook had exceeded all bounds by attacking the symbol of sovereignty—the head of state. So, I promised I would open Facebook and combat them. I almost hung up on him but instead waited till I heard him address someone else. Then he hung up on me.

It was after seven p.m., and Mona was seated on the floor, leaning back, chewing qat, smoking, and watching cartoons. I washed my face and scrutinized it in the mirror. Then I sat down beside her. She handed me a wad of qat. I set it aside and started to caress her. Another call from the executive editor—may God never create another person like him among the Muslims! He said the newspaper had rented a furnished apartment for me and that I was to move there in the morning. Then he gave me the address.

Mona asked me what was troubling me. I told her we would move tomorrow into a furnished apartment. In her eyes I saw a sorrowful look and on her sweet lips a suggestion of anxiety. I asked her, "Why are you glum?"

She drew a fervent sigh all the way from her ribcage and replied, "I'm afraid they will separate us."

The burst of pain I felt in my heart was like an electric shock. I was reminded that our situation was impossible, that we would, inevitably, be separated. I asked, "Do you love me, Mona?"

She responded, "I love you more than I love myself." I sensed the veracity of her words; she meant what she said. I removed the small box from my pants' pocket and opened it. I removed the cheap plastic ring from her ring finger and replaced it with the platinum one I had purchased for her. She leaned her head against my chest, and her tears flowed down it.

Thursday

Chapter 55

We ate our last meal in the hotel with voracious appetite and packed. Mona felt super and laughed at anything. On the way to our new apartment, we stopped at a bookstore, and I bought all the day's papers.

I told Mona that *al-Sha'b* had published my report about Shaykh Bakri and handed it to her to read. While she did, I flipped through *al-Nidal*, which was published in Hodeida. It had dedicated the two center pages to a lengthy interview with Jalila's attorney, Shu'ayb al-'Ujail. Skimming through this dialogue, I found my name mentioned slightingly in one of his answers. He referred to me as "an insect" and threatened to ask the public prosecutor to summon me for an investigation of my false representation, my fraud, and for misquoting of the words of the child Jalila in the interview I conducted with her. I did not have the patience to read any more. So, I put down the car window and tossed out the newspaper. I turned to Mona, who was looking at the color picture of the shaykh. What do you think of the report? It's all a shameless lie, isn't it?"

She bowed her head and replied, "I don't know how to read." Then I felt that I had unintentionally humiliated her by asking her to read something. I did not know how to apologize and was tormented by regret. So, I took the paper from her and tossed it out the window too. Then I took her hand and kissed it.

We entered the furnished apartment as the noon call to prayer was sounding. Mona said she had been in this apartment before, pointing out the kitchen, two baths, and three bedrooms, and providing some additional information. I was amazed that a village girl like her could have set foot in a place like this. When I inquired further, she refused to reply at first. When I pressed her, she said she had spent a night here with the shaykh. I asked her why the shaykh had brought her to Hodeida. She said that she had entered puberty two years earlier and that when the shaykh learned that she was menstruating he had taken her to a physician in this city and had her fitted with an intrauterine device.

I inquired, without hiding my anger, "Mona, when did that happen for the first time?"

She asked, "My periods?"

I countered, as I unintentionally spoke even louder: "No—that thing."

She looked far away and replied: "Five years ago." I realized then that he had begun having intercourse with her when she was only ten. Something snapped in my conscience, and the world seemed a very bleak place. I felt I was in the wrong—collaborating with the man who had robbed her of her virginity and her childhood. My eyes filled with tears, and my lips began to tremble, in spite of me. Turning my back toward her so she would not see how upset I was, I told her I would go buy some lunch and qat and left hastily. I sat behind the steering wheel and spread out a newspaper, which I pretended to read as my tears flowed spontaneously. I could feel her sense of subjugation in her words and the amount of pain sheltering behind her eyelids from five years of sexual assault and humiliation—a child in the bloom of youth, forced to endure terrors would be too much even for the hearts of adults to withstand. As if that weren't already too much, she had been forced to swallow her pain and the oppression inflicted on her silently without daring to complain to anyone.

My phone rang. I saw that the call was from my wife. I hesitated to take her call because my psychological state wasn't appropriate. At the last minute before she was going to hang up, I pressed on the button to take the call. She did not ask me how I was or when I would return. She blamed me and accused me of compromising her and ruining her reputation. We had a pointless debate. I tried to explain to her that this was a temporary situation that would be resolved soon, but she wouldn't listen to me. She kept trying to teach me a lesson. I told her that I had done what I did to make money. Her commentary on that was harsh: "Let them screw your butt then to make more money." That comment floored me. It wasn't like her. I knew how much she loved money. This language was borrowed from a different, middle-class person with leftist tendencies. She wasn't speaking to me from her own script; she was speaking with the voice of friends she had made during her years in university. She ended her condemnation by threatening that if I did not return the following day to Sana'a, she would take the children and move back to her family's house. Then she terminated the call. Her voice was harsh, denuded of any trace of affection. She had spoken in a commanding, defiant manner.

I purchased a bounteous lunch and high-priced qat. I wanted to bury my sorrows and quandaries by chewing qat, which would make me oblivious to the world around me.

Friday

Chapter 54

Mona woke me up very early—at three a.m.—and suggested we go to al-Kathib to eat breakfast there. She had prepared everything for this outing, leaving me barely enough time to wash my face.

There were no vehicles in the streets, and we reached the cape in minutes. There was a warm breeze from the sea, and she guided me to a little frequented part of the shore. We removed our shoes and street clothes and ran into the sea in our underwear. We immersed our bodies in the water, which was pleasantly cool. We swam and played around under cover of darkness. At dawn's first light we left the water, shivering from cold. We dried off and dressed, after changing into fresh underwear. We spread out a quilt and sat there to watch the sun rise.

Fishing boats were visible out to sea, and Mona placed her head on my lap, retreating into her own special world. I respected her silence, feeling that she wanted to preserve these moments in her memory as something precious—a happy memory that could not be effaced by future ordeals or the passing years. The sun, whose affection we sought, appeared first dark red—like coffee beans, but minutes later we started to sweat from its force and heat. So, we climbed back into the vehicle and departed.

Three vehicles were parked at a restaurant composed of beautiful, square-shaped pergolas. We chose one and sat down on its concrete benches. We could hear the waves, and that made us feel peaceful and tranquil. The young waiter, who was only nine, cleared his throat before intruding on our privacy. Then I gestured for him to approach. He asked us, "Butternut squash?"

I said, "Yes." Then he nodded and left. This restaurant offered only one breakfast. I asked Mona how she knew about this magical place, but she threw me a look of censure. I realized that I shouldn't distract her from the present moment, which was filled with delight and sweetness, by forcing her to recall a past I reckoned she wished to forget. She wanted to smoke a cigarette. So, I obeyed her request and fetched a pack from the car. We started smoking with satisfaction. I noticed that she was imitating the way I held my cigarette between the index and middle fingers of my right hand when I inhaled and then resting it between the divide between the index and middle fingers of my left hand. When I pointed this out to her, she retorted that I imitated many of her gestures. She was right. Without being conscious of it, we were both imitating each other's hand gestures, facial expressions, and even our respective vocal ranges.

The boy brought two fish that had been grilled over charcoal. They resembled a pair of juxtaposed skiffs immersed in red spices. They were accompanied by flat crepes with a bubbly upper crust—*khubz mulawwah*—a hot tuna, tomato, coriander, zaatar, and mint salad—*sahawiq*, and two cups of tea. We attacked the food like prisoners of war, leaving nothing for the cats that prowled around our nest. If the brass implements had been edible, we would have eaten them too; we were that hungry. I thanked Mona for choosing this place, because I had just eaten the tastiest meal of my entire life.

The boy returned with a plastic bucket for the empty plates and cups. Before he departed, we asked him for two more cups of tea. From her handbag Mona brought out hand sanitizer and a bottle of perfume. She washed my hands, and I washed hers. Then we spritzed perfume on our hands and clothes to kill the aroma of the fish.

We smoked another round of cigarettes, which we found had acquired a legendary taste after this unique meal. With an embarrassed look, Mona asked me what my wife's name was. Without meaning to, I touched the silver wedding ring on my ring finger. I had never mentioned to Mona I was married, but she had apparently figured that out. I said her name was Houriya. We fell silent, sensing suddenly the presence of a censorious phantom between us. The boy brought the tea and left.

She looked up and asked me, "Do you have children?"

"Three: Habel, Najat, and Karama."

"Their names are beautiful—especially Karama."

Her cheeks quivered, and she looked away, toward the sand that extended endlessly. I thought about Karama, a girl like the one whose honor the shaykh had violated when she was ten and kept as his concubine—a fact that all the inhabitants of her district knew. She brushed the edge of her left eyelid, perhaps to prevent a tear from escaping and falling to the concrete table. In a trembling voice, she asked, "Do you love her?"

I replied immediately, "Yes."

She lifted her cup and sipped slowly, holding the tea in her mouth. Then she began turning the cup around in her hands. "I've never heard you call her from the hotel or the apartment."

Closing my eyes, I said, "I called her yesterday."

She stared straight at me and asked, "Who is more beautiful: she or me?"

Her question seemed childish—or perhaps the problem was that I had forgotten her gender and that this was a common question for women. I happened to move my right foot, and it encountered her feet, which were raised and dangling. I sensed that she was tense and that her nerves were stretched like a meteor caught in the gravitational field of some planet.

I told her, "My wife was the most beautiful woman in the world until I saw you." I could tell from her face that she did not find my answer convincing.

She asked, "Is she a mountain woman?"

I laughed, confirming her guess. She unclenched her fist and requested: "Show me her picture."

Troubled by this request, I began tapping thoughtfully on the hard table. I was uncomfortable by the direction the conversation was taking.

I told her, "She is about my height and wears prescription glasses. She is full-figured and light complexioned. Her hair is black."

Mona took my hand and kissed it. She said apologetically, "Forgive me for comparing myself to your wife."

I kissed her hand, and my tongue proceeded down her wrist and forearm.

We toured Hodeida's districts by car, and from Suq al-Hunud I bought her a paper cone filled with jujubes as well as a garland of fresh jasmine blossoms, which she loved more than anything else.

The executive editor Riyad al-Kayyad called and asked me to turn on the radio. I did and selected the Sana'a station. The preacher delivering the Friday sermon was criticizing civil society organizations and characterizing their work as harmful to Islam, etc. I turned off the radio, and we returned to the apartment.

Mona opened the window that faced the sea and stretched out in bed. I wanted her very badly and removed her clothes. The voice of the preacher delivering the Friday sermon could be heard from a nearby mosque. He mentioned Salam Mahdi by name, calling her an infidel and an apostate from Islam. He labeled her murder a licit act. When I heard the preacher deliver this dreadful verdict against her, my agitated heart was filled with sympathy for her. I pictured her psychological state when she heard that hundreds of preachers had pronounced her an infidel in mosques throughout Yemen.

My lust slipped away. I withdrew, put my clothes on, shut the window, and turned on the air conditioning. I apologized to Mona and told her I needed some time to myself to write an essay for my daily column in *al-Sha'b*. She asked if I wanted some tea or coffee.

After thinking it over, I said, "Both!"

She laughed, kissed my cheek, and left for the kitchen.

I turned on my laptop and began to browse the news sites. I found an electronic campaign directed against the rights activist Salam Mahdi. These attacks varied between casting doubt on her, accusing her of treason, and outing her as an infidel. I went on Facebook, where the battle was even more horrific and the war drums were sounding ever more loudly.

Mona brought me the three glasses—one of tea, a second with coffee—and the third held cold water with ice cubes floating in it. Then she withdrew, on tiptoe.

I turned on some classical music and forced myself to write an essay for my daily column. I'm not sure when I finished it, but afterwards I threw myself on the bed and fell fast asleep.

I was changing clothes in a shared, student dorm room, and my roommates were doing the same thing when the alarm siren blasted a terrifying warning that an attack was imminent. I went up on the roof with another roommate, and then it became clear that I was living in a foreign city—in Europe—where there were bushy trees. The roofs of the houses were pyramidal and made of tile. When I looked up at the sky, I saw a hot air balloon shooting flames and dropping bombs on this city's residents. My roommate suggested we descend to the air raid shelter, but I objected and stood there, staring at the hot air balloon.

I was awakened from my dream by the telephone's ring. With my eyes closed, I crawled to the nightstand and felt its wood surface, searching for my phone. Once I found it, I turned it on. The caller was the executive editor Riyad al-Kayyad, the single greatest source of trouble in my life. The damn hot air balloon I saw in my dream may have symbolized him!

I asked curtly, "What do you want?"

"Sorry. I can tell from your voice that you were sleeping."

"Yes, I was experiencing a dream as sweet as honey."

"The young girl appears to have exhausted you! Ha-ha!"

"What's on your mind?"

"The Russian physician, Tatiana, is now in Hodeida."

"God willing, she'll drown in the sea. What is she to me?"

"Tatiana is a beautiful young woman with a complexion as white as snow. She has hair as blonde as gold. Your favorite type."

"How do you know what type of women I prefer? Have you been rummaging around in my heart?"

"By your Lord, Mutahhar! I'm like a father to you and know what's in your soul. Tell me whether you have had lunch?"

"No."

"Excellent. I want you to bathe, put on your best suit, and go to Rose Moon Park. You will find her there."

"What should I do?"

"I want you to interview her for the newspaper."

"But I don't know Russian."

"She knows some Arabic and English, and I leave the rest to you, Hero."

"Huh! An interview conducted in sign language!"

"Listen: I want you conclude the interview by inviting her to a sumptuous dinner. Demonstrate your Arab hospitality, Bro."

"What's the point of all this outlay?"

"Frankly, we want you to bond with her."

"What kind of talk is this? Has my body also become a commodity that is traded on your exchange?"

"Don't yell at me. I'm not the one plotting the strategy. I am just a pawn. Who do you think ordered that you be compensated with the beautiful girl Mona? Don't think you merely made a positive impression her. The dark gem who lay beneath you would have been traded back and forth in ancient times by kings as a precious delight common men were not allowed to touch."

"Was Mona was just a test to see whether I was willing to engage in extramarital affairs. Isn't that so?"

"Since you've cheated on your wife, how will it harm you to add one more woman to your list? Praise God, Bro. A thousand young men would covet what we're providing you."

"I'll do the interview for the newspaper. As for the rest: no. I'm sorry."

"Is this your best offer? The Shaykh will become angry and withdraw his present. In any case, you are free to do as you like."

He hung up on me without waiting for my response. He knew that his allusion to me losing Mona had touched a sensitive nerve. I opened the bedroom door and looked for my princess. She was sitting on the floor in the living room watching television. She had bathed and donned the stunning red dress we had purchased during our morning outing, and a fragrant perfume emanated from her. She told me she had been out and bought lunch from a nearby restaurant. The carryout plates were on the floor and had not been touched: rice, fish, and *fattah*: bread with clarified butter and honey. I looked at the clock; it was four-thirty in the afternoon. "Why haven't you eaten lunch?" I asked her critically.

She replied, "It wouldn't be a proper meal without you." I noticed that she had set a place for me. She continued, "I washed the qat and put it in the fridge so it wouldn't wilt." She moved closer to the dining mat and waited for me to sit down.

There was no way I was going to disrespect her plan. I told myself I would eat quickly and go out. She talked and ate, but truth be told I wasn't listening to her. I was preoccupied by suspicions that she was part of the vile conspiracy that had ensnared me. I thought she didn't love me and was an actress who had performed her assigned part brilliantly. A voice echoed in my head, repeating that she was cunning and that her deception had easily conned me. My mind entered a labyrinth of foul suspicions as I imagined nasty machinations. I decided privately that, when I returned, I would try to draw her into a conversation to discover how involved she was in the drama in which I had been cast.

I stood up abruptly and told her that I was going out on an important assignment and might be late returning. She was so surprised by my sharp tone and the change in my facial expression that her jaw dropped. She replied with a single word: "Fine" and bowed her head. She said no more but looked sad.

I removed all the money from the drawer, not leaving her a single rial. I returned to my room and prepared my briefcase for my assignment. Then I left the apartment without saying goodbye to her.

While I drove the car, crazy thoughts stormed through my head. I attempted to calm my nerves and expel the depressing suspicions from my mind. One of these ideas was to gun my vehicle, plunge into the sea at high speed, and drown myself.

I phoned the executive editor Riyad al-Kayyad, and he provided me with some advice. He asked me to purchase a chess set and commented that the Russian woman would not refuse if I offered to play a game with her. He told me she spent her free days at this park, smoking a hookah. He asked me if I had tried them, and I said: "No."

Then he said, "Then the time has come for you to try." He hung up.

I drove to a large bookstore in the Bab Mushrif market and bought the day's papers and a wooden chess set small enough to fit into my bag, which had started to resemble the belly of a woman in the last week of her pregnancy.

I parked my vehicle near the entrance to the park and applied some of the lavender cologne Mona had left for me in the glove compartment. I followed the executive editor's instructions to look for a guy named Iwad Abdallah. Once I located him, I introduced myself. Then he smiled at me and said he was at my service. I asked him to show me where a Russian woman was sitting and described her for him. With a smile that tilted to the right, he asked, "Tatiana?"

I replied, "Yes."

He told me, "Come."

He picked up a copper brazier, and I followed him. We headed to some concrete benches that were separated from each other by reed partitions a meter and a half high. These granted a person seated there a reasonable amount of privacy.

We reached the bench where Tatiana was seated facing the sea, smoking a hookah with her back to us. I asked Iwad to introduce me and tell her I wished to interview her for a newspaper.

Iwad went to her and placed fresh coals in the container on top of the hookah. Then he leaned forward and whispered to her while gesturing toward me. She rose and looked at me. She seemed perturbed as if she didn't know how to reply. I drew the best smile from my quiver, clasped my hands together and bowed entreatingly. My gesture succeeded in melting her reserve, and she welcomed me with a gesture of her hand. I asked Iwad to bring me "light" nargileh, and he started to laugh! I did not know whether I should offer to shake her hand; so I introduced myself, personally and professionally. I handed her my card that identified me as a member of the International Federation of Journalists. She accepted it and proceeded to read it attentively. Then she returned it to me and shook my hand heartily and invited me to have a seat. I explained to her that I would like to interview her regarding the case of the girl Jalila. She drew her head back as she reflected. Then she looked me in the eye again and said, "OK." I praised God privately that I had just overcome the largest stumbling block in my assignment. I turned on the recorder and asked her ten questions. The interview, which was conducted entirely in English, lasted half an hour. Then I inquired whether I could photograph her. She did not object. So, I photographed her from in front and both sides. She remarked jokingly that I was photographing her the way the police photograph a criminal! She was extremely beautiful. A lovely she-genie from the storybooks! I was incredulous that such exceptional beauty had escaped the eyes of the world to be buried in a small country far from her homeland.

I was ready to leave then but she told me: "You haven't touched your nargileh!"

I replied, truthfully: "I'm afraid I will disturb you with my smoke."

With a merry expression on her face, she said, "I won't be disturbed if the smoke only comes out of your mouth and nostrils."

I laughed wholeheartedly. Then I inhaled a few times extremely cautiously. Nevertheless, I was overwhelmed by a mighty cough, my eyes protruded, and I almost checked the box Tatiana had warned me not to. But God smoothed over everything. I did not need to bring out the chessboard, because she had an excellent sense of humor, and her spirit was lighter than a morning breeze.

We were surprised when the sun set, because we hadn't felt time passing. When she prepared to depart, I invited her to dinner. But she rejected my offer, explaining that she needed to return early to the town of al-Jurum. I took a risk and offered to drive her there in my car. She agreed to let me take her as far as the depot for the Peugeot vans, where she would catch a shared taxi.

I winked to Iwad for him to alert the cashier that everything should be charged to my (government) account. When Tatiana reached the till and opened her handbag to pay, the cashier told her that her bill had already been taken care of. Then she chastised me and said she would like to pay for herself. I told her that I was indebted to her for agreeing to the interview without any prior notice.

We climbed into the vehicle, and I took her to the depot. Travelers had deposited their bags along the sidewalk, because the Peugeot vans had been deserted by their drivers. The situation was totally abnormal. I climbed out with Tatiana, and we learned that the drivers were on strike and demanding that their union raise the rates. Tatiana looked anxious, and she started to bite down on her lower lip. I could tell from the look in her eyes that she was afraid of spending the night far from her residence in al-Jurum. I repeated my offer to her, and her pride prevented her from accepting. She refused and said she would look for a hotel. I entreated her and insisted, Finally, she relented after she noticed that several travelers had stopped to stare at her. Her beauty merited their attention.

She climbed back into my car, and we headed to al-Jurum. Before leaving the city of Hodeida, I purchased some shawarma sandwiches, which we ate in the SUV. I told her about my work at the newspaper, and she told me about her job at the hospital. We exchanged telephone numbers, and our friendship was consolidated. Praise to God for this success! Luck had served me by allowing me to appear a chivalrous gentleman in her eyes.

I returned to the apartment at 11:30, and Mona was still awake. She opened the door for me before I could put the key in the lock. She embraced me longingly and helped me remove my shoes and socks. I treated her coldly and entered the WC without saying a word. When I emerged from it, she said that dinner was ready. I told her I had eaten dinner. She followed me, humbly and downcast, unnerved and disheartened by my sudden hostility toward her. I told her I was tired and would go straight to sleep. I turned out the light and stretched out on the bed. In fact, I was exhausted, and it took me less time to fall fast asleep that it would take to blow out a match.

Saturday

Chapter 53

When I woke at nine a.m. my eyes were swollen from having slept so long! I flipped over to Mona's side of the bed but found she wasn't beside me in bed. I felt the mattress and found it was cold there. I searched my phone but didn't find any missed calls or texts messages. Speaking frankly, I admit I was expecting to find a text from Tatiana thanking me for the ride.

When I opened the bedroom door, I was surprised to find Mona asleep on the floor of the living room. When she heard the door creak, she woke and sat up. She did not raise her eyes toward me. She reminded me of a dog guarding its master. I was overwhelmed by an enormous feeling of regret for the atrocious way I had treated her the previous day. My transformation from a madly infatuated lover who almost worshipped her to a rogue whose eyes were filled with doubt and jealousy had no doubt been a bitter blow for her. As I stood in the doorway, I gazed at her and silently found fault with myself. I was waiting for a word or look from her to abandon my froideur and advance toward her apologetically, but she ignored me and concealed her apprehension behind her fingers. When she could bear it no more and raised her head wanting to see me, I approached and sat down facing her.

I asked her, "Why didn't you sleep on the bed?"

She turned her face away and replied in a weak, broken voice, "I felt you wanted that."

I would have liked to say something and defend myself, to deny that, but was not capable of mistreating her; the scent of weakness emanating from me was detectable in every breath I exhaled. I drew her to my lap and embraced her. Then she burst into tears and sobbed. I dried her tears, humored her, and suggested that we breakfast in the sand dunes. Then she came back to life, and a smile returned to her face.

I entered the bathroom and shaved. I was bathing and my body was wet with suds when Mona knocked on the door to tell me my phone was ringing. I told her I would deal with it once I had bathed, thinking that the caller was either the executive editor Riyad al-Kayyad—and this was impossible because he would not wake in the morning even if people kidnaped his mother—or it was my wife! I was feeling upset when I emerged from the bathroom. Then Mona handed me the phone. The caller had been none other than the executive editor. I dressed quickly as my level of anxiety rose. Mona had readied herself quickly, put on her jacket, and picked up her handbag as joy pulsed in waves through her. I embraced her, kissed her on the mouth, and for some moments forgot my separate existence as we merged into a single being more exalted, noble, and pure than anything I could be alone. The executive editor interrupted me—may God never reward him—by calling again. He asked in a gruff, grumpy voice: "Are you still alive? Open the internet and read the news!" Then he hung up. This time the matter seemed important. I picked up my laptop, and we left the apartment.

The sun was radiating heat and dazzling light. I turned on the engine and the air conditioning and was about to drive off when the executive editor Riyad al-Kayyad rang again. "Listen, I want you to write an immediate rebuttal of the news."

"What news?"

"Good morning! Are you drinking?"

"Not right now. Tonight, God willing."

"Son, you are a born alcoholic. There's no need for you to add any more moisture to your wet clay!"

"Some of it's from you!"

"Your tongue's grown as long as a cat's tail! Fine, that's why we need you. Shove your tongue at them till it drags on the ground. I'll call you again in half an hour."

He hung up. I apologized to Mona and explained we would not be going to al-Kathib. I informed her that developments required me to stay in the apartment and work. She tried to hide her disappointment and said she would make me bean sandwiches and a cup of coffee.

We returned to the apartment feeling defeated. I turned on my laptop and started to browse the net. I found that several Arab newspapers carried stories about the rape of the girl Jalila in their editions for the day and a brief report on the human rights activist Salam Mahdi being declared an infidel because she supported the raped child. The biased slant of these news reports was not encouraging, and the source of these stories was a reputable international news agency. I followed this coverage in English and was thunderstruck to find that more than five hundred news agencies and foreign newspapers from five continents had published the story. This meant that the case had gone international and spread beyond our limited local region.

An hour elapsed as I moved from one site to another. The executive editor appeared to be busy with something besides me, and that was good, because he was shredding my mind with all his calls. Mona took my empty coffee cup, and I asked her to fix another one.

I was smoking ravenously now that my nerves were shot. I quickly drafted a bombastic news release that denied the accusation against Shaykh Bakri Hasan and affirmed that the person accused, according to the police investigations was a teenage boy who was still a fugitive from justice. I denied that the advocate Salam Mahdi had been declared an infidel. I mentioned that imams in some mosques might have raised concerns about her conduct, without stooping to the level of mentioning any woman by name. I reread my draft several times and deleted the personal references to Salam Mahdi. Then I emailed my release to the executive editor.

I went next to Facebook, where our front was looking feeble while the other side was advancing forcefully and confidently, garnering unprecedented sympathy. I entered my Twitter account where I found demoralizing tweets, including this one from a friend: "The people who have dragged Mutahhar into the case of the girl Jalila want to destroy him in order the avenge themselves on his late father." This friend's words stung me like a bee sting that had penetrated my skin and infected it.

It was past noon and the sound of the call to prayer rang out from nearby mosques when Mona brought my third cup of coffee. Then I gave her some money to buy us lunch and qat. The executive editor Riyad al-Kayyad rang me while I was nervously waiting to hear what he thought of my release.

"You did great! I shake your hand firmly."

"I think the release should be translated to English and distributed to the international news agencies."

"We've just finished having it translated and will send it out in an hour."

"Excellent."

"What did you do about the interview with the Russian woman?"

"I'll finish that this afternoon."

"Send it in the way it is—in English. Send it, and the translation department will edit it."

"Won't it be published in Arabic?"

"No, we will publish it in the magazine "The Queen of Sheba" and not mention your name."

"Whether my name is on it or not doesn't matter. The important thing is for me to receive several copies of the magazine to serve as my excuse for contacting her again."

"Don't wait for the issue to appear. Devise any pretext to stay in contact with her. By the way, your bill for the meeting with Tatiana has been paid."

"Great."

"You have another assignment now."

"May God grant that it is for the best!"

"Ha-ha! Don't get your hopes up. This time the interview is with a man with mustachios long enough to link Asia and Africa."

"So, I guess he molests boys."

"Mortada Abd al-Jabbar is the toughest colonel in the police. The Minister of the Interior personally selected him to track down the accused boy in the lands of the Banu Musa'ib."

"When will he be appointed?"

"The decision to name him Chief of the Bab al-Minjal Police Department was made recently. He is on his way now to the airport or he may be soaring in the air. You need to welcome him at the Hodeida Airport and take a statement from him."

"What about Colonel Ahmad Fatini?"

"He has been placed in retirement. The change will occur today, as well as the transfer of command from him to the new Chief. . . . Where are you now?"

"In the apartment."

"Head immediately to the airport."

I did not know whether I should wait for Mona to return or depart. If she had known how to read, I would have left her a note. When I returned, I intended to buy her a cellphone and a SIM card in my name—exactly for situations like this. I told myself that I was pressed for time and sped downstairs. I drove the car recklessly toward Kilometer 16.

I passed through the checkpoint and entered the airport. The parking spaces were empty. Five vehicles were parked near the gate of the only waiting room, and the few porters resembled flies beating their heads against glass. When I stepped out of my airconditioned vehicle, the scorching heat from the asphalt was so heavy my hand could almost grasp it, and I felt that my face was roasting.

I strolled to the waiting room, expecting it to be airconditioned, but it wasn't. I asked when the plane from Sana'a was arriving. They told me it would land in ten minutes. I looked through the glass at the runway. There were no planes there—except for an old, brokendown plane, which resembled a dead mule.

The plane from Sana'a arrived an hour and forty minutes later. Since there was no bus from the plane to the terminal, passengers walked that distance. I recognized the colonel easily by his uniform, which had stars that glinted in the sunshine. Executive Editor Riyad al-Kayyad had lied to me or had never met the colonel in person, because Colonel Murtada Abd al-Jabbar had not a single hair beneath his nose. Both his chin and his lips were cleanshaven, and his face was as smooth as a mirror. Two other surprises were his dark brown complexion and his pot belly, which resembled a balcony. He did appear to be someone with a forceful personality. I rushed to greet and introduce myself to him. He embraced me very warmly and kissed me on the cheek. This was off-putting for a typical Yemeni man, because what we normally do is touch cheeks and send kisses through the air. I asked if he would provide me with a statement while we were standing, and he suggested that we sit down! He explained that he would need to sit in the waiting room of the airport until his car and guards arrived from Sana'a. I recorded his statement and took some photos of him. He asked to see them. So, I sat beside him and began to display them. Then he placed his hand on my thigh. His fingers weren't cut from the same cloth as his stern, military appearance.

They were short and round, in fact supple and soft enough to belong to a young woman! When his fingers slipped down inside my thigh, I couldn't take any more and stood up and prepared to depart. He invited me to have lunch with him, but I apologized that I needed to dispatch news of his appointment as quickly as possible to the newspaper. When he asked me to select the best pictures, he winked.

As I left the airport, I remembered that, in jest, during our telephone conversation about him, I had suggested to the executive editor that he was a pedophile. Now that I had met him, I felt my hunch was correct!

I passed by a kiosk and purchased the day's papers. Then I stopped at the first shop that sold phones. I purchased a first-rate phone for three hundred dollars as well as a SIM card. The vendor promised he would have the SIM card ready in an hour.

I returned to the apartment. Mona wasn't there. I searched all three rooms. Then I entered the kitchen and found that she had bought lunch and the qat, but had just left things there and departed. I felt anxious and depressed. What had happened? Frightening suspicions assailed me. I decided to go down and drive around streets in the area searching for her. I wished at that moment I had a revolver. A disturbing thought occurred to me: a miserable gang of supporters of that leftwing teacher Husayn al-Battah might have kidnaped Mona to present her to the international media as a young girl who had been subjected to sexual exploitation. A treacherous accusation like this could ruin my career and destroy my family's reputation forever.

As I was descending the stairs, barely able to see where I was going because I was so upset, my phone received a text message. I opened it and found it was from Shaykh Bakri Hasan: "Excuse us, Sir. We have taken Mona temporarily. We need her for my sister's wedding, which will take place next Thursday. She will return to your service on Friday. We hope you will be able to attend the ceremony."

I sat down on the stairs as contradictory feelings assailed me. I was happy that Mona was safe. I mocked myself for thinking that an assemblage of fools would kidnap Mona and employ her as a card in the struggle.

I returned to the flat, feeling lonely. I was overwhelmed by a deep, indescribable despair. Words could not express what being parted from Mona meant to me. I saw her in every corner of the apartment. These images wounded my memory, which began to bleed the beautiful moments we had experienced together: her words, her touch, the way her slender body swayed, the coquetry of her gestures, the grace of her walk, the sweetness of her spirit, and her light sense of humor. I lost my appetite and put the food in the fridge. I rinsed the qat three times and then sat down at my laptop. I placed my fingers on the keyboard but could not move them. My right hand had gone dead. I rested my cheek on my left hand and wondered whether this was my real life or a troublesome dream?

Sunday

Chapter 52

My phone rang nonstop for twenty minutes. I felt anesthetized—conscious of my surroundings but paralyzed. I found it hard to open my eyes. The sun's light dazzled my eyes and gave me a headache. I remembered tossing and turning on the bed for hours without dozing off for a second. The insistent caller was the attorney Hammoud Shanta, who brought me up to speed on the latest developments. He told me that Jalila's lawyer, Shu'ayb al-'Ujayl, had obtained from the public prosecutor a writ summoning me for a deposition regarding the charges made against me of deliberately altering the statement of the girl Jalila with the intent of perverting justice, in the interview I conducted with her and published in *al-Sha'b* newspaper. He reassured me that I could avoid it, if I wanted, but should avoid setting foot in the building housing the public prosecutor in al-Jurum. He also said that this impudent attorney had submitted a memorandum to the court requesting that Shaykh Bakri Hasan be barred from leaving the country. Enraged, I asked him, "And you? What are you going to do about that? Will you stand by and watch them give us a drubbing?"

He replied that his efforts were focused on delaying the transfer of the case file from the public prosecutor to the court. He said that the judge of the court in al-Jurum was a senile old man who had been left behind after the Ethiopian invasion of Yemen in the sixth century CE, that he lacked "flexibility" and wasn't "cooperative." Then Hammoud Shanta asked to meet me, saying he would be in Hodeida that afternoon to take care of some business and would be available once his chores were finished. I begged off, saying I would be busy writing my daily column for *al-Shaʿb*. He asked me to name a time. I responded, "Let's leave that open."

He then made a remark I didn't fully comprehend: "Only blindness and deafness come free."

I asked, "What do you mean?"

He said: "Just look around you. You'll see what I mean. Goodbye."

I headed to the kitchen and stood at the refrigerator while I held its door open and consumed whatever I found on the shelves. I was so hungry I was trembling. I had not eaten a bite since the previous morning. Since I did not feel like remaining in the apartment, I evacuated my bowels, but did not shave or wash my face before I left.

I shot off in my car to a nearby bookshop on Harbor Street and bought the day's newspapers. Then I headed to the Corniche where I parked near the shore. I turned off the air conditioning and put down the vehicle's windows to allow the warm, humid breeze to provide a sauna and restore life to my circulation.

All the government papers printed the news about the appointment of a new chief of police for Bab al-Minjal and published his picture. At the end, these stories had a passing reference to the early retirement of his predecessor for negligence in fulfilling his studies. I studied the new chief's face again; he was neither handsome nor ugly, but there was something about his mien that did not please the eye or reassure the heart. I reflected that they might have selected him for his dark complexion, wishing to give people the impression that he was a native of the coastal region. I heaved a sigh when the image of Colonel Ahmad Fatini flashed through my imagination. I had no doubt ruined his life, but that was inevitable. Circumstances had placed us on different sides.

The opposition newspaper *al-Ayyam* republished the report from the international agency and included a supplement about declarations of apostasy in Yemen. The Hodeida newspaper *al-Nidal* had wide journalistic coverage about the investigation of Jalila's case—including a scathing attack on Shaykh Bakri Hasan published under the nom de plume of "the Hodeida Rose":

Around the residence and farm of the shaykh hover girls between eight and fourteen. Their faces are covered with makeup to lighten their complexion, their lips are a shocking red, and they carry little handbags. These very young girls, dispatched by their impoverished families, are easy prey for Shaykh Bakri Hasan, who loves to have sex with underage girls and gives them large sums of money in exchange for deflowering them.

This daring column was by someone who seemed to be a local from the Bab al-Minjal region itself and knew precise details about the private life of the shaykh. I reckoned the author might be Sami Qasim. If he had written the column, he had just dug his own grave with his pen. I tossed the papers under the seat and tried to call my wife to reassure myself about my children, but she did not pick up. I took out my laptop and browsed the net. I opened YouTube and found numerous TV interviews that local and international satellite channels had conducted with the girl Jalila and the rights-activist Salam Mahdi. These interviews had a high number of viewers. I watched all of them and noticed that Salam Mahdi was deliberately inciting public opinion against the authorities. The attacks against the government on Facebook were continuous, and the balance of the battle had shifted to their side since that ill-omened news was published.

Time passed quickly, and now the sun sat securely on its throne in the middle of the sky. I was hungry and had been waiting for noon to arrive for some time. It was stupid, but I felt uncomfortable going to a restaurant early. I drove till I found a restaurant that looked crowded. This is a practical guide to the excellence of its food. I ordered *hanidh*: braised chunks of lamb, with rice. I received a call from a number I did not recognize, wiped my fingers on the paper napkin, and answered. The caller was Colonel Mortada Abd al-Jabbar, who thanked me for the news release and the handsome picture published in the newspapers. Then he said he was happy to bring me great news: "We have captured the suspect Ata al-Musa'idi who is accused of raping the girl Jalila."

I congratulated him on this significant accomplishment. I was about to say: "And I send you a firm handshake," but pulled the words back off the tip of my tongue. He asked me if I was coming to the station for this scoop. I asked, "When did you arrest him?"

He replied proudly, "An hour ago. Our patrol spotted him when he came to Wadi al-Dud. We pulled him out of the water naked. Ha-ha!"

I told him jestingly, "I'll come, but on condition that the boy has put his clothes back on."

He replied in a softer tone: "His body is beautiful. You'll enjoy seeing him naked!"

I finished my meal and drank a bottle of sparkling water to help me digest the lamb I had eaten. I started my car and shot off toward the town of al-Jurum. From there I headed to Bab al-Minjal. I reached the police department and drove inside the courtyard.

Colonel Mortada Abd al-Jabbar was in the interrogation room questioning the boy al-Musaʻidi, and the soldier refused to let me enter. I expected to hear screams and cries for help if he was being tortured, but the silence was absolute. It was so total it was frightening. The soldier graciously ordered me to wait in the office.

I headed to the office but could not bear to sit down. I was anxious for the boy, especially since I sensed the Colonel might be sexually aroused by lads. Strolling the corridors of the police station, I spotted the massive black policeman of Akhdam heritage in a holding cell. I greeted him, but he did not reply and looked away. He seemed to recognize me. That column about Colonel Ahmad Fatini must have reverberated throughout this region. I asked the soldier on guard duty what the prisoner's name was, and he said, "Saʻd Musa." Then I brought out my camera and took his picture. When he saw the flash, he realized what I was doing and became enraged. He tried to attack me like a jinni, and I moved away from the steel bars in alarm. The nasty insults he hurled at me shook the walls of the police station, and my heart began pounding with terror. He was shaking the bars, trying to pull them loose. Even the guard sensed the danger and grabbed his rifle, which he loaded threateningly, attempting to subdue his prisoner's rage.

I fled to the office with a dry throat. Colonel Mortada Abd al-Jabbar caught up with me there, sweating profusely. He opened a small fridge and brought out three cold bottles of mineral water. They were so cold that slivers of ice were forming in them. He offered me one. The second was for his assistant and the third he kept for himself. After we had a sip, he smiled and made a triangle on the desk with his hands.

Then he said, "I have good news for you: the accused, Ata al-Musaʻidi, has confessed and we have recorded his confession in the official report."

Observing the assistant's furtive, straying glances, I exclaimed: "So quickly!"

Colonel Mortada laughed and replied, "I have a tried-and-true method that makes any accused person confess to committing whatever crime I suggest."

Hideous forms of torture flashed through my mind. I brushed them aside and tried to gain control of myself so he wouldn't notice the effect his words had on me. Then I said, "The news will be printed in all the paper tomorrow."

He raised his arms, flexed his muscles like a wrestler demonstrating his strength, and said, "Print my names in large letters, because the credit for solving this case goes first and foremost to me."

I rose, starting to feel nauseous, and said, "I want to take some pictures of him to publish with the news." He narrowed his gaze, emitted a little snort that was accompanied by a fleeting, smarmy smile, and asked his assistant to accompany me to the interrogation room.

The soldier opened the door for us as my heart began to beat faster. I entered and saw Ata curled up in a corner like a frightened caterpillar. His face had turned yellow, and the blood had drained from it. I asked the assistant to leave us alone for a few minutes. He stroked his shoulder as if afraid of losing its single star and objected: "That's against the law."

I scolded him, glaring at him obstinately: "Brother, leave. You're keeping me from doing my job."

He lowered his gaze, cleared his throat in an embarrassed way, and said, "I'll tell His Excellency."

I took out my camera and prepared to shoot a picture. The boy was watching me with eyes filled with tears. I told him I wished to take pictures that would be printed in the newspaper. There was no reaction from him. I asked him to stand up, but there was no response from him. I told him if I photographed him in this demeaning and pathetic posture and published that picture in the newspaper, readers would get a poor impression of him and his people, the Banu Musa'id. Some concern showed in his eyes. I continued: "I want your picture to show you in the paper as noble and honorable." He seemed to have finally heard what I was saying. Spotting a bottle of water in my bag, he asked to use it to wash his face. I handed it to him. When he had finished, I handed him a paper napkin to wipe his face. He rose, trying to hold himself together, even though he was physically and mentally exhausted. That was obvious in how he moved. I took four pictures and stopped.

He retreated to the corner. I squatted beside him and whispered, "Did they torture you?" He nodded his head in the affirmative. I asked, "What did they do?"

He needed to vent his travails to anyone and spoke in a broken voice, trying his hardest to keep from weeping: "They fettered me, stripped my clothes off, threatened me, and I fainted."

Glancing at the door and hoping no one was listening, I asked: "What did they threaten to do?"

He replied in a tearful, quavering voice: "They threatened to sodomize me."

I felt that someone had hit me over the head with a hammer and struggled to control my feelings. "What happened then?"

As tears flooded his cheeks, he said, "They poured water over me and continued to ask me to confess, but I refused. When I felt **it**, I passed out again. When they poured water over me, I came to. Then I confessed that I had assaulted Jalila."

I wiped away the tears that had formed around my eyes, kissed him on the forehead, and left. My steps were so unsteady I almost fell and was forced to steady myself with my hand to keep from falling.

Monday

Chapter 51

I found an email from my wife asking for money. I began cursing her as if she were standing before me. I had already given her a sum equivalent to eight months of my salary, and she had spent it in two weeks. Bloody hell! I tried to phone her, but she didn't answer. I had no appetite for breakfast. I turned on my laptop and looked over the internet site for the newspaper *Al-Sha'b*. I found that my material had been published as important news: "Arrest of Ata al-Musa'idi for taking indecent liberties with the minor girl Jalila establishes innocence of Shaykh Bakri Hasan of the charge of rape." The photo of Ata did not show up on the site; the internet connection was lousy. I decided to go out to buy the papers and some qat.

I passed by a supermarket and purchased several boxes of chocolates. Whenever I felt hungry, I ate some. Seated behind the steering wheel, I flipped through the papers. The picture they had printed of Ata was not the best one. I thanked God they hadn't printed it upside down— something done occasionally to rape victims. I leafed through the Hodeida paper *al-Nidal*, which contained information about Ata's arrest and concerning a demonstration planned for this morning in front of the public prosecutor's office in al-Jurum. The executive editor, Ghalib Zubayta, had written an editorial denouncing the entanglement of young Ata in Jalila's case. He mentioned that the boy's confession had been obtained from him by torture. I felt a kind of curiosity to meet this journalist who had demonstrated a lot of courage in siding with the child Jalila, or at least to see him from a distance, since we lived in the same city. I checked Google to see if I could find a picture of him but was surprised to find very few results for him. He seemed to have sprouted overnight.

I called Nasama, the executive editor's beautiful secretary, and she told me that Mr. Riyad al-Kayyad sent me his greetings and wanted me to go to an address she then gave me.

I started the car and drove immediately to that address. I tried to figure out what was up, but my mind did not proffer any reasonable explanation. I reached the Bab Mushrif Market and, with some difficulty, after numerous attempts, located a wholesale distributor of foodstuffs. I disembarked and found the Hajji whom the secretary had described to me. He was seated cross-legged on a daybed with a rope seat, smoking *titin*, a type of tobacco with an unpleasant, acrid aroma that streamed out of the shop into the street like a swift racehorse. I asked him for "the consignment," and he requested my identity card. I handed it to him, and he examined my photo for a long time before returning it to me. He called one of his "boys" and whispered to him. The worker returned in a minute with a carton sealed with brown tape. I opened the rear door of the vehicle for him, and he shoved the carton inside and walked away. I thanked the Hajji—not knowing what I was thanking him for—and departed.

Once I had driven a safe distance, I pulled the car to the side of the road, because curiosity was killing me. I got out and opened the carton. I could not believe my eyes. The gift was not only precious; it was beyond my wildest dreams: twelve bottles of vodka. The noon call to prayer suddenly erupted. I began to tremble, feeling that the muezzin had caught me red-handed! I closed the rear door tight and drove the vehicle to an excellent restaurant. I was feeling hungry, and my tummy was purring happily.

That afternoon the executive editor Riyad al-Kayyad contacted me. The moment I answered his call, he began to laugh. I laughed too! Attempting to keep himself from guffawing, he asked, "How are you feeling"

"Sublime! You could use my brain as a nuclear reactor."

"Excellent, my boy. Wouldn't you like a drinking companion to share the pleasure?"

"Ha! Who?"

"Tatiana."

"I wish I could reach her, even on my hands and knees."

"God bless vodka, ha, ha. Why don't you contact her and invite her for a trip to Kamaran Island?"

"I doubt that she would agree."

"She will agree. We have learned from our sources that she has been wanting to visit Kamaran Island but hasn't been able to find anyone who will go there with her."

"Praise to God Who has exploited me for her!"

"I will transfer half a million rials to you to cover the costs of the trip."

"Ye-e-e-s! That large a sum could topple a fortress. Ha-ha!"

"Consider Tatiana the last of the Communist fortresses. Have at her!"

I called Tatiana. She had just left the hospital and was on her way home. I proposed the idea to her. She was hesitant and could not decide. She asked for time to think it over. I told her I would call back at nine that evening.

I went to collect the funds from the exchange company and transferred one hundred thousand rials to my wife's account in Sana'a. I did not do that because she had asked. That was for my children—because I wanted to hear their voices.

I passed by the supermarket and stocked up on food: various types of cheese, olives, mortadella, mixed nuts, and more boxes of fancy chocolates. I had a strong hunch that Tatiana would agree to the trip and that we would enjoy some excellent times in my apartment.

I ate at a restaurant that served a banana fritter casserole made with sesame oil. This is an astonishing dish that provides the body with lots of energy. I waited anxiously for it to be nine p.m. "Hands" was the wrong word for what was circling the clock. They were tortoises!

I dialed her number. She quickly responded. I realized that she had been awaiting our conversation as impatiently as me. She said she would go to the hospital the next day and submit a request for a one-day leave. If her supervisors agreed, then she was fine with going. I asked her when I should ring her again. She said at one p.m. I wished her a good night, and that was the end of our conversation.

Tuesday

Chapter 50

I learned from the internet that a huge demonstration had been staged in the town of al-Jurum and that demonstrators had encircled the public prosecutor's building and demanded the release of young Ata al-Musa'idi.

Colonel Mortada Abd al-Jabbar had anticipated the demonstrators and handed the boy over to the public prosecutor at seven a.m., absolving himself of any responsibility.

Some internet sites said that the crowds had attempted to storm the public prosecutor's building. During that scuffle, many people were injured. There were contradictory reports without any confirmation from independent sources. I opened the internet site of the newspaper *al-Sha'b* and found a column by the politics editor. He accused the opposition of aggravating the situation on the Coast. I told myself that the political editor's reaction and shrill rhetorical attack weren't based on nothing. Some clashes must have occurred. It was unusual for our political editor to turn his attention to local cases. This only happened rarely and indicated that matters were threatening to become dangerous.

I wrote an essay for my daily column and then called my wife, who did not answer this time either. I tried again using the SIM card I had purchased for Mona. This attempt succeeded, and she answered. But once she heard my voice, she hung up on me. I felt an enormous rage and began to think seriously of divorce. A rotten spendthrift, who could not hold on to money and who had driven me, against my will, to soil my hands and ignore my conscience, was now treating me disdainfully and faulting my conduct—as if I were filth that might stain her fragrant life. I reflected on our relationship and decided it was devoid of love and had survived as a duty, nothing more.

At precisely one p.m. I called Tatiana, and she replied cheerfully that the administration had granted her two days off. She added that her supervisor himself had suggested the extra day! She was delighted to have three days in a row to relax and recover her strength. She told me I was a lucky man, because her supervisor was a stubborn person who typically refused to give her any vacations. This time, though, he had unexpectedly seemed generous. We agreed that she would travel to Hodeida the next morning and I would meet her at the bus stop. From there we would go directly to al-Salif and hire a motorboat to the island.

I went out to have lunch at a restaurant and on the way picked up the day's papers. I was happy and didn't need anything external to cheer me. For a long time, leafing through the newspapers had been my favorite pleasure in life and to some extent I had become addicted to reading them and did not feel comfortable until I had a dozen or more under my arm. I would carry them home to keep up to date on current events and to read what the pens of political elites of different persuasions and parties were writing.

The sky clouded over, and rain poured down copiously. Then the weather changed and became nice. Cool refreshing breezes were blowing. I began to drive around in my vehicle to enjoy seeing the city after rain had cleansed it. I parked by the beach and placed selections of zither music in the cassette deck. I pulled out a cigarette and lit it. I took out the newspapers and began to leaf through them in an excellent humor. It felt to me that the world was proceeding down its destined course and that a man should accept the conditions placed on his existence without grumbling.

Wednesday

Chapter 49

I waited at the bus stop. Tatiana was late. I busied myself by cruising the net. At some distance from my vehicle, I noticed an electric transformer thirty centimeters from the wall. A young man in filthy clothes was kneeling behind it, pretending to urinate while instead displaying his tool within the eyesight of a swarm of young beggar girls. The windows of my vehicle had a reflective coating that prevented him from seeing me. The girls, who had noticed him, had averted their eyes. I felt disgusted and nauseated. There was a fleet of white clouds on the horizon. The summer rainy season would soon begin. I feared that the sky would darken at any moment and a rainstorm would blow in while we were on the water in the motorboat; then Tatiana and I would drown. I suddenly heard a tap on the window. I looked up and turned. It was Tatiana. I gestured for her to climb in on the righthand side. She opened the door, took her seat, and greeted me in Arabic. She had brought an athletic bag with a strap and a large water bottle. I turned on the car, and we shot off toward the harbor at al-Salif. I noticed that she seemed glum and was sighing. I felt that she must have encountered some problem.

I turned off the music and asked, "Are you okay?"

"Yes?"

"Are you having second thoughts about this trip?"

"Oh, no.... Forgive me. I didn't mean to look sad."

"What's happened?"

"Don't worry about it. It's not right for me to spoil your happiness."

"Please. I want to know."

"I'll give you a full account, because you're a journalist and may want to write about it."

She removed her sunglasses and began to clean their lenses with a cloth. Her expression was perturbed, and her eyes were swollen from weeping and red from a lack of sleep. She began: "Yesterday at two in the morning, they woke me and asked me to come quickly to the hospital. There was an emergency case—a seven-year-old girl had been raped. It's hard for me to relate the rest of the story, because it is so disgusting. I asked who had done this to her. A woman who had accompanied her said it was her husband. I started screaming at her like a mad woman, and my blood was boiling I was so furious. She had already lost a lot of blood when they brought her in. I did everything I could, but it was already too late. She died in my arms."

Tatiana began weeping and put her dark glasses back on, to hide her tears.

"I asked her who had done this to her, and she said, 'It was Abboudi,' meaning her husband Abdallah. I learned from her that she loved him! He had given her lots of money to buy ice cream, chocolates, and cookies. He had bought her a doll and marbles. She said he played with her and allowed her to invite the neighbors' daughters to play with her. She admitted that he would remove her clothes when those girls were present and explain to them how babies were conceived. She said that the last time the devil had caught him off guard and that he had injured her. Her friends—there were three of them—had seen everything. I told her he was a criminal and would be imprisoned. She defended his innocence. She said it wasn't his fault. . . it was the devil's. She asked for him and repeated his name as she was dying. Unfortunately she died without it ever occurring to her to think ill of him. The girl told me during the last moments of her life, with extraordinary joy sparkling in her eyes, that she could see children seize her hands, wanting to raise her up to play with them."

She turned her face away and wept.

She turned on her phone and showed me the girl's picture. She was a brown-skinned child with a rather long face, a wide mouth, and an upper lip that was fuller than her lower lip. Her nose was somewhat flat, and on her right cheek there was a small scar, a dimple from an old wound. It became her, making her look even more beautiful. I swallowed and wondered what Tatiana would think of me if she knew I was living with a girl who was only fifteen.

It took us an hour to reach the harbor at al-Salif. We hired a motorboat and set off. Because of the emotional maelstrom into which Tatiana had introduced me, I forgot to ask if she had eaten breakfast. Now that we were out on the sea, it was pointless to ask. Tatiana's face was as red at the flesh of a watermelon, and her face showed she had been crying. The boat belonged to a brown-complexioned young man with a bushy mustache. He watched us attentively with furrowed eyebrows. He seemed to be wondering whether I was kidnaping this white woman. I became even more nervous when I unintentionally broke the piece of wood I was sitting on.

Within a matter of minutes, we caught sight of the unpretentious buildings of the city of Kamaran, where a white minaret gleamed in the sunshine. The boat owner asked me, "What did you do to her?"

I replied, "Nothing. She's a doctor who works in the hospital at al-Jurum, and she's sad because a young girl died, and she could not save her."

He asked her in English if what I had said was true, and she replied that it was. I was surprised he knew English and wondered whether he had learned it from associating with foreigners, whom he took back and forth to the island. Casting me a look as penetrating as an arrow, he told me, "Praise the Lord, man. I was planning to throw you into the sea for sharks to eat, because I despise men who abuse women." He wasn't kidding and meant every word he said. His features attested to his zeal, courage, and dignity. The two creases around his lips afforded the impression of a forceful and determined personality. I was forced to confess I secretly envied him his toxic masculinity!

We reached the wharf, and I tried to pay him the amount we agreed on, but he refused to accept it. Pointing to Tatiana, he said, "In honor of this fine woman, the ride's on me." I tried to insist, but he cast me a fiery, threatening look. Tatiana thanked him, and we left. I hated him for showing me up as a dwarf devoid of virility.

Snapping photos, we walked down the community's streets, which seemed deserted. The houses, weighted by the burden of antiquity, spoke of declining economic conditions. The ancient wooden doors seemed to be weeping for the departure of the English colonizers from the island. The residents of the island now seemed to be few and sad. They had grown used to ignoring the tourists who rambled around their island without paying any attention to them.

We looked for a restaurant but could not find one. Passersby told us that on the north side of the island there was a camp with huts and lots of food for tourists. There weren't any taxis, and it was extremely hot. It would have been hard for us to walk all that way on foot. So we hired a boat to skirt the island.

The restaurant resembled an upside-down ceramic bowl with five or six arbors near it. We ordered fish with rice. They took their time preparing our meal. While heading back we amused ourselves taking photographs. Clouds that resembled a flock of sheep appeared, and the weather moderated as the temperature decreased.

Tatiana took a brief nap. They served us lunch that afternoon. We were almost faint from hunger by then. The owner of the boat we had hired ate with us. He was a boy of thirteen, or perhaps younger.

Then we continued our boat trip, feasting our eyes on the mangrove forest on the north of the island. We picked a suitable place and left the boat to walk. Thousands of crabs were strolling there to molt their shells. Sea turtles gazed at the horizon as if contemplating migration from the island. The beaches were so enchanting that anyone would wish he had a house or shack there and could spend the rest of his life in it. We took hundreds of pictures in an impossible attempt to capture this fascinating natural beauty.

By sunset, we had circled the entire island. Once we were near the town of Kamaran, the skiff changed course and headed toward land even as our eyes were trained on the island that we hadn't tired of admiring.

While we were heading toward Hodeida, I suggested to Tatiana going to the Rose Moon Park to smoke nargileh. She had no objection. Her mood had improved, and there was a gleam in her eyes from having achieved one of her cherished goals. The trip had washed the sorrows and bitterness from her spirit.

From time to time, I stole a glance at her enchanting face, which I never tired of regarding. There was a nobility to its lineaments, and her thick, level eyebrows suggested dignity and majesty.

Iwad, the waiter, greeted us warmly and selected an isolated spot for us, far from prying eyes. Then he brought us two water pipes from which wafted the fragrant smell of muʻassel. We discussed the late Soviet Union, and I told her that we Arabs look back at it with nostalgia and regret its passing. She said that Russians don't regret its demise. She used a comparison that I may not have grasped properly. She compared the former Soviet Union to a person who makes a show of being wealthy by spending his money on banquets while the members of his family are racked with hunger and forced to steal teaspoons from their neighbors!

Time passed quickly, and we both felt a desire to remain near the sea for as long as possible. Tatiana said she would like to fall asleep here to the monotonous roar of the sea. I said to her, "You must be used to snoring!"

She laughed and said she was from Saint Petersburg and that love of the sea was in her blood. I told her I was staying in an apartment that overlooked the sea and invited her to spend her holiday as my guest. Her cheeks blushed scarlet, and she was slow to respond.

I told her I knew magnificent beaches for swimming far from the city's hubbub. A gleam appeared in her green eyes, and I asked her encouragingly, "How long are you going to be satisfied with greeting the sea from afar? Let's do it! You'll have an opportunity to enjoy the warm sea water whenever you want."

She sighed gently with a slight nod of her head, announcing her consent in this refined, reserved manner.

We headed to the apartment, and I asked her on the way if she would like to dine in a restaurant. She said she would rather carry out shawarma sandwiches from the place we had previously purchased them. We went there and bought all we wanted. I passed by a bookstore and purchased the day's newspapers, not thinking I would have time to read them. This had become a habit that was hard to drop.

Tatiana inspected the apartment and liked it. She opened the bedroom windows overlooking the sea and, with her eyes closed, began to listen to the wash of its waves. That resembled a lover's whispers. When she entered the kitchen, she gasped with astonishment at the number of vodka bottles there. As I filled her glass, she exclaimed, "I don't believe I'm in Yemen!"

We ate our sandwiches greedily, standing up, as if we had just come from a famished land. I told her, in response to her statement: "If the sea were wine, the Yemenis would drink all of it in one night."

Tatiana laughed and replied, "On one occasion I visited the Russian ambassador in his residence and noticed that his bar lacked any alcoholic beverages. I asked him why, and he said he had invited Yemenis to a get-acquainted party, feeling confident that they were Muslims and did not drink alcoholic beverages. Then he discovered that they drank more than Christians and had drained all the alcoholic drinks he had stocked in his bar, not leaving him a single drop. He commented that his supply, which was intended to last for the next five years, was exhausted in two hours, and that his guests were still searching the bar, looking for more. He said that had it not been for diplomatic protocols, they would have searched his pockets!"

We spent an enjoyable evening by the window, which was open

to the sea. We did not turn on the air conditioner, enjoying instead the warm, sweet breeze wafting generously from our compassionate friend. We agreed that Tatiana would sleep in the bedroom and that I would sleep in the living room on a foam mattress.

It was a virginal night; there was absolutely no physical contact between us.

Thursday

Chapter 48

On opening my eyes, I looked at the clock. I went to the bathroom, where I shaved and bathed. I felt very energetic, and my morale was high. This was just the right humor to be in to write my daily column. So, I immediately began drafting it on my laptop.

I wrote two columns and saved them. Then I began a third. Ideas were traipsing into my mind with amazing alacrity. I was interrupted by the ringing of the apartment's doorbell. I opened the door and found Bakhit, the Shaykh's driver there. He gave me the Shaykh's greetings and handed me a sealed envelope with my name on it and a fancy box with a clear glass cover. Inside was a circular honeycomb the color of milky tea. This honeycomb was floating in honey the color of thick, red tea. Ali was licking his mustache with the tip of his tongue and ducked his head to the left once and then to the right as he tried to see over my shoulders into the apartment. This rude behavior was totally inappropriate, and my head apparently had become—so far as he was concerned—an obstruction or pillar that blocked his vision. I asked him to give my best wishes and greetings to the Shaykh and dismissed him. I closed the door in his face while he was still searching the apartment, using his brown irises in lieu of radar. This fellow provoked me and got on my nerves in a manner I did not understand. If I carried a revolver, I might have shot him without any regret. My desire to kill him tormented me like an itch in my brain and felt as real as a rough patch of skin. What, I wondered, did this scumbag know that made him feel entitled to act so insolently toward me? I was overwhelmed by a strong suspicion that his behavior served some purpose. From the Shaykh, or by some other means, he must have known that Tatiana was in the apartment with me.

I put the honey in the kitchen and opened the envelope. In it I found an ornate invitation to the wedding of the Shaykh's sister and a letter written in an elegant hand:

Brother Mutahhar Fadl, may God preserve you. With regards to the girl Mona, we inform you that my sister has bonded with her and wishes to retain her. You may have learned how trustworthy she is and what dedicated service she provides. With God's permission, my sister will move to her new husband's home in the city of Midi tonight. Mona will go with her. We will find an excellent servant for you at the earliest opportunity. Your brother, Shaykh Bakri Hasan.

This letter notified me that my separation from Mona was final. I felt as if a pane of glass had shattered in my spirit and serrated shards of that glass were slicing into my throat and windpipe, draining blood into my lungs. I could not speak or breathe. I left the apartment and walked toward the sea. I walked down to the beach and stood on sand as soft and smooth as Mona's enticing cheek. Each wave rose till it broke at my feet. Then it would retreat, whispering consoling words. The sun's rays fell directly on my bare head as sweat oozed over every hair on my body. I wanted to punish myself and plunge my silly head into the sea until it exploded. I was stung by regret and blamed myself for not fleeing with Mona to a city far from the eyes and antennae of the Shaykh. I was besieged by the thought that Mona deserved the sacrifice of my wretched, misspent life and that we could have traveled to any country in the world and begun a new life together, far removed from the spider's web that had prevented us from spreading our wings and flying free and instead bound us in its sticky, poisonous strands. Losing Mona was the worst defeat I had ever suffered.

I returned to the apartment feeling drowsy, my eyelids drooping, and I could scarcely keep them open. Tatiana began to speak to me with a towel wrapped around her head. I felt an irresistible urge to sleep. I entered the bedroom and dropped onto the bed like a dead man.

I experienced dense, obtuse dreams from which I could not break free. In each one, I found myself in desperate situations I could not resolve. I could not even utter a word. I encountered an extraordinary number of dreams that lasted millions of hours. I seemed to have expanded chronologically into a life lasting ten thousand years. Amidst this galaxy of dreams, I felt an intense heat that did not disturb me. In fact, I was refreshed by it and enjoyed it. I felt that I had finally been sent to hellfire to suffer punishment for my worldly deeds. An idea like a shooting star penetrated my consciousness and informed me I was melting down—like a star that was about to explode.

When I opened my eyes, I saw Tatiana withdrawing the syringe from my arm. I attempted to rouse myself but soon returned to my deep and troubled sleep.

When I woke, I found that night had fallen. I felt cold. The air conditioner was running, and the door and windows were closed. I was surprised to find that I was clad only in my underwear, because I did not remember removing my clothes before I fell asleep. I felt very energetic and mentally alert—with an enviable intellectual clarity. I remembered the nightmares that had beset me like a poorly cut movie in which scenes were so mixed together that it was impossible to decipher a coherent plot.

Tatiana entered the bedroom and appeared happy to see me sitting up. She turned on the light and approached me carrying a thermometer, which she placed beneath my tongue. When she drew it out, she said my temperature was 39 centigrade.

I asked, "What happened to me?" I poured myself some water and started to drink it, but she took the glass away from me.

She said I had suffered sunstroke and that my temperature had soared to 40.5 centigrade. She removed my clothes from a drawer and placed them on the bed. She said, "You were feverish and raving. I was forced to remove your clothing and lower your temperature by turning on the air conditioning full blast. I placed cold compresses on you. Then I went down to the pharmacy and purchased a 250 ml of a saline solution, which I administered to you."

I told her I was lucky to have had her in the apartment. But for her, I would have been roasted by my fever! In fact, had I been there alone, the angel of death would have dropped the final curtain on my life's futile melodrama. I was incapable of telling her this, even though she richly deserved this praise, for I really did owe her my life.

She said my phone hadn't stopped ringing and then left the bedroom.

I put on my clothes and drank a glass of water. My body was awake, and I felt more than usual energy pulsing through it. I seemed to have just emerged from Dante's purgatory—in other words to have been purged or purified, which of course is what my name, Mutahhar, means. Dante described purgatory in the second part of his famous book *The Divine Comedy*. I smiled when I realized the correspondence between my name and the name of his book.

Tatiana returned with my cell phone. All the missed calls were from executive editor Riyad al-Kayyad. God knows I saw him in hell; how was he able to escape the inferno and call me? Has Satan erected cell towers or run fiber optic cable for his estimable guests?

Tatiana inquired if I was hungry. Then I asked her if she had heard of the whale that devoured the Prophet Jonah.

She replied, "Yes."

Then I said, "If that whale were placed before me now in a skillet, I would devour him including his bones."

Tatiana laughed and drew me by the hand to the kitchen, where she had placed a table and two chairs and laid out a feast. She took some bread from the fridge and heated it. We ate it with honey, cream cheese, slices of mortadella, olives, and a variety of other dishes. Tatiana really liked the honey the Shaykh had sent and ate a large piece of the comb. We drank two glasses of vodka, and then I looked at my watch. It was ten p.m. I suggested to Tatiana going to the Rose Moon Park to smoke nargileh. She did not agree. She said it was too late. I apologized to her for wasting a day of her vacation by forcing her to look after me and provide me medical care. She told me I would make it up to her the next day—on Friday.

I had also missed the wedding of the Shaykh's sister. I had nourished a miniscule hope of seeing Mona there, even if only for fleeting moments, or at least of being able to gain a last wave of farewell.

Tatiana talked about her boss, saying: "He suggested I convert to Islam. When I told him I don't believe in any religion, he began to treat me more ferociously, refusing to grant me any holidays."

I told her, now that my mood had improved, "The next time he suggests you convert, you should agree but on one condition."

She inquired with interest, "What condition?"

I said, "That he leave Islam!" She laughed heartily. Then I told her, pretending to be serious: "You will be doing us Muslims a big favor if you relieve us of that individual!" We had downed an entire bottle of vodka by this time, and even the appearance of a fly before our noses was enough to produce gales of laughter. When it was bedtime, I forgot our pact and headed to the straight to bedroom, quite innocently, instead of the living room.

Since I am shy and find it hard to take the first step, this unintentional error benefited me, and I enjoyed one of the most delightful nights of my life. I remember the time, which was 10:10, as a good omen, when happiness welled between my lips.

Friday

Chapter 47

My son-of-a-bitch cell phone kept howling. So I rose and took it away while cursing the inventor of this device, which has destroyed the peace of mind of modern man and his happiness once and for all. I left the bedroom to avoid disturbing Tatiana. The wall clock in the living room indicated it was 12:30. This meant that most men in the city were in a mosque enjoying the Friday sermon.

The caller was the executive editor's secretary, Nasama: "A blessed Friday to you!"

"Humm. To us and all of you."

"Is Tatiana with you?"

"What are you saying? I don't know anyone by this name."

"Just a moment. Mr. Riyad al-Kayyad wants to speak to you."

I felt angry. How could this creature tell his secretary the most personal details of my private life? He was devoid of morality and paid no attention to the privacy of others! The executive editor's words were punctuated by a belch: "There are developments."

"For the good?"

"Tatiana must not return to al-Jurum."

"How so? Her leave ends today."

"I know. We'll think of a workaround. We still have a few hours."

"What has happened?"

"What's in play is the death of the girl with whom her husband tried to consummate their marriage."

"Tatiana told me that story. The girl was named Muhsina."

"Many worthless journalists are searching for Tatiana for her to corroborate their pipe dreams with her statements."

"What about the medical report?"

"It no longer exists."

"Tatiana has saved a picture of the girl on her phone."

"Hm . . . . This isn't good. Your assignment is to choreograph her movements and prevent anyone from getting near her."

"Understood."

"I'll call you back in an hour with your instructions."

He hung up on me. I suspect that hanging up on people is something he learned from **his** government handler. I felt anxious, and sick to my heart. I had been afflicted by one calamity; now a second disaster was being added to the previous one. I looked out the window at the street below and noticed a taxi parked in front of our building. Security forces had entered the fray; we were being watched.

I went to the bathroom, shaved, and showered. Then I entertained myself by scanning the internet while waiting for Tatiana to wake up. I clicked on various news sites but found no coverage of young Muhsina's case.

Tatiana appeared at the bedroom door and wished me a good morning. I advised her: "It's afternoon now!"

Fixing her disheveled hair, she asked, "Do we still have a deal?" I nodded in the affirmative, and she retreated, chirping what I assumed was a Russian song.

The executive editor Riyad al-Kayyad rang me earlier than he had promised: "What's your schedule for the day?"

"We're going south of Hodeida and getting out at a beach far from the city."

"Great! Don't leave any possessions of value in the vehicle. We'll send a couple of agents on motorbikes to steal Tatiana's phone. Don't forget to leave the doors unlocked."

"What if she leaves her phone in the apartment?"

"If she doesn't take it with her, contact me. Say: 'Bab al-Mindab.' Then we'll send someone to break into the apartment. He hung up, as haughty as ever.

My God! Thanks to my despicable betrayal of you, Tatiana, they're going to steal your cell phone. What a villainous wretch I am! After you offered yourself to me, Tatiana, I repay you by conspiring against you!

Tatiana brought me coffee and a pastry. I ate silently, incapable of looking into her serene green eyes, which were fit for an angel.

We took towels and large plastic bottles of water to use to wash the salt off our bodies after we swam. I was jumpy but tried hard to keep Tatiana from discerning that I was. She brought a bottle of vodka with her, some snacks, and placed her cell phone in her elegant purse before we departed.

I drove south till we were outside the city and beyond its suburbs and then chose an isolated beach. I mocked myself, thinking: *This is isolated enough to make the thieves' job easy!*

I parked the vehicle on a hill far from the beach. Tatiana removed her jeans and white blouse and ran to the sea in her underwear. I ran after her, leaving the driver's side door wide open, and removed my clothes near the water. The car key was in the pocket of my trousers. I swam after Tatiana.

We were oblivious to everything else while sporting in the water. With my body immersed in the water, I was able to enjoy the sun's rays, which I had learned to fear.

When we got out, we headed to the car, where Tatiana discovered that we had been robbed: her small purse had disappeared, and the glove compartment was open. We searched our remaining possessions, and she remarked that the thieves had also taken the bottle of vodka. I shouted without meaning to: "God curse them! Islam no longer exists in this country!"

Tatiana asked if I had lost anything from the glove compartment. "Some money: a hundred thousand rials."

Tatiana was sad I had lost such a large sum. I had lied about the amount so I might seem in her eyes to have also suffered. She asked me where the car keys were, and I said they were in the pocket of my trousers on the beach. Trying to console me, she said, "That's lucky. Otherwise, they might have easily stolen the car."

We washed with the fresh water, put our clothes on, and returned to the city.

I selected an elegant restaurant that served contemporary dishes. We were hungry, and our bellies were as hollow as jellyfish. We enjoyed the meal. Tatiana was happy and quickly forgot the theft of her phone. As we left the restaurant, the sun, which was descending toward the sea was beginning to remove her glowing garments in preparation for a swim.

We headed to the Rosy Moon Park and ordered apple mu'assel. We lovingly watched the sun set with reverent silence—as if seeing off a dear friend leaving on a journey. Tatiana looked at her watch, and said she wished to return to al-Jurum. I did not say anything then but asked to be excused to go to the restroom.

I called the executive editor Riyad al-Kayyad, wishing that I could curse him. He had forgotten to phone me while I was sitting on pins and needles with Tatiana.

"I have delightful news."

"What is it?"

"Tatiana, the rising, full moon, will remain in your embrace for an entire week, you rogue. Ha-ha."

"How? She wants to leave for al-Jurum now."

"We have arranged everything. Do exactly as I say. Tell her you spoke by phone with the hospital's director, Salim Muqahqah, and made a deal with him to write a laudatory profile of him and the hospital of al-Jurum in exchange for him granting Tatiana leave for a week. The written order authorizing the leave has been sent and will reach the exchange office at the depot around eight. You can go with her to pick it up. If she asks to return to al-Jurum to pick up some clothes or accessories, take her straight to the nearest shopping center and buy her whatever she wants. We will cover the bills."

"What if she insists on returning to al-Jurum? I can't compel her to do anything against her will."

"That's sissy talk, and I find disgusting it. Watch out, my son. Neither I nor you can control things in this country. If you want to help Tatiana and preserve her life, prevent her from traveling to al-Jurum."

I returned to Tatiana weighed down by worries. Her life was in danger, and I was not able to warn her. If anything happened to Tatiana, I would never forgive myself. I wished I had the courage to explain to her frankly what was happening and discuss the dangers encircling her as well as the despicable things I had done. But I am a coward who fears being killed, dreads poverty more than death, and cannot bear to lose his social status, which is now underpinned by corruption and dishonor. A man says: "It's just one small step and then the matter will be wrapped up." But a first wrong step leads to many others, and eventually we find we have lost our way and are wandering in a labyrinth.

I told Tatiana. She was incredulous at first and thought I was kidding. Then she asked me to swear a solemn oath, and I did. Contrary to my fears, she was happy and grateful. She said, obviously overwhelmed by emotion: "I provided medical assistance to you without expecting anything in return, but you're a chivalrous and generous man and return a single favor with two." As I listened to her words, I felt even more ashamed of myself. I wished I deserved the praise she was showering on me. Back when I might have deserved such praise, there was no occasion for it. Once destiny brought the opportunity, it was way too late.

At 8:30 I picked up an envelope with my name on it from the exchange office and showed Tatiana the official memo, which was signed and stamped, granting her leave for a week. Tatiana looked at the signature and confirmed that it was genuine. "Yes, this is his signature, which looks like nothing so much as a cockroach with antennae!"

I told Tatiana I had a second surprise for her, even though she had not requested it. I had decided to buy her a new wardrobe to recompense her for her stolen cell phone. I, myself, saw nothing wrong with exploiting the rogues I worked for and spending their money.

We headed to al-Mitraq Street and spent three hours shopping there. We bought cosmetics, shoes, handbags, pairs of jeans, and blouses appropriate for summer and others for winter, bras, changes of underwear, hair conditioner, and shampoos. I spent close to three hundred thousand rials.

Back in the car, Tatiana said with astonishment, "You bought me enough to last me for a visit lasting three years!"

I don't know how I blurted out: "I wish you would stay with me forever." Tatiana kissed me on the cheek, and all the way back to the apartment her cheek rested on my shoulder while she sang a Russian song with a beautiful melody.

Saturday

Chapter 46

At noon I received a call from executive editor Riyad al-Kayyad. An hour earlier I had sent him an invoice for the expenses, expecting him to admonish me for them—not because there wasn't enough money to cover the costs but because he was a jealous person who would envy me spending as if there was no tomorrow and enjoying the company of beautiful enchantresses as if I were Yemen's James Bond. In fact, his chest was filled with rancor and hatred because I had expected him to fork out the cost of my pleasures without him grumbling about them. "My son, what is this? You spend fifteen hundred dollars in one night!"

"Isn't the nation's honor worth that sacrifice? Huh?"

"My son, frugality is advisable in everything. If God were a spendthrift, He would have provided man with one tube for urine and a second for semen."

"But, how do you account for His granting man two testicles instead of just one? Huh?"

"You're a demon and will be my companion in hellfire, God willing."

"Speaking only for myself—I'd rather go to paradise."

"In your dreams, Mutahhar! You've purchased a ticket on a jumbo jet bound straight for hell and have a reserved window seat so you can see the sinners welcoming you there by raising their middle finger at you."

"Nonsense, I won't be able to see any finger they raise while I'm inside a jet plane at a high altitude!"

"My son, my son, don't you have any imagination? Pharaoh's middle finger, for example, after millennia of torture, will be the size of Great Britain! It's lucky you didn't try to write novels!"

"If I ever turn my talents to literature, I'll write a novel about you."

"I know, and you'll depict me as an effeminate Sodomite."

"No, I will portray you as a revolutionary combatant!"

"That's worse. My son, you are very evil."

"Assuming I do become an author, I will consider this statement of yours to be extraordinary praise for my talents."

"My son, the only thing you're good at is fucking women. That means even stray dogs share your special talent."

"All the same, any dog would hope to be in my place!"

"You're insulting me, Wretch, ha-ha. Your bitch is extremely beautiful. I saw a folder of photos of her on her phone. You ought to be paying us, you ingrate, ha-ha. Listen, you have a big assignment today."

"Almighty Benefactor!"

"Ha-ha. No more pillow talk for you! We want you to go

immediately to do a report on Dayr Bani Musa'id and interview their Shaykh."

"Praise the Lord! What has happened?"

"There's been a major development: three thousand men and women from the Bani Musa'id tribe announced yesterday that they are joining our party."

"What about Ata al-Musa'idi?"

"He was released an hour ago. All the charges against him have been dropped, and his name has been permanently expunged from that case."

"That means we're back to zero."

"Yes, and the Shaykh is a suspect again. We need to build a different defense strategy to win the case."

"Fucking prick! I've felt this case was ill-omened from the start."

"Ill-omened, how? What are you talking about? We have gained thousands of new supporters for our side, and painful blows are falling in quick succession on our foes' heads. Politics is a grist mill that never stops turning."

"Who negotiated this alliance with the Bani Musa'id?"

"Your uncle, Jabir Shanini."

"That's incredible. He doesn't even know how to pronounce the name of their tribe correctly."

"Add this to your workload: interview Jabir Shanini."

"Blessings! Are you considering him for some post?"

"No idea. The interview you conduct with him will cause important figures in the state to notice his services."

"One camel squeezes the juice for another to drink."

"Take good care of Tatiana. Don't even think about compensating her for her lost phone with another one. You need to sever her ties with the world for as long as possible."

He hung up. What a bastard! How could he know I was planning to give her the phone I bought for Mona?

At Tatiana's request, we went to a restaurant known for its local specialties. We ate *hanidh*: mutton wrapped in tinfoil and cooked over a wood fire. I told Tatiana that I was leaving for a reporting assignment, and she chose to spend the remainder of the evening at the Rosy Moon Park smoking nargileh.

I gave her a copy of the key to the apartment and told her I would be out late and might not return till midnight. I passed by a large bookstore and bought the day's papers and an English-language magazine to entertain Tatiana. I dropped her off at the gateway to the park and continued. I felt sleepy after eating such a rich lunch.

I encountered some congestion. People were bumping into each other, and parked cars were lined up every which way. Realizing there must be a qat market nearby, I pulled my car over and got out. The qat was inexpensive, and this indicated there had been daily rains in the mountainous highlands where it was grown. I purchased three sacks and returned to the car, where I started to chew qat and flip through the newspapers. My attention was drawn to a brief report in the opposition newspaper from Aden, *al-Ayyam*, about the death of the girl Muhsina, who had been married as a child to a man who was almost thirty. He had penetrated her violently and caused her to bleed profusely. She had taken her last breaths in the hospital in al-Jurum. No picture accompanied the article. In *al-Nidal*, a newspaper published in Hodeida, I found a very brief reference to the girl's death. The report didn't even mention the child's name. I felt very uncomfortable and had chest pains. I was having trouble breathing. Nausea was moving up my throat and ruining the taste of the qat. What I feared had happened: Muhsina's case and its aroma had found their way to the media. It would be hard to halt its repercussions. Matters were becoming increasingly dreadful. As usual, I would find myself embroiled in defending the dirty bastard who had killed his child bride. What upset me most was Tatiana's role in the case. I hoped that destiny would be compassionate to her.

Sunday

Chapter 45

In a dream I heard Mona call my name. It wasn't like someone calling me from far away; her voice sounded nearby: strong and loud, angry and scolding. I awoke with her voice ringing in my ears. I remembered the timbre and register of her voice, and this nightmare version was a perfect match.

I rose and searched unsuccessfully for Tatiana. On the door of the fridge, I found a note saying she had gone to the market.

I turned on my laptop and entered Facebook. The rights activist Salam Mahdi was beating her battle drums, demanding the arrest of the husband of the dead girl Muhsina, of her father, and of the judge who had drawn up the wedding contract. I wrote a post criticizing Salam and spinsters like her:

Now, because of the incident involving Muhsina, the human rights activist called Salam Mahdi has opened her market. She will receive millions of dollars from foreign nations and organizations for mobilizing to prohibit the marriage of minors in Yemen. Here is another opportunity for Salam Mahdi to practice her favorite hobby of sticking her nose into sex cases. Does this old maid suffer from some sexual inhibition? I counsel her to get married and obtain some sexual gratification in a healthy and direct way—not in this convoluted one.

Half an hour later Salam Mahdi replied with a very long text. I will copy down just its opening passage:

Mr. Mutahhar Fadl has forgotten that he is a human being—not a political animal. He has transformed the legal case of the child Muhsina, may God be merciful to her, from a human rights case that should shake the world's conscience into a struggle between the political ruling elite and the opposition. His nonchalant portrayal of the slaughter of the child Muhsina and the position of those who condemn this crime as enemies of our nation is a form of political prostitution unparalleled in the history of mankind. . . .

Tatiana returned with large quantities of fish, meat, vegetables, and salad makings that she had bought with her own money. She placed her purchases in the kitchen and then went to the window to gaze down at the taxi outside the building. She complained that the vehicle's driver had stared at her strangely. I patted her on the shoulder and reassured her: "I've noticed him too. He's an ignorant country bumpkin who isn't used to seeing beautiful, blonde women."

Tatiana smiled and hugged me. Then she asked if I was a good cook. I told her, "If I had not become a journalist, I would have been a cook!" Tatiana laughed, took my hand, and led me to the kitchen, where we began preparing a feast fit for the late Czar of Russia. I cooked a fish cutlet stew, a *sanuna*, and rice and meat pilaf. Tatiana cooked pasta with a meat sauce, and Russian cabbage soup, which she referred to as *Shchi*.

The doorbell rang, and I felt apprehensive, not knowing whether to answer the door or not. Unfortunately, the door did not contain a peephole so I could determine the visitor's identity. I asked Tatiana to stay in the kitchen and remain silent, while I went to the door, listening carefully for any sound. The visitor stopped knocking and called me by my name. He called to me in a nasty way, pronouncing my name derisively, mockingly, in a voice that deprecated the person he was calling to—as if his vocal cords had been tuned to say my name meanly. I felt the name being called wasn't mine, that it was a low-class sobriquet that wasn't appropriate for me. There was no way I would use a ludicrous name like this.

Through the door the visitor said, "Open up, Mutahhar. I know you're in there." I recognized the man from his voice. It was the Shaykh's attorney, Hammoud Shanta.

I was obliged to open the door, grudgingly, and stood there blocking him from entering. All the same, he brushed me aside rudely and entered the apartment. He was carrying qat stems under his arm, and they were wrapped in a thin plastic cone that was tapered at the top and wide at the bottom, as if it were a locally manufactured nuclear rocket.

I asked him what he wanted, and he headed toward the living room, where he sat down, draping one leg over the other. "I've been asked to coordinate with you. The situation is very grave, and we need to stand shoulder to shoulder."

His last phrase made me laugh—but I may have been laughing at myself and at the circumstances that had placed me in the same skiff with an unbearable man. He asked me if we had eaten, and I said "No."

Then he replied: "Then I'll eat with you."

I felt anger welling up inside me. When I saw him armed with qat, I assumed he had eaten lunch and had come to chew the qat.

I told Tatiana the sad story and pointed out that we had only two chairs. She said that didn't matter and that she wouldn't mind eating on floor. We spread out some newspapers as a dinner mat and then brought the dishes to the dining room. Hammoud refused to use the spoon provided and began to eat rice with his hand. He would raise a hand like a backhoe to his mouth and then shake the grains of rice sticking to his fingers back on the plate he was eating from. After he bit the meat off the bones, he sucked the bones, making awful sounds. When Tatiana served the cabbage soup, and he began to pluck the cabbage and vegetables out of it with his fingers. He consumed the crème caramel with his forefinger! The way Hammoud ate was familiar to me, but I noticed Tatiana wasn't eating anything. I asked her in English why she was refraining, and she replied that when she saw someone eat in this disgusting way, she lost her appetite and was unable to put a single morsel of food in her mouth. A disapproving look passed across her face, but she immediately succeeded in erasing it. I felt sorry for her, because after she had spent hours preparing the food, she was unable to touch it. She would go hungry and throw the leftovers in the trash. What a very sensitive temperament she had! Doubtless, if she stayed in Yemen for the rest of her life, she would starve to death, God willing, the sooner the better.

Even though Hammoud did not understand a word of English, he guessed that we were talking about him. Then, looking at Tatiana, he recited:

Yemen (*al-yaman*) tempers

Those not tempered by Time (*al-zaman*).

He laughed at his bon mot with a guffaw as cacophonous as a motorbike. Then he began to lick the crème caramel plate with his tongue. Tatiana picked up the empty dishes and departed for the kitchen. Hammoud filled me in on the latest developments, saying that "the Organization for the Defense of Minor Girls, which Salam Mahdi heads," had presented a brief to the public prosecutor in al-Jurum demanding that the husband of the minor girl Muhsina, her father, and the religious notary public who had performed the marriage all be prosecuted.

I told him: "You should submit a brief on behalf of Muhsina's family and will certainly prevail, because there is nothing in the Shariah or Yemeni law that forbids the marriage of a minor girl."

He replied: "Actually, I have been commissioned to represent them. They are simple folk overpowered by the creatures of globalization—male and female activists who are the agents of imperialism in our land. They want to impose the ethical standards that dominate the West in our country. Marrying off a young girl protects her from deviance. But, according to the standards of the Licentious West, the marriage of minor girls is a form of deviance!"

I realized that he would give me a headache pontificating about early marriage, so I picked up the remaining dishes and left him rambling on to himself. In the kitchen Tatiana and I agreed to go swim at the beach in an hour. Then I carried chilled water and an ashtray to the lawyer, who was already plucking qat leaves from the stem, even as a cigarette still burned in his mouth. Grasping a handful of qat stems, he tossed them in front of me and said, "Chew!"

I returned them and said, "Not today, I'm going out shortly with Tatiana." The right side of his mouth quivered. His hopes had been dashed. He may have expected that I would enjoy the siesta with him; he may even have fantasized that Tatiana would sit and chew qat with us. I got this idea from after noticing that he had shaved his beard and mustache. The nicks on his face suggested that he had shaved within the past hour. He had spruced up and donned a suit jacket, even though it was a very hot day, and added a touch a normal attorney would never have thought of wearing: a brown shirt with light green trousers and a jacket.

Sighing, he said, "I have bad news. The file for Jalila's case has been submitted for judgment, and the first session is scheduled for next Saturday."

I yawned and asked, "Why are you sighing? You're an attorney, and this is your chance to make lots more money from the Shaykh."

He smiled broadly. Then he resumed playacting the role of a dedicated advocate for the Shaykh. "The problem is that the Shaykh is very busy and doesn't have time to attend all the court sessions. Speaking frankly: the judge of the court in al-Jurum is a strict person and may issue a restraining order that would prevent the Shaykh from traveling." He fidgeted and was speaking more loudly than there was any call for, since I was seated right beside him. "The Shaykh is upset about any restraining order that would keep him from traveling. He likes to spend a week every month in one of his apartments outside the country."

I remarked, "Then, Mr. Genius Attorney, you need to demand that Jalila should also be barred from traveling. Ha-ha."

Hammoud frowned. He may have thought I was implying something dirty. From his bulging shirt pocket he pulled out some folded papers and reading glasses with slim lenses.

"They have asked me to give you a file on Judge Tahir al-Darrak and the questionable rulings he has made on cases." He spread out the pages, cast a quick look at them, and handed them to me.

I objected: "You said a file!"

He raised his middle finger to me and smiled sarcastically at his own extreme niggardliness.

Tatiana and I departed, leaving Hammoud Shanta to enjoy his siesta with our flat's afreets.

I went to a bookstore to buy the day's papers. The newspaper *al-Shaʿb* had published the report on the Dayr Bani Musaʿid region, spread over two color pages, with twenty photos of the tribe's dignitaries and an interview with the tribe's shaykh. It was accompanied by a large picture of him. Their requests for more public services were also printed in large type. The interview I conducted with Jabir Shanini took up an entire page, and his picture occupied at least a quarter of the page.

Tatiana saw a man selling *makhluta*—fried balls of dough mixed with potatoes, leeks, and coriander—from a stand in the street and asked me to stop. She got out to buy some. The man scooped ten balls out of the oil, placed them in a paper container, and gave her *sahawiq* hot sauce in a plastic bag. Once she climbed back in the vehicle, she began eating them greedily. I told her I was surprised she ate food prepared by street vendors—food exposed to the sun and dust and of questionable cleanliness whereas not so long ago she had been queasy about eating food she herself had prepared. As her face grew flushed from eating hot pepper, she huffed, "I'm not a picky eater. I have a strong stomach that can combat germs, but your friend was eating in a disgusting way. This is a psychological sensitivity that I can't control or treat."

I kidded her: "Tatiana, don't be so hard on him. He asked me whether you are married. He seems to fancy you!"

Tatiana frowned and cast me a piercing look. "Please let me enjoy my *makhluta*!"

So, I smiled and kept silent.

After she had finished her meal and cleaned the oil off her hands with a damp paper napkin, she exclaimed, recalling his appearance in her imagination: "My God! He looks like a slave trader!"

Monday

Chapter 44

The satellite channels, international newspapers, and news agencies spread accounts of the death of the girl Muhsina throughout the world like a pandemic. Billions of people learned about her tragedy, and the source for all these reports was the Organization for the Defense of Girls' Rights. The reputation of Yemen tanked.

I wanted to hear the voices of my children and phoned my wife, but she did not answer. This woman who complains about our married life and says she isn't happy with me—two months ago I discovered she was taking antidepressants! Naturally, I asked her why, and she responded that she had repeatedly considered killing herself! I was shocked. I thought I had supplied her with everything she needed to be happy: lots of money, thrilling sex, a dinner table spread with the finest types of food, and a large daily allowance. On our bed, I paid my debts to her once or twice a day! I gave her three children, each one as beautiful as the moon: healthy, bright, good looking. What did she lack? I have no idea!

She says she wants "feelings" from me! Phew! Doesn't this pampered woman understand that my "feelings" were lost somewhere in the congestion of life?

She's always longing for her days in the Faculty and wishes we were still in love the way we were back then! This is a demented woman! She wants us to live a life composed of nothing but love and Romantic sighs. She forgets that there are practical demands in life and that money does not grow on trees. There is no way to escape from plunging into the life's struggle every day to grab a living from other people.

She expects to live a comfortable life but at the same time wants me to devote myself exclusively to loving her, courting her, exchanging love letters with her—as if we were teenagers whose shoulders are not weighed down by duties and responsibilities. She even wants me to do chores at home: to work as a servant, while also fulfilling her emotional needs! In other words, she allows me no time to rest, no opportunity to forget my duties in life. She wants everything from me: my body and my spirit. This is a pathological obsession, which will result in one of us being committed to an insane asylum.

Tuesday

Chapter 43

The public prosecutor in al-Jurum opened an inquiry into the case and interrogated Ibrahim Belghayth, who confirmed that he had married off his seven-year-old daughter but denied that she was deceased. He said she was alive and flourishing and that he could bring her to the prosecution any time they wanted to check for themselves.

I attended his interrogation and recorded his words. The deputy prosecutor cooperated fully with me and provided me a private room where I could write up a quick report. As soon as I completed a draft, I emailed it to the executive editor Riyad al-Kayyad. In an hour, the official rebuttal of the death of young Muhsina appeared on all government news sites.

I ate lunch with the deputy prosecutor, Colonel Dibwan Haider, in his office, which was fully mobilized, as calls for the public prosecutor streamed in like flies, mainly from correspondents for foreign news outlets, requesting a statement from him. He replied to each of them that young Muhsina was currently in a state-controlled building and that media representatives could see her whenever they wanted.

Some correspondents did flock to the public prosecutor's office, each hoping for a scoop. Sami Qasim, the correspondent for the paper *al-Ayyam*, was not among them. I was told that he was spending the day, safely, somewhere as a "guest."

Teams of photographers for government-affiliated television channels arrived from Sana'a with all their cameras and gear, and each crew was keen to interview young Muhsina on TV for immediate broadcast.

I asked the deputy prosecutor if he knew the correspondent for the newspaper *al-Nidal*. Among the scrum of journalists present, Colonel Diwan Haider pointed out a brown-complexioned, tall, lanky young man, who wore prescription glasses with square frames. His hair resembled a juniper's foliage, and he was clean-shaven. His cheeks protruded, his lips were thick, and his manner of dress suggested a stylish young man about town. I asked the deputy prosecutor if he knew this correspondent's name. After scratching his cheek and reflecting, he replied, "Ghalib Zubayta."

I was astonished: this youth was that newspaper's editor—someone I had been keen to see! But I felt a huge disappointment. I don't not know why I rejected his appearance. Perhaps twenty-five years old, he resembled any other young man and seemed a guy keen to look sharp and attract girls' attention. He did not look like a daring champion who devoted his time and energy to serving others. I observed from his gestures and motions, from how he smiled and spoke and thought, that he was modeling himself after a Hollywood movie star—but which one precisely? I did not know American actors well enough to say, but any savvy person would have known immediately at first glance that this young man was no longer the same person he had begun life as. He had reduced himself to a deformed chimera by aping someone else.

Following the afternoon prayer, we were driven in large buses—provided by the state—to a fancy building with five stories. Its façade was composed of exorbitantly expensive, polished, white stone. A huge sign had been placed on the structure to designate it as: "Al-Jurum Center for the Temporary Protection of Minor Brides." This placard had clearly been hastily produced—as evidenced by its copybook calligraphy and the use of the technical term "Minor Brides," which was an unforced acknowledgement by the State of the prevalence of marriage of minor girls. Worst of all was the word "temporary," which seemed to imply that the state would keep underage girls here until they were old enough to be handed back to their husbands!

We shoved against each other to enter the portal of the Center, which was packed with armed soldiers. I don't know why they searched us! We found Muhsina by a mound of toys in a vast room that obviously had a new carpet. Everyone competed to ask her questions, and television cameras besieged her from all sides. Blinding lights overwhelmed her. Her father, Ibrahim, embraced her as he tried to shove away the microphones thrust at the terrified child's mouth like so many male organs. It was bedlam as many people tried to speak to her at the same time. With some effort, I was able to take a picture of her. I tried to record her answers, but her voice was lost in the hubbub around her. I noticed that this substitute child looked very much like Muhsina, even down to the scar, which they had copied, although it was clearly a recent wound, because the blood was still clotting on top of the skin. That was the limit of their competency!

Two journalists quarreled and exchanged words, causing the girl to cry. Then Colonel Dibwan Haider ordered us leave the room.

Out in the portico, Ibrahim, the girl's father, declared to the media that he would sue the Organization for the Defense of Children's Rights for releasing false information that had caused material and psychological harm to his family. After he made this statement, the soldiers expelled us roughly from the building.

As we were preparing to board the buses, Ghalib Zubayta addressed us in a loud voice: "Folks, do you believe Yemen is wealthy enough nowadays to dedicate a huge building to one child? Why aren't there centers like this in our large cities? This is doubtless the only building of its kind in all of Yemen. Moreover, it is dedicated to protecting victims of child marriage for only a single day. The moment we turn off this street they may evict that girl in the worst possible manner and even confiscate her toys." He spoke in such a theatrical way, flaunting himself, his clothing, and his brilliance, that he resembled a peacock spreading his tailfeathers.

We returned to the public prosecutor's offices, which had been transformed into newsrooms. I dispatched an urgent report to my paper, *al-Sha'b*, attaching a photo of the girl who had been substituted for Muhsina.

I finished work around nine p.m., when I learned from Colonel Dibwan that the human rights activist Salam Mahdi had that morning attempted to interview the Indian nurses at the hospital where young Muhsina had died but that sisters of the fugitive husband had attacked and beaten her. Then the police had come and arrested Salam Mahdi's attackers, who, after being held all day, had just been released.

I left the public prosecutor's building feeling like a self-satisfied soldier who had just won a battle. I quit al-Jurum, heading for the city of Hodeida, yearning for Tatiana, whom I had not seen since that morning. Clouds released hail and then a downpour that lasted all the way—as if a tap the size of the entire celestial sphere had been turned on. I was forced to stop repeatedly to wait for better visibility. I was amazed at this rain, which was pelting down at night as if to torment us. It should have come during the day, when we really needed its protection against the glaring sunshine and scorching heat that had been so fierce it almost made a person forget modesty, strip off his clothes, and walk around naked.

I bought some of the shawarma sandwiches Tatiana loves on my way to the apartment. I drove fast, trying to reach her as soon as possible. I parked my vehicle in front of the apartment and found that the "taxi" Tatiana had complained about was gone. I bounded up the stairs, rang the doorbell to warn her, and then opened the door with my key and entered.

When I did not see Tatiana's shoes by the door, I was upset. Then I noticed the black flipflops of the lawyer Hammoud Shanta—covered with dust from the street—and a pair of cheap plastic women's shoes that were a rosy red color. Removing my shoes, which Tatiana had shined herself that morning before I left, I felt dizzy and smelled an unfamiliar fragrance in the apartment—not that of my shared life with Tatiana.

I entered the living room and asked Hammoud without any preliminaries: "What are you doing here?"

He was chewing qat, and his cheeks were swollen with the huge wad in his mouth. He said, "I have a letter for you."

I left him and searched the apartment. In the kitchen I found a young girl washing the utensils. Anger flared up inside me, and I returned to Hammoud. I yelled at him: "Where's Tatiana?"

"Calm down."

"I won't calm down. Where is Tatiana? Speak!"

"The police arrested her."

"For what?"

"She allegedly performed hymen reparation surgeries."

"That's a lie. Where is she now?"

"She was taken by airplane to Sana'a. From there, she will be repatriated."

"Impossible! You have Tatiana locked up. I'll contact the Russian Embassy and inform on you."

"Believe. This is the truth. Don't get all worked up."

I didn't listen to anything else he said. I left the apartment, slamming the door behind me, hard. I felt strongly that she was being held somewhere in the city.

I drove my car to the Intelligence Services, to the building where I had dropped Hammoud Shanta on an earlier occasion. My blood was boiling. A siren pierced my hearing, like a warning siren. I almost caused multiple traffic accidents. My entire body was convulsed by anger, rage, and a sense of defeat.

When I arrived there, I screamed insanely at the guards' faces, demanding to meet the officer in charge. They arrested me and threw me into a cell by myself.

Wednesday

Chapter 42

They released me in the morning, and the commanding officer came to apologize in person. He reassured me that Tatiana had reached her homeland and advised me to forget about her. Then he invited me to have a cup of tea with him in his office.

I started my car, which they had parked in the courtyard, and drove to the seashore. There I sat behind the steering wheel and gazed at the clamorous waves, while brooding about my life, which was now a depository for despicable deeds. Concern for Tatiana overwhelmed me, and I decided to return to the apartment, turn on my laptop, and see if any news sites had published something about her.

I passed by a bookstore and asked for the day's papers, but they hadn't arrived from Sana'a yet. So I bought a copy of *al-Nidal*, which was published in Hodeida. A picture of Muhsina's child-double occupied half of the front page. It was accompanied by a banner headline: "International Appeal to End Child Marriage." The newspaper's executive editor had printed the statement that he made yesterday, but with additional curses against the government. He demanded that the constitution be amended to include a clause specifying the minimum age for marriage for girls as eighteen. He spoke out against clerics who opposed such legislation and described them as lascivious men addicted to copulating with nymphomaniacs and underage girls. He addressed a shameless question to religious scholars: "In paradise, will you dare ask God for houris seven years old?"

Drawing a connection between this editorial and his Occidentalist posture as a person keen to imitate everything Hollywood, I felt disgusted. He was nothing more than a parrot who repeated the talking points of foreign, international organizations. I crumpled the newspaper and tossed it out the car window.

I was so hungry, I felt faint. I had not had a bite to eat since lunch the previous day. I stopped at the first cafeteria I saw and ordered a cheese and tomato sandwich with lemonade. After silencing my hunger, I smoked my first cigarette of this mournful day.

I returned to the apartment. As I opened the door, I heard someone washing clothes. I noticed the girl's plastic shoes, but the attorney's flipflops were no longer there. My suppressed resentment suddenly rose inside me like a poisonous vapor from my bowels. I did not remove my shoes at the entrance and walked to the bathroom, where the door was open. The girl, who wore a diaphanous nightgown that showed off her body, did not notice me, because she was leaning forward, soaking clothes in the tub.

I screamed at her in a reverberating voice: "What are you doing here?"

She released a shriek of terror and retreated into a corner, trembling. No doubt my frowning visage and unshaven beard added to her panic.

I shooed her out with my hand, saying, "Go on. Get out of here."

The poor girl ran to the bedroom and put her few belongings in a bag. She slipped into a tunic of a type popular with old women and a black abaya, covered her hair with a yellow scarf, and departed.

I returned to the bathroom to see whether she had left any of her clothes in the laundry only to find that all the clothes she had been washing were mine. I went to the kitchen, opened a bottle of vodka, and poured myself a glass. I opened the freezer and found a full tray of ice cubes. I did not remember filling the trays the last time. The girl I had just thrown out of the apartment had filled them. I took four ice cubes and tossed them in the glass.

I went to the bedroom. It had been tidied, thoroughly cleaned, and now had a thrilling feminine fragrance. I took my laptop out of its black case and turned it on. I noticed how clean its keyboard was. The keys themselves were as gleaming as if they had just come from the factory. "What's all this?" I asked myself. "She seems to be a very skillful housekeeper, even though she's only thirteen or fourteen."

I opened the website for *al-Sha'b* newspaper and found a report about Tatiana: "Russian doctor arrested for performing hymen restoration surgeries." They had also published a picture of her. I pulled up the websites of other government-affiliated papers and found the same information published on all of them, although they were phrased differently, and there were different photos that had been taken from her stolen cell phone. Tears flowed from my eyes. This was how we rewarded her for the medical services she had provided to our country!

I fetched the bottle of vodka and refilled my glass. I went on Facebook, cursing, swearing, and giving free rein to my rancor, like a drunkard stammering in his inebriation. If there had been a Facebook site there for comments, I would have peed all over them and their publications.

Once I had emptied the bottle, I lost control of myself and wept fervently. I sobbed loudly, indifferent to whether the neighbors could hear me. I don't remember when I disappeared from the world and surrendered myself to slumber.

Thursday

Chapter 41

I rang my wife, who finally accepted my call. She did not speak to me and handed the phone to Habel, who talked to me for a long time. Then I spoke to my daughter Najat, who told me about the bikes her mother had bought and other toys. The last grape in the cluster—Karama—did not say a word. She just laughed. Her pure laughter brought life back to my ailing heart and the way she crooned and chortled transported me from the suffering that had overwhelmed me to delight and relaxation.

Feeling agile and energetic, I shaved off my beard, which was starting to grow, trimmed the hair from my body, and bathed. I realized that my apparently reformed wife would not have allowed me to hear my children if she did not plan to ask me for more money.

I browsed the net and found that Ibrahim Balgheeth, Muhsina's father, had lodged a complaint with the public prosecutor's office in al-Jurum against the Organization for the Defense of Minor Girls and that Salam Mahdi would appear before the prosecutor the next Saturday for a deposition. The newspaper *al-Ayyam* from Aden published the full name of Muhsina's missing husband and mentioned that he had traveled to Mecca for the minor, umrah pilgrimage!

I went on the Facebook site where the fires I had set the previous day were still raging, as male and female Facebook cadets howled like whipped dogs.

I entered the kitchen and prepared myself a cold meal, planning to rest at home today. I would have time to write several essays for my daily column.

When the call to the noon prayer rang out, I decided to eat lunch in a Sana'a-style restaurant and have quiche-like Yemeni *saltah*, which I had not eaten since my descent to the coast. I would also buy some qat and the day's papers.

When I opened the apartment door, I was thunderstruck to find the girl, whose name I did not know, sitting below me on the landing, hugging the sack that contained her clothes. I gasped and struck my forehead with my hand. Approaching her, I asked, "When did you return?"

She replied, "I never went anywhere." I had trouble keeping myself from crying. I picked up the bag of her belongings and invited her to enter. She climbed up two steps and staggered. I steadied her with a hand beneath her armpit and helped her climb the rest of the way.

I sat her down in the living room and brought her some water. When I noticed how exhausted she was, I asked her, "Why didn't you go home?"

She replied, "I don't know the way."

I asked her, "Where are you from?"

She said, "From Dayr al-Dumu'."

I scratched my nose. I had never heard of a village by this name. Then I asked, "What's your name?"

"Khatima," she said with a sigh.

I went to the kitchen and fixed a quick meal for her: salty cheese, olives, and sesame halva with bread. I offered this to her; it was clear that she had eaten nothing since yesterday morning. I told her to eat. She stretched out a hand and gnawed on a dry piece of bread. Then she stopped. She said she felt nauseous. I did not know what to do for her. I did not fancy taking her to the hospital. What would I tell the nurses there? That she hadn't eaten for a day and a half? I told her I was going out for a drive and would be back in an hour. She looked at me with expressionless eyes.

I left, feeling upset. I went to a restaurant called al-Salta but did not enjoy the meal because I was tortured by pangs of conscious. I felt guilty for allowing someone who depended on me to go hungry, a person who had every right to expect me to respect her weakness and loneliness. I asked the waiter to put aluminum foil over the clay casserole dish so I could take the meal home, paid the proprietor, and left.

I bought qat and cigarettes and obtained, from a bookstore on Sana'a Street, those of the day's newspapers that had arrived. In the paper called *al-Thawri*—"The Revolutionary," which is published by the Yemeni Socialist Party, I found news that attracted my interest: "Death of Comrade First Deputy Sa'd Musa in Murky Circumstances." When I studied the picture, I recognized him. He was the huge, black Akhdami soldier who had challenged the Shaykh and his supporters in the police station of Bab al-Minjal. The report said that the body of Sa'd Musa, a Party member, had been found abandoned on one of Bab al-Minjal's roads. His head and limbs had been chopped off. Suspicions centered on Shaykh Bakri Hasan, who had previously threatened to kill the comrade in the presence of a group of citizens of the region. The writer of the report was my former friend, who no longer liked me: Sami Qasim.

I remembered the death threat this reporter himself had received, and a chill swept down my arms and legs. I wondered if I, who had not been threatened, felt frightened, how alarmed Sami was now?

I returned to the apartment with the clay casserole dish and a sack of round loaves of *kidam* bread. I went to the kitchen where I found Khatima washing my dishes, which had accumulated in the sink. I scolded her and asked her to skip her chores and rest. She continued working without even looking up at me. I grasped her arm and ordered her to rinse the soapsuds off her hands. She obeyed me but contracted her narrow eyebrows and pursed her lips. I drew her to the living room and ordered to her sit in the place I indicated until I returned. She sat down and crossed her arms. She was not happy sitting still when there was work she hadn't completed. She was upset because she had not finished her chores. I started heating up the casserole and went to the bedroom to change my clothes. I found the washed clothes hung on lines on the balcony. I told myself: "This girl knows no mercy for herself."

I opened the refrigerator and found the interior just as I expected. She had put all the food I had offered her back in the fridge, untouched, except for the round piece of bread; she had eaten half of it. I took the casserole off the heat and dished out a reasonable portion. I carried that to the living room, placed it on the floor, and told her, "Come, eat."

She replied, "May God be generous to you! I'm full."

I scolded her, "Khatima, listen to what I say and come here."

She crawled toward me on hands and knees. I began to eat, and she took the hard crust of the *kidma* bread and chewed on it, dry. I was obliged to dunk a morsel of it in the *salta* and feed it to her with my hand. She objected and refused to open her mouth. Then I threatened to beat her—I was just kidding, naturally, but to my astonishment she immediately obeyed. I seemed to have uttered the magic word. I continued to feed her by hand until she burped because she was full. We left the dish as empty as a mosque after worshippers have quit the communal Friday prayer. I felt happy and relieved because she had eaten. I sensed that I had compensated for my sin. She asked if I would allow her to clear away the dishes, and I forbade that. Then she returned to her previous position and crossed her arms. I cleared away the dinner mat and went to the kitchen, where I washed the dishes. I plucked the fresh, qat leaves, which were as red as raw meat, and washed them three times.

My plan was to withdraw to the bedroom and write my essays. I offered Khatima some qat, but she said she didn't chew it. So I turned on the television and handed her the remote control. Then she said that she didn't watch TV! I asked her, as my temper flared: "Do you know how to sit quietly on your rear end?"

She replied, "Yeah."

I told her in a threatening tone: "Fine. Don't make a sound. I'm busy. I want to write." I left her and went to my room, telling myself that the best thing about this girl was how obedient she was.

Friday

Chapter 40

I found my shirts and trousers ironed and hanging in the closet. My underwear had been folded and placed in a drawer. I was astonished that Khatima had been able to pass through my room to the balcony, take the clothes off the line, iron them, and arrange them in the closet without me sensing her presence at all. Did she have a deft hand, or had I been fast asleep? I turned off the air conditioner and opened the window. A hot breeze from the sea entered the room and sucked the unhealthy air up from my ribcage, oxygenating me. Then my lethargy immediately left me, and I felt I was fine, perky, and in excellent health.

I opened the internet and went on the Facebook site, where I found a quarrel about the girl Jalila. Some were demanding that people pack the courtroom tomorrow—Saturday—morning in support of this girl, but there were also calls for the media to attend the trial so that the general public would know what transpired there and exert public pressure till justice was done.

I added a post in which I said that publication of the details of the trial in media of all forms was tantamount to whipping the assault victim and harming her reputation for years to come. The sexual predator, on the other hand, if the Shaykh had committed the assault without the child's prior consent, would, by contrast, be considered very manly by our Eastern society, and his reputation would not be besmirched in the least. To the contrary, women would rush to him in response to his virility!

The voice of the imam preaching the Friday sermon reached my ears as he threatened and chastised the West. He was utilizing all the registers of his voice, like a mangy old tomcat confronting a younger, tougher cat. I closed the window and went to the kitchen to fix myself a snack.

I discovered that Khatima had fixed me a boiled egg, broad beans, and a pancake with oil and had also prepared tea, which she had poured in a thermos. I ate the pastry with sips of tea. The pastry tasted delicious! Its layers were crisp and not oily. That demonstrated her extraordinary skill in kneading and frying pastry. What Khatima did not know about me is that I never touch broad beans. I'll admit I avoid *ful*, because I consider it a working-class dish and a sign of poverty. I shun beans for reasons of class. I feel I belong to the middle class and reject being ranked with the lowest rung of the proletariat. I understand that I sacrifice many ethical principles and maxims by renouncing this dish.

I looked for Khatima in the living room, but she wasn't there. She was in the third room, cleaning the carpet with a rag soaked in water and disinfectant. I asked her chidingly: "Khatima, what are you doing? This place doesn't belong to me or you. Why are you cleaning the carpet when we will eventually move out?"

She stopped rubbing and bowed her head but did not reply. I looked at the walls and found they were sparkling clean. I pursed my lips regretfully. Then I asked her, "Have you eaten?"

She replied, "Yeah."

I sighed with relief. I told her: "You eat the egg and all the beans, because I'm going to have lunch in a restaurant."

I walked out of that room but then reflected that I should thank her for washing and ironing my clothes. When I returned, I found her silent and motionless. I surprised her by asking, "Khatima, what's come over you? What are you thinking?"

She looked at me, focusing on my feet. "I'm thinking about the way you walk."

I scratched my knee, assuming that she was criticizing me for walking on the carpet when it was still damp. "What about the way I walk?"

"You walk like a mountaineer. You lift your foot as though you were climbing a mountain."

Her observation made me laugh. I did not feel insulted. "So how do you all walk?"

Looking me in the eye, she said, "We walk causally. We advance our feet without raising them much at all."

The look in her eye suggested to me that she was unusually bright. Overwhelmed by curiosity, I asked her: "Have you attended school?"

She said, "As far as third primary."

I inquired, "So, do you know how to read and write?"

She replied, "Yeah."

Complimenting her, I observed, "If you had continued in school, you would be in junior high now." She suddenly rose and started imitating the way I walk. We both laughed. I asked, "Don't you see how manly that way of walking is? Doesn't that look better than the sliding forward way like you all?"

She rejected my suggestion: "No—the way you mountaineers walk suggests you are trying to look forceful. We don't need to demonstrate our power."

Her statement reverberated in my ears. This young girl possessed discernment superior to that of most politicians and cultured people. I left the apartment praying that no one would give her books by Karl Marx or Lenin, because, quite frankly, she would be a force to be reckoned with and might overthrow our nation's primitive capitalism. Walking down the street I stamped my feet on the ground as if I were in a military parade. Once I reached my car, I looked up and saw her at the window watching me leave. I offered her a military salute, and that made her laugh and hide inside. Near my car was a four-wheel-drive Toyota Hilux, parked with the driver inside it. After I climbed into my vehicle and turned on the engine, I looked at him carefully and recognized him as the same detective they had previously sent to watch Tatiana. I mocked the security forces then for switching vehicles but not the man! It naturally occurred to me that I was under surveillance. This was odd but did not worry me. I convinced myself, instead, that I had joined the ranks of important people who are provided security, frequently without their consent.

I ate lunch and relaxed through my siesta at a park that offered nargilehs. I observed the give and take on Facebook. My ancestors had been horsemen who fought with swords, and I was still loyal to the chivalric code but conducted my battles with a keyboard. In this age, people were slain psychologically, not physically, and wounds did not scar the skin—they went straight to the spirit. In the past, duels were nobler and more honorable, and kills a more convincing proof of courage. Today, the world's duels are hypothetical and teach a man to be vile and weak. They turn the most cowardly man in the world into a hero.

After sunset, Executive Editor Riyad al-Kayyad called and asked me to go the next day to the court in al-Jurum to cover Jalila's trial.

I returned to the apartment a few minutes before midnight and found Khatima asleep in the sitting room. I went to the kitchen, heated up the green bean stew, and finished it off. I told myself that she was a perceptive girl who, once she learned that I would die from eating green beans, would always cook them for me. I put out some money for her with a note telling her to buy all the necessary supplies for the kitchen and set the alarm on my phone to ring at precisely seven a.m.

Saturday

Chapter 39

The courtroom in al-Jurum was packed with people, and the percentage of journalists among them was high. The atmosphere suddenly became tense when the judge, Tahir al-Darrak, ordered the Shaykh placed in the defendant's cage. After some give and take and an entreaty from the public prosecutor, Shaykh Bakri Hasan obeyed the command and entered the cage. Jalila and her grandfather, together with several other relatives were seated in the front row. Outside the courthouse, the Shaykh had assembled ten vehicles and more than one hundred armed men to frighten the court. This may have provoked the judge to treat the Shaykh severely and order him restrained in the cage. I looked at the Shaykh's attorney, Hammoud Shanta. His face reflected his client's deteriorating situation.

The girl's attorney, Shu'ayb al-'Ujayl, presented an eloquent plea at the end of which he sought life imprisonment for the Shaykh. The defense attorney protested that the medical report was inaccurate and requested that the girl Jalila receive another virginity examination. He presented to the judge documents confirming that Dr. Tatiana was unfit to offer an opinion, since she was suspected of deeds that violated the customs and traditions of the country including hymen repairs. It came as a huge surprise when the judge rejected the defense attorney's request, on the grounds that court had validated the medical report prepared by Dr. Tatiana and that a verdict rendered against this physician in another case did not negate the report's validity. Attorney Hammoud Shanta's defense collapsed then, and he was at a loss for what to do.

The judge ordered that the Shaykh be forbidden from traveling outside the country until a verdict was rendered in the case and set the date of the next session for August 10th.

Supporters of young Jalila exited the courtroom feeling elated and shouting: "Long live justice!" The Shaykh was escorted from the defendant's cage shaking his head as if warding off an invisible blow. His subdued supporters whispered to each other and moved anxiously and nervously. The journalist Sami Qasim trailed the judge like his shadow and exchanged a few words with him. I thought about taking a photo of the judge but hesitated. He passed near me as he departed. A man in his seventies, of awe-inspiring majesty, he strolled forward, greeting people, pausing to shake hands with some. He asked an adult man how he was and inquired of young fellows how their father and family were. If someone bantered with him, he did not take offense. He seemed modest now, as if on leaving the courtroom he had become an ordinary citizen. He had an unusual, lovable, magnetic personality unlike any I had witnessed before. The prosecutor appeared before me and asked me to come with him, each man in his own vehicle, to the prosecutor's office. When we arrived there, I asked what was the matter? He told me that the rights activist Salam Mahdi, who had come that morning for an inquiry into the allegation that she had released false information, had refused to post bond and that he had been obliged to detain her. I was stunned and asked why she hadn't. He replied that pride had blinded her. She had assumed he would not dare arrest her. He asked me if I would like to photograph her. I replied I would just like to see her.

He led me to the holding cell. The moment I set eyes on her, she blurted out: "So, you've come to gloat, you foundling."

Since she had obliged me to defend my lineage, I retorted, "No, by God, I'm not a foundling bastard—I descend from a line of tribal shaykhs. Your grandfathers worked as herdsmen for mine."

She seemed to have been waiting for this opportunity to vent her rage. So, she began cursing me with the foulest, backstreet, gutter terms chosen to melt the brain of any free-born man! I brought out my camera and snapped several pictures of her. She became even more ferocious and began beating on the bars while giving full rein to her tongue.

We left her and went to the prosecutor's office. He laughed and said, "I don't know why she went crazy when she saw you. Did you see how she was beating on the bars? You would almost think a jinni had possessed her."

I excused myself to fetch my laptop from the car so I could write an article about her. He said he would order lunch for us. Influenced by my rage, I wrote a report, which was accompanied by photographs, with the title: "Jailing of Rights Activist Salam Mahdi for Inquiry" and sent it to our newspaper.

The executive editor called in a few minutes and said, "I shake your hand." He volunteered that the photos I had submitted were priceless and then laughed. Finally, he said he was sending me three hundred thousand rials to support my free mind. Then he hung up.

I ate lunch with my mind at ease, because I had expressed my anger and been handsomely recompensed. Colonel Dibwan brought the prosecutor a bunch of qat wrapped in a banana leaf, and we chewed qat. I wrote coverage (slanted toward the Shaykh) of the day's court session and sent it to the paper along with a photo of the judge on the dais of the court.

A diminutive man came and whispered to Colonel Dibwan.

His words almost made the colonel choke on his qat. I noticed his expression change. He had been leaning back but now sat up straight. After the informant had left, the colonel said, "That Communist, Husayn al-Battah, is goading people to join a demonstration to march on us tonight."

I felt a tremor strike my body like lightning and asked, "Do you expect a riot?"

Rocking in his seat, he replied, "Husayn al-Battah is a daredevil who could incite the riffraff to attack the public prosecutor's headquarters, vandalize the offices, torch the files, and perhaps open the detention cell and free the prisoner."

I asked, "What will you do?"

Standing up, he said, "I don't have enough manpower to confront them. I just have a few individuals. I'll request reinforcements from Hodeida."

He headed to the phone and picked up the receiver. He was tense, and I noticed that his hand shook as he dialed the number from memory. We were obviously jittery. Our lives were exposed to severe danger. During these disturbances, we might be killed in a wave of violence for which no one would be held accountable. Colonel Dibwan received a reassuring response and told me that a detachment from the central police station was on its way.

I shared my thoughts with Colonel Dibwan: "What if you released that ill-omened woman and robbed the rioters of their opportunity?"

"Salam Mahdi defied the law. Do you mean to imply that she's more important than me and this establishment?"

"I believe she deliberately got herself arrested to draw attention to herself. She craves notoriety. Don't you agree?"

"I am very familiar with these little games and how some people seek to provoke others by placing themselves in conflict with us so they can be said to be combatants. But this matter goes beyond my authority. I could only release her now with an order from higher up my chain of command."

"So, this wicked woman, who plotted all this in advance with her friend Husayn al-Battah, will achieve her objective and make her arrest a cause célèbre. She will gain more fame and renown outside of Yemen. She will surely receive support and sympathy from foreigners. I beg you to consider all this."

"Don't pressure me, my friend. Even if she has been plotting to stir up a disturbance, she will not depart till she submits to the law. I am sure that I've made the correct decision."

"All the same, I'll stay with you to photograph whatever mayhem erupts."

Colonel Dibwan sighed with relief and cast me a grateful look. Just after sunset vehicles arrived from the central police station with dozens of soldiers, brandishing weapons, who encircled the building.

The cold wind that blew in from the east indicated there were strong downpours of rain on the mountain heights. Following the evening prayer, bunches of young men started to assemble at the entrance to the public prosecutor's office. Colonel Dibwan phoned the head of electricity for al-Jurum and asked him to cut off power on that street. Then the entire neighborhood was plunged into total darkness, and several snipers climbed onto the building's roof. The demonstrators lit candles. There were thousands of them, and they began to chant slogans.

I climbed to the roof and began to photograph them. They filled the street, and the roar of their shouts was heart stopping. I told myself that Salam Mahdi, who could no doubt hear their voices, must be bursting with pride and would become crazed with a feeling of self-importance. The demonstration concluded peacefully and without any disturbances worth mentioning. At ten o'clock, the demonstrators departed.

The electric current was turned on half an hour later, and I wrote a quick report about the demonstration and filed it. I had closed my computer and was starting to leave, when Colonel Dibwan came to me with a nervous smile on his face: "Glad tidings. They have arrested Husayn al-Battah." I shook his hand to say goodnight and headed to my car.

All the way to Hodeida, my mind was preoccupied by the series of ill-omened mistakes the authorities were committing. These unforced errors transformed dunces into heroes in the eyes of the people. I may also have felt slightly jealous of Salam Mahdi and her colleague Husayn al-Battah.

This is a weird feeling—what kind of soul do I harbor inside my ribcage? I seem to have inherited some heroic, audacious genes from my ancestors. That would explain why my soul longs to confront forces greater than me and demonstrate the strength of my resolve. Now I acknowledge that being taken captive is a secret hope stirring deep inside me, because the descendant of any great warrior is never free of that. What enrages me now is that history has granted this gift to two insignificant individuals without the least link to chivalry.

Sunday

Chapter 38

I opened my eyes and hippity-hopped to Facebook! I have become addicted to Facebooking. Just as I thought: Facebookers are circulating news of Salam Mahdi's arrest. They have turned her into a martyr of liberty and a heroine of civil rights—as if she were Yemen's Martin Luther King!

I wrote a post and published all the photos I had taken of her in detention with the caption: "Lovers of imported freedom, feast your eyes on your prophet Salam Mahdi languishing behind bars." An idea for my daily column came to mind, and I drafted it quickly:

With reference to the imprisonment of the social butterfly Salam Mahdi, this woman who operates with the mentality of a hypocritical voyeur and delights in being photographed with victims so she can vaunt her claim to being a humanitarian and who runs her suspicious organization like a family shop, this woman who has hung out a placard larger than the size of the modest apartment she has rented for her organization in order to dazzle the eyes of foreign eunuchs who oppose the marriage of young girls, you all should understand that it is impossible for civil-society organizations to emerge in a country that is dominated by a rural character and which has not yet produced a civil society. This means that her organization is nothing more than a Western concoction that serves only to give Yemenis the impression that it is fit to circulate in their environment.

I heard knocking on the door and was surprised, because I had told Khatima firmly not to disturb me. When I gave her permission to enter, she opened the door, showed me the newspaper in her hand, and said, "I found this thrust under the door." I took it from her and found that it was a copy of *al-Nidal*, which is published in Hodeida and therefore is available by seven a.m. On the front page they had published a large picture of the Shaykh standing in the defendant's cage. The red banner headline said: "Shaykh Bakri Hasan finally in the dock." They also published news of the arrest of the rights activist Salam Mahdi. Husayn al-Battah's arrest wasn't mentioned, perhaps because it had occurred late that night—in other words, after this edition went to press. On an inside page, I was shocked to see they had printed a photo of me with the naughty caption: "Sophist/journalist Mutahhar Fadl, whom the authorities in Sana'a have put in charge of covering up the crimes of the Shaykh and improving public perception of him." The executive editor of *al-Nidal* was a fool descended from men who copulated with jennies. He had started this fight, and I would not remain silent. I would find a way to repay him.

I asked Khatima if she knew who had brought us the paper, and she shrugged her shoulders. From the glint in her eyes, I grasped that she had read it and seen my picture and what was written about me. Once this idea ambled through my mind, my nose turned red, and I felt uncomfortable. So, I asked her to prepare breakfast. She said it was ready. Then I decided to finish my essay some other time. After closing my laptop, I headed to the bathroom.

In the bathtub I found a strange black insect with very many feet. Its head and back were round. It resembled a centipede but was bigger and shaped differently. I killed it with the handle of the mop, lifted it up and examined it. It looked scary because feelers protruded at the bottom of its feet and provided it with a dark yellow halo. I tossed it in the open toilet and flushed it away. A feeling of pessimism settled into my heart: when unfamiliar insects enter someone's house, that's a warning of unpleasant events to come.

Khatima set out the breakfast mat in the living room. The breakfast she had prepared consisted of beans, crispy, crunchy pastries with olive oil, and tea with milk. I asked her to sit down and eat with me. She said she had already had breakfast. I insisted. So, she sat down and started to eat shyly. I looked at her palm and nails. They were rough and thick like a man's. She was a hardworking girl and perhaps had been performing heavy labor since she was seven or six years old. Her face, which the sun had scorched, was an adolescent's. The lower eyelid of each eye was dark and wrinkled. I touched the skin of her face with my fingers, and she cringed. I closed my eyes and continued to feel her face. Her face was rough, and the skin was taut and lacked the freshness of youth. To my touch, it felt dry and hard, like a plank of wood. Khatima sighed twice. I opened my eyes and withdrew my hand. I gazed into her eyes, where I detected a life weighted with cares and a personality replete with an astonishing world of secrets, magic, and mystery. She was ten years more mature than her chronological age. She had experienced life, men, and the vagaries of fate—perhaps more than I had, and I was thirty-three. I felt no sexual desire for her. Without any doubt, she was a pretty girl who possessed an attractive figure and a seductively thin waist, but there was something about her that repelled me. I'm not sure what.

We heard chants and ran to the windows that overlooked the street. Buses packed with schoolgirls were passing. They held photoshopped pictures of Husayn al-Battah. I realized that there was going to be a demonstration and these students were heading to it. I dressed for work, picked up my bag, and went down to the street.

I caught up with them at the governorate building, where

I witnessed the oddest demonstration in Yemen's history. Five thousand girls stood in protest in front of the governorate building and demanded the release of Husayn al-Battah and of the rights-activist Salam Mahdi. They threatened that they would not abandon their vigil till their demands were met. I slipped inside the governorate building, which was chaotic and crowded with a crush of security officers, in uniform and in civilian attire. I learned there that Husayn al-Battah had been moved to Hodeida overnight and was now held by the intelligence services. A trustworthy officer informed us that a comparable, synchronized demonstration of approximately three thousand girls was taking place in al-Jurum at the prosecutor's office.

The executive editor Riyad al-Kayyad called to ask me to provide immediate coverage of these events. I set to work writing a report that I drafted without much concentration and sent off.

I was surrounded by crazy people and rumors sputtered like broth in a pot over an open fire. What was certain was that the allied leftwing parties had organized this demonstration. Their obvious logistical ability in printing all the leaflets and photos was astonishing as was the precision of the organization. Their major coup was in assembling so many members of the "gentle sex" to demonstrate with such extraordinary speed, since the world had barely heard about this news before the area was teeming with cameras and microphones reporting on this event, one unique in the Arab world!

Given the influx of dozens of journalists and correspondents from the satellite television channels, it was not possible to disperse these female demonstrators forcibly.

At two p.m., the Governor, who was under extraordinary pressure from the schoolgirls' next of kin, issued an order to release Husayn al-Battah and Salam Mahdi immediately. The girls responded with such deafening trills of delight that our African neighbors across the Red Sea may have heard them.

At three p.m., Husayn al-Battah arrived at the square where the demonstration was held and made a statement, using a megaphone, to the students. When he finished, they made their hands smart applauding him. What a majestic moment! Who would have imagined that such an insignificant man would receive such an ovation? This was a day that made us look bad! We received a painful blow then, and our enemies emerged the victors.

I could not bear to write a report, despite the executive editor's insistence. My morale had sunk to rock bottom, and tears were forming in my eyes. I wanted to smash and break things to express my feeling of defeat. No one understood me, not even my executive editor. What was crushing my heart was not losing a round. No, it was caused by loss of my sense of being a hero. I had seen a real hero here. The crowds had surrounded and applauded him. Regrettably, someone else emerged as the hero I thought I was. Husayn al-Battah had stolen this role from me. I should have been that hero. That was my throne; I deserved it more than that schmuck. But, cursed destiny had turned everything upside down and granted the hero's role to someone who didn't deserve it.

Any goal we set for ourselves we will achieve, sooner or later, if we devote our time, effort, and spirit to it. The difficulty is always for us to acknowledge deep inside ourselves the goal we have set, because we're not truly conscious of it till it's too late!

I bought qat for an absurd price and returned to the apartment. Khatima greeted me and took the bunch of qat and my heavy bag from me. She said lunch was ready. I lied to her and told I had eaten. I asked her to wash the qat three times.

I entered my room and turned on the air conditioner. I felt tired. I told myself I would recline my head on the pillow and give my eyes a little rest. But sleep carried me away on its wings and then dropped me down a well of dreams.

Monday

Chapter 37

I woke feeling very hungry at three a.m. and went to the kitchen where I ate the mixed vegetables Khatima had cooked. My qat leaves had been plucked from their stems and placed in the fridge as well. I felt restless and decided to go to the beach to breathe the fresh air. I poured vodka into a metal thermos, picked up a pack of cigarettes, and departed.

I crossed the street to the sea with quick steps, approached the water, and sat down on the warm sand. After I had drunk some vodka and refreshed my heart, I rang the executive editor Riyad al-Kayyad. I knew he would be awake and still at work in his office, revising, and updating news on the front page.

He answered and said jovially, "What do we want?"

"I'm tired and want to return to Sana'a."

"Don't be hasty. We're arranging even bigger things for you."

"I trust you but really can't take any more. I need to rest after all this deleterious nervous pressure."

"I understand, but withdrawing you from the battlefield now would not just mean our defeat. It would mean you're a coward. Would you like that to be said of you?"

"No."

"Then stand strong, my son. In a few days you will see how the tide of battle changes to favor us."

"Just a few days?"

"I swear on my honor. We are working night and day. There's no way that matters can get out of control."

"I would give my life to know what whore of a plot we're working on."

"Ha-ha. Rest assured that our cause will triumph. Would you like me to share a secret with you to calm your nerves?"

"I wish you would."

"We are conducting a crisis management drill."

"What's the name of this drill?"

"Hot air balloon."

"Now I understand."

"What have you understood?"

"Ahhh. It's to prepare plots when you're floating high overhead."

"Right. You're very clever. Don't let lethargy dull your soul. A bright future awaits you, my boy."

"God willing."

"It's great that you called me, Hero; you have a new assignment."

"What is it?"

"Judge Tahir al-Darrak—this senile, white-haired man who is a thorn in our throats."

"What am I to do?"

"That's up to you. Take care of him. By now you have started to learn the tricks of our trade. Find a bright idea to topple him."

"The information that Hammoud Shanta supplied me doesn't cut it; the man has a very clean slate."

"Find some other avenue."

"To tell the truth, I can't think of anything else."

"Have you heard of the 'Drunks Only' Restaurant?"

"No."

"Go there now. I'm sure you'll find the ideas you need."

"Do you know what time it is? It's almost dawn."

"My son, this restaurant opens at 11 p.m. and does not close till sunrise."

"Ha-ha. That's why it's called the 'Drunks Only' Restaurant!"

"Get a move on. They will quiz you. Tell them you are looking for someone who has gone missing. Ha-ha!"

He gave me the address and hung up.

I tarried a bit to finish the rest of the vodka. Then I headed to the restaurant.

I drove slowly, even though there were no other vehicles on the streets. I parked in front of the restaurant and got out. I walked cautiously, trying to maintain my balance. I was shocked to find that the restaurant was jampacked with patrons. I paused in the center of the dining room as puzzled as an ass whose master has disappeared! A huge waiter with a potbelly noticed me standing there like some dimwit. He took me by the arm and seated me. He stared at my face for a few seconds and then released a resounding cry: "A order of liver with sides!" Then another waiter with red eyes and a frowning face placed a cup of coffee before me.

As I sipped the coffee, I glanced around at the other patrons. They were a rowdy lot and spoke in loud voices, laughing so uproariously the walls shook. A third waiter, whose eyes were even redder than the two previous ones and whose expression was stormy and glum, placed bread before me. When I was bold enough to thank him, he assaulted me with a fierce glance, as if he wanted to devour me. The first, pot-bellied waiter placed before me a large quantity of liver fried with onions and tomatoes. I thanked him. He looked at me disdainfully without uttering a word. I expected that people so stern and with lips sealed as tight as a tiger's would never succeed in preparing excellent meals. But when I tasted the liver, I found that it was very delicious and melted in my mouth like chocolate and that the wavy flatbread (*khubz mulawah*) was as crisp as potato chips.

When the man sitting next to me left, another patron took his place. The pot-bellied waiter approached him and glared at the man's face—as he had done with me—and then shouted: "An order of eggs. . . . He's just eating." The second waiter brought him tea. I was nonplussed by the protocols of this restaurant, where customers did not place orders. Instead they sat down with arms crossed, and were content to eat whatever dish the pot-bellied waiter selected. No one here seemed to dare to object. The expressions of the men running the restaurant did not augur well, and their rippling muscles showed they had served their time in prison lifting weights. They might even have broken out of jail. That would be why they did not have a day job and preferred to work under the cover of darkness! The pot-bellied waiter set down a flat, cracked plate with a small amount of egg on it—perhaps a half-portion—in front of the newcomer, who had a sparse beard. I told myself: they must not appreciate his looks!

I moved closer and asked him where the airport was. He laughed and replied, "You must really be drunk! You can't tell your head from your foot!" When he spoke, he did not reek of alcohol, and I realized that he didn't drink. That was why the pot-bellied waiter was annoyed with him.

Unfortunately, this young man with a scrawny beard did not inspire any thoughts in me, but a table in front of me did. A disagreement had erupted between two drunk men; each one was insisting that the other fellow pay the bill. They were dressed in a typical Coastal way: an unbuttoned shirt with a sarong: an *izar*. One man was middle-aged and had curly gray hair. His face suggested that he was a cultured person with an earnest personality. The second was a young fellow around twenty, and his face showed that he was a conceited peacock. I followed their debate with interest.

The adult said: "Either pay the bill or do a somersault like a monkey."

The young man retorted: ". . . . your mother! You have piercing vision! How did you know I forgot to wear underpants?"

The adult: "That's your problem: you're always forgetting things: your money and your underpants!"

We all laughed—except of course not the young peacock and not the waiters who stood there like boulders, as if a smile would lower their prestige among the customers.

Looking at the pot-bellied waiter, the youth: "If the lads will agree, I'll pay tomorrow."

The pot-bellied waiter replied: "On one condition."

Our heads all turned toward him, and our eyes locked on his lips, waiting for what would emerge from them.

The pot-bellied waiter: "That you do a somersault like a monkey!"

We all burst into laughter, and some of us even fell to the floor. I laughed so hard my belly hurt, and my face turned a bright red.

The youth: "God damn you scoundrels! When I publish my odes to the nation and become rich, I'll pee down from far above on all of your heads."

One of the customers: "Praise the Lord, he's going to turn into a damn crow!"

The middle-aged man (pushing the young peacock to rise): "Go on: do a somersault! The nation will not be harmed if you turn one somersault!"

The young man stood up, looking very flustered. We trained our eyes on him and held our breath as an expectant silence reigned. We could even hear the flies buzz. He raised his hands on high and then somersaulted onto them. He was propelled forward by his momentum and landed on his feet. We all clapped warmly for him while we dissolved into laughter. Some men started to whistle. The young man sat back down, virtually melting from embarrassment, because everyone had seen his genitals wave in the air like a flag! I paid my bill and departed, praising God that I had not forgotten to put money in my pocket!

I returned to the apartment as the morning's light glimmered. Opening the door of the sitting room, I did not find Khatima. I noticed that the TV was shrouded by a white curtain. I told myself: this wild child hasn't adjusted herself to civilization yet. I opened the door of the third room and found her sleeping at some distance from her pallet. She must have been doing somersaults in her sleep. When I remembered the youth somersaulting like a monkey, I almost laughed out loud. I closed the door again and went to the kitchen. My mood had improved, and I felt like working again. I took the qat and a bottle of mineral water from the refrigerator and went to my room. The executive editor had hit the target; the "Drunks Only" restaurant had inspired me with an idea more lethal than dynamite. When it was published, Judge Tahir al-Dirrak would explode into body parts.

I turned on my laptop and began writing an article entitled: "Just Between the Two of Us: The Story of the Dissolute Judge." In it I discussed the attraction a judge of the court in al-Jurum felt for adolescent males. I did not mention his name but said this perversion was influencing the justice of verdicts he pronounced. In several cases he had judged, this proclivity had biased his ruling. I asked for a review of his judicial file and holding him accountable. I cited, for example, that he went to bathe every Friday morning in Wadi al-Dud, where a troupe of boys came to skinny-dip. When they emerged from the water and donned their sarongs—since they were rural boys and did not wear underpants—he would offer them money to perform somersaults like a monkey. Then these adolescent males would compete to perform somersaults for him, oblivious to his motivation, and he would give each boy a hundred rials. His practice was well known in the wadi, but men there turned a blind eye to it, judging it to be harmless enjoyment—an entertainment that was limited to looking. In their opinion he was a Platonic lover whom God had afflicted with a love of boys!

I completed this article in one go, without dallying, and sent it off. I was sure the executive editor Riyad al-Kayyad would go crazy with delight when he read it.

I left my room and found that Khatima was awake. I hugged her and kissed on the part of her hair. Then I asked her to cook some broad beans and prepare pastries fried in olive oil.

I went to the bathroom where I shaved and washed. Then I oiled my hair. I was happy and did not know what I would do during the hours until the executive editor woke at noon.

I went to the living room, removed the white curtain from the TV, and turned it on. Several satellite channels were broadcasting news reports about the massive feminine demonstrations that had been held in both Hodeida and al-Jurum. Salam Mahdi and her face, which was as long as a squash, appeared, thanking the daughters of Yemen. Khatima brought in breakfast. I commanded her to sit down and eat with me. I kept changing channels while I observed her eat slowly and watch the television. I noticed the subtle way she turned her head toward the TV and deliberately avoided looking at me. She would, however, glance at me out of the corner of her eye where I was within the range of her eye, and she could observe me without making me feel that she was. She did not dare look directly at me, even though I was frankly gazing straight at her. When I was done eating, she put a hand on her forehead and her face was contorted by pain. I asked her what was wrong, and she said: "A headache and a pain in my stomach."

I asked her to change clothes and prepare to go out. Then I took her to a private hospital. The physician examined her. He took me aside and told me the girl was fine and merely suffering from symptoms of puberty—menstrual cramps! He suggested that she has pretending to be ill to garner my interest and compassion. I reckoned that I had neglected her and treated her like a domestic animal without paying any attention to her feelings.

When we climbed back in the car, I asked if she needed anything. She shook her head: no. She asked me what the physician had told me. She arched her eyebrows and gave me an intense, predatory look like that of a lioness. She no doubt suspected the naughty slander that had been spoken at her expense.

I said in jest, although with a serious expression: "The physician said you are suffering from an internal fever."

She said with her fine, coal-black eyebrows meeting in the middle: "Then why didn't he write me a prescription?" I pressed down on the gas pedal, and we shot off.

"He said the best treatment for you is ice cream. Ha-ha!"

There was an ice cream shop on al-Mitraq Street. We went inside it and chose a "family" booth with curtains. They served us mango-flavored ice cream with two packs of cookies. I had noticed that all the time she had been in the apartment she had worn the same old-fashioned blue blouse with red flower buds, of a type favored by old ladies, and never changed it. I asked her, "How many blouses do you have?" She held up four fingers. I told her I had only seen her wear one. Then she replied that she had only brought this one blouse from her village.

I took her on a tour of clothing stores and bought her four blouses of a contemporary style. I noticed she was casting a long look at a store that sold beauty products. So, we entered it. I'll admit that I have no expertise in these matters. I drew the salesclerk aside and told him, "This girl is going to be married next week. I want you to doll her up like a bride."

The salesclerk raised one eyebrow and said, "May God help her husband!"

I bought her makeup, French perfume, skin lotions, a deodorant, a depilatory, hair conditioner and shampoo, and various accessories. I paid the clerk after my assistant, Khatima, helped me bargain the price down by tossing the merchandise back on the glass counter and threatening to walk out.

Once we left, Khatima told me that I did not know how to bargain. I admitted I usually did not bargain when I shopped. I would simply pay the amount requested. Hugging our purchases to her chest, she said, "The first thing you need to remember when you are buying something is: don't smile. Instead, you need to look the clerk in the eye as if he had killed your mother."

I laughed and asked, "What's the second?"

She said, "You must point out the defects of the merchandise you intend to buy and estimate its value at a quarter of its true price."

Looking at her askance, I commented, "I wish the idiots who buy weapons for billions of dollars could hear you talk."

We were feeling very thirsty, because the sun was directly overhead, and its flaming rays were scorching our heads. So, I suggested we return to the ice cream shop. Khatima agreed with great delight. We left our purchases in the car and hurried back to that shop, bathed in sweat. We ordered chocolate ice cream, and Khatima and I devoured our portions swiftly. Then I asked for water, which we drank till we had quenched our thirst and felt a delightful chill flow through our bodies. We loved this shop and did not want to leave it.

I looked at Khatima and reflected that she might speak more openly now that I had spent a lot of money on her. "You said you're from Dayr al-Dumu'?"

"Aye."

"Who is your shaykh?"

"Shaykh Bakri Hasan."

"Are your parents still living?"

"My father is, but my mother died when I was three."

"What does your father do?"

"He's a shepherd."

"Are you engaged?"

"Engaged! Ha-ha. I got married when I was eight."

"Why the rush?"

"The proverb says: You know you can trust a girl when she's eight."

"Where is your husband?"

"He divorced me two years after our marriage and went to work in Saudi Arabia."

"Why did that idiotic donkey divorce you?"

"Please don't curse him; he's my cousin."

"Amazing; do you still love him?"

"He was forced to divorce me."

"What? Did Saudi Arabia impose that condition on him?"

"No. My master did."

"Who is your master?"

"The Shaykh."

"Oh!"

She was scratching the table with her fingernails, and a mournful pout was traced on her lips. I forgot to flirt with her lips. Her beauty was more apparent when she was sad! Her delicate upper lip was gently raised in the center, and her lower lip was full and bowed like a cupcake.

Conscious that we had reached a restricted region, I asked her, "Did he marry you?"

"No, I'm licit for him without that."

She began to nibble on her lower lip anxiously after that slip of the tongue. I immediately guessed the secret she was keeping from people like me, perhaps out of fear for her father's life and those of other relatives.

Thinking the Shaykh had a harem reminiscent of men in olden times, I asked in a low voice, "Are there many of you?"

. . . .

"Do you know a girl named Mona?"

Khatima had turned into a mute boulder and ceased talking. Her expression was sullen. I paid the bill, and we left.

When we were on our way to my favorite restaurant, the executive editor Riyad al-Kayyad called and told me he shook my hand. He praised the article and promised to transfer to me lavish compensation once the piece was published. I realized that he would need attestations from leading figures of the tribe Banu Musa'id. So, I promised to work on that. To celebrate this success, I ordered a fine lunch. We ate till we could eat no more, leaving some dishes untouched. Khatima insisted on wrapping the extra food and taking it home with us. I dropped her at the apartment and told her I might be home late.

I passed by a bookstore and bought the day's papers. Then I made my way to al-Jurum. I called Jabir Shanini and told him what was up. He said he would meet me in Dayr Bani Musa'id and be there when I arrived, after preparing the atmosphere for me and choosing suitable informants.

Tuesday

Chapter 36

The newspaper *al-Shaʿb* published the article with the accompanying investigative report on two pages in the middle, together with thrilling titles and photos of everyone included in the investigation. Executive editor Riyad al-Kayyad called to congratulate me. His felicitations were especially strong this time because important figures had called him and praised my piece. At the end of our conversation, he asked me to go and collect a money transfer. When I stood in front of the exchange window, I was stunned by the size of the remittance.

Khatima was wearing one of her new blouses and had applied kohl around her eyes and lipstick to her lips. She had oiled her hair and dabbed on perfume. She had removed the slight amount of hair from her forearms. She truly looked an enchanting maiden, but I wasn't attracted to her.

I retreated to my room where I busied myself writing essays for my daily column and pursuing Ghalib Zubayta, the executive editor of the paper *al-Nidal* on Facebook, slamming him with sarcastic comments. I included photos of extremely ugly women whom I described as the childish old spinsters who financed his paper. By midnight he had banned me. So, I went on Twitter and continued my artillery attack against him till dawn broke.

Wednesday

Chapter 35

This is the final day of the month, and I received a letter from my wife asking for money! She isn't a normal woman. Not even a mother rat would smell money at such a distance! I went on the internet and spent a brief time on Facebook. When the noon call to prayer resounded, hunger's bell chimed in my stomach. I thought of taking Khatima to a restaurant to eat fish cooked in a traditional Yemeni *mofa* oven.

I found her stretched out in bed with a high fever. I offered to take her to the hospital, but she refused. Then I brought her ice and a towel to improvise a cold compress for her forehead. Within minutes she was feeling better, and her temperature had gone down.

I went to the restaurant. Once I returned, I cut up a cucumber and sprinkled salt on it, but she refused to eat. She said she felt nauseous. When I pleaded with her, she agreed to eat one slice. I placed pillows beneath her neck, raised her up a little, and fed her three more slices. Then she asked for a bucket. I ran to the bathroom and got it. She vomited into it. My day was spent nursing and caring for her.

Thursday

Chapter 34

The opposition newspaper *al-Nidal* published a serious report about the complicity of the governor of Hodeida in the trafficking of child brides. It mentioned that he ran a network that arranged for minors to marry Yemeni and Arab millionaires. As I read the report, my heart rate increased significantly because I realized that Mona was one of these child brides the article was discussing and that we were in the summer holiday season when wealthy Arabs flock to Yemen to enjoy legally sanctioned sexual gratifications. My heart was haunted by a suspicion that the Shaykh had taken Mona from me to marry to an elderly man only steps from his grave.

Dark thoughts assailed me. I imagined Mona being sexually assaulted by an aged millionaire with wrinkled skin. My soul was revolted and almost fled through my gullet. My blood pressure probably increased, because I felt a tingling spread through my body—as if I were a fish in a skillet! I wondered whether this journalistic attack on the Governor of Hodeida was in retaliation for our vicious attack on Judge Tahir al-Dirrak.

The health condition of Miss Khatima had not improved. I purchased a remedy for nausea and another for her fever. She no longer ate anything except what I hand fed her and then only a few, small morsels. To raise her spirits, I gave her the cell phone I had purchased for Mona, trying to raise her spirits. She busied herself with it for a brief time only to set it aside. I offered to take her in my car to her father's house in her village. She rejected that idea fiercely and wept.

I went to the grocer's and bought her sweets, chips, and many types of cookies and cake. She loved the chips and ate a lot of them with red pepper. She seemed to feel better while I stayed with her but relapse whenever I left for however short a period to attend to my affairs. That night I was obliged to stay with her and share the bed, because she refused to release my hand. I felt she would leave the world overnight, and we slept with our fingers intertwined.

Friday

Chapter 33

Unprecedented international concern was expressed about the trafficking of child brides in Yemen. It was the most widely disseminated news story about Yemen of the past five years! Even political developments in this nation had not been granted the same amount of coverage in the international media. With an unexpected stroke of luck, a modest local newspaper had scored a resounding success around the world. I assumed that executive editor Ghalib Zubayta must feel all puffed up with admiration for himself. He was no doubt swaggering around, cracking farts at his enemies.

Khatima was still sick. She complained of a headache, nausea, and a high temperature. I decided, without telling her, that I would take her to the hospital the next day, even against her will.

After the Friday prayer, I went out and bought a takeout lunch, qat, cigarettes, the day's papers, and a carton of Pufak snacks. I spoon-fed her broth into which I had squeezed lemon juice. I also fed her a few spoonfuls of rice and a small piece of meat—no bigger than a fingernail. Then she closed her mouth.

She would not respond to my pleas—not even with one word. She would also turn her eyes away as if she did not hear me.

I ate my fill and then gave her the medicine. I fetched the newspapers and leaned against her. She would doze off and then wake. Her breathing was occasionally troubled.

Executive Editor Riyad al-Kayyad called. I sensed from his voice that he was upset and that his nerves were frayed. "We must mount a journalistic campaign in defense of the honor of our governor."

"What do you suggest?"

"Go tomorrow morning to the governor and conduct an interview with him. Focus on getting him to deny the reports circulating about him."

"Absolutely."

"Sunday, I want you to do a very lengthy report on the Governor's achievements and explain how Hodeida has become the 'Pearl of the Red Sea' during his term in office. We will publish the report on four, color pages."

"Wait for me to jot this down."

"On Monday, survey public opinion across different segments of society about citizens' opinion of the Governor. I am looking for praise that will restore honor and recognition to this man. Don't forget that he is one of the President's key supporters. We need to fight with our bare teeth, if necessary, to extricate him from this crisis."

"I understand."

"Please don't disappoint me."

He hung up on me, leaving me shocked at his change of tone. This was the first time since he hired me that he had used the word 'please' when addressing me. The matter seemed to be serious. Perhaps for the first time, things were out of control.

Khatima woke up and moaned. I asked her how she felt, and she said she had a headache. I told her I would go down to the pharmacy and get some Panadol for her.

I bought a strip of pills and gave her one. But she did not get better. I suggested going to a walk-in clinic, but she refused. She asked me to help her walk to the window to look out at the Red Sea. I helped her stand up and walk there, leaning on me. When we reached the window, she seemed to be incapable of standing erect. So, I put my hand beneath her arm and supported her with my body to keep her upright. She rested the weight of her body on me and moaned.

Her desire was searing, and she was about to melt in my hands like butter. I lifted her off the ground and carried her to the bed. Then I provided her the remedy that cures an ailing heart as spurts of juice continued to spill forth till the appearance of the first light of day. She was so totally cured that if she qualified to participate in a race, she would have won an Olympic medal.

Saturday

Chapter 32

After the end of the workday, I conducted an interview with Governor Hamza Shu'ayl, who seemed to be a fine person and someone who had been maligned. Personally, I was convinced he was not linked to trafficking underage brides. On many occasions during my interview, he quoted verses of Arabic poetry. He was a member of a tribe famed for bravery in warfare and for a tendency to rebel against the central government. With that background, you might expect to see the earth shake beneath his feet. Contrary to that imagined stereotype, he was a cultured, demure man and as a meek as a dove.

I returned to the apartment in the afternoon, prepared the interview in record time, and sent it off. After that I did not have time for the day's papers, the satellite TV stations, or even a quick glance at Facebook, because a gazelle with lethal, aromatic musk sparred with me, and I skirmished with her with my spear until dawn.

Sunday

Chapter 31

I agreed to bathe with her, and for the first time in my life someone bothered to give me a sponge bath. She was excellent at this too. Then I took her with me for a tour of the city of Hodeida. I photographed the gardens, parks, paved streets, schools, hospitals, shopping centers, university, seaport, and airport.

We ate lunch in a restaurant that served fish, which had been baked in a traditional oven, with wavy flatbread. Then Khatima said she would like some ice cream; so, we went to al-Mitraq Street and ordered new flavors we had not tasted before. I took advantage of this opportunity to click many photos of the most famous commercial street in the city.

Next we headed to a distant beach, where I told Khatima I would stay in the vehicle to work and suggested that she swim. She said she did not know how to swim but would go into the water up to her waist and play there. In two hours, I produced a report on the city of Hodeida, and attributed all its fine features to the leadership of the Governor. After a quick review, I chose some pictures and sent the material to the newspaper.

The sun had set, and darkness was ramming its horns into the day's cracks as anger and vengeance flared in its eyes. I sounded the horn. Then Khatima rushed back to the car with her clothes all wet. She was very happy and almost leaping with joy. She said it was the first time she had ever been in the Red Sea! I placed a blanket on the seat for her and we shot off for the apartment.

We both felt a strong desire for the other person, as every square centimeter of skin of one person longed to unite with its counterpart on the other one.

Monday

Chapter 30

I purchased a man's shirt and pair of trousers for Khatima, in her size, and a broad-brimmed "straw" hat made of palm fronds and taught her how to use the camera. Her chest was a flat as a boy's and that made it possible for her to walk the streets disguised as one.

I chose people at random and asked them questions while Khatima photographed them. We were a brilliant team and did our work energetically and vibrantly. Laughter bubbled from us like water from a spring.

We returned to the apartment and washed off the sun's sweaty rays. She shoved me into the tub and rubbed my body with soap while kissing me nonstop. She was overflowing with happiness, enchanted by her experience as a journalist in the field. That had aroused in her a kind of intoxication and rapture unlike any she had experienced before. She no longer knew how to thank me or to express her gratitude.

Tuesday

Chapter 29

We woke to a catastrophe. The European Parliament had issued an edict against Yemen, condemned the marriage of minor females, and called on the Yemeni government to pass legislation specifying eighteen as the minimum age for marriage.

The executive editor called and asked me to write a series of essays for my daily column in defense of the social customs of our conservative Yemeni society. He said that Yemeni journalism was in a state of extreme mobilization and that all pens were being employed to defend the Yemeni constitution and our national sovereignty.

Wednesday

Chapter 28

Multiple governmental decisions were announced today, one of which was the announcement that Hamza Shu'ayl would be replaced as governor of Hodeida by Mr. Jabir Shanini. Another was the suspension of Judge Tahir al-Darrak and his referral to the High Commission for Combatting Corruption. Miqdad al-'Addad was appointed to replace him as judge in the court at al-Jurum. In addition to these decisions, there were many others concerning other judges and governors.

We launched a huge information campaign to convince the ambassadors of the states comprising the European Union that our announced changes addressed the statement from the Parliament of the European Union and demonstrated that Yemen was advancing on the path of modernization and civility and ending barbaric customs and traditions. What could we do? We had to bow before the storm until it passed, because these nations granted Yemen many loans and grants that were crucial for our economy.

Once I had completed all my journalistic chores, I went to the sea that evening with Khatima to teach her how to swim, as I had promised. Afterwards, we spent the most enjoyable night of our lives, and I fully satisfied her.

Thursday

Chapter 27

The transfer of power from the outgoing to the incoming governor was completed in the morning, and I went to the governorate building that afternoon to greet and congratulate my friend, Governor Jabir Shanini.

When he saw me enter his office, he jumped up from his chair and leapt to embrace me, his face was brimming with delight. He wore an expensive black suit, which was very elegant, and his red necktie added the finishing touch to make him look grand enough for his post. He excused an employee who had been sitting in the chair beside his desk and had me sit there. He ordered a cold drink for me. As he sat in his comfortable swivel chair, he kept turning it right and left like a child delighted with his new toy. He deftly slipped some black chewing tobacco behind his lower lip and relaxed. His mood immediately improved, and he smiled broadly.

I kidded him: "I'm asking for my cut."

"How so?"

"If I hadn't descended the mountain from Sana'a and turned the coast upside down with my newspaper columns, you would not have become governor."

"Well, I'm ashking you for the right to ushe your name."

"How so?"

"Yeshterday wash the happiesht day of my life, becaushe I wash appointed governor and my wife gave birth to a shon I named Mutahhar after you, shir."

"A thousand congratulations! God willing, this boy will prove a blessing to you."

"You have alsho proved a bleshshing for me, shir. I shpent twenty yearsh sherving in local cooperativesh and counshilsh and had deshpaired of ever reshieving any promotion."

When I left him, I found I was infected by his slur, replacing each "s" with "sh." I wash incapable of shtraightening out my tongue!

Friday

Chapter 26

The electricity cut off, and the air conditioner stopped running. The room quickly heated up. I woke to find myself floundering in my sweat. The communal Friday prayer had ended, and it was almost 1:30. I groped around for Khatima, who had shared the bed with me the previous evening. I found her awake and lively. She apparently had been awake for some time and was in the mood for love. I did not disappoint her desires.

The executive editor called and asked me to meet him immediately! I was confused by his request, until he explained that he was in Hodeida, staying in the Thuraya Hotel. Then he hung up.

I was totally astonished that an important man government ministers fear, someone like Riyad al-Kayyad, would leave his eagles' eyrie and descend in person to the Coast. This suggested that matters had deteriorated and gotten totally out of control. I was afflicted by anxiety and negative expectations. I prepared to depart, feeling flustered. I told Khatima I had an emergency assignment and might be out late. She brought a small pair of scissors and trimmed my mustache. Then she brushed my shoes. When I was on the stairs, she brought me the car keys, which I had forgotten. Then she zipped my zipper, which I had neglected to close!

I set off in the car toward the hotel while reminiscing about my few brief happy days there with Mona in room 307. I entered the lobby and asked the desk clerk to call the room. He asked my name, and I told him. Then he looked at the sheet of paper in front of him and asked me to go to Suite 505.

Riyad al-Kayyad welcomed me with open arms and sat me down at a table that held a bottle of whisky, a glass a quarter full, and a laptop. He asked if I was hungry, and I said: "Yes." He picked up the receiver of the house phone and ordered a multi-course lunch for the suite.

I heard a hairdryer running in the bathroom, although its door was closed. When he noticed me raise my left eyebrow as I glanced at the bathroom door, he cleared his throat loudly, to inform the person inside that I was present.

He sat down, stared straight at my face, and burst into gales of laughter. I contracted my eyebrows and asked why he was laughing. Putting his pinkie finger up a nostril, he said, "It's obvious your mother's been praying for you, because tomorrow you're going to join the adults."

I leaned forward like a cat and remarked, "Man, I'm happy where I am."

The bathroom door opened, and a beautiful young woman, two or three years my junior, emerged. Her complexion was the color of butter, she had big boobs, and her belly protruded slightly with a supple, gathered paunch. When she caught sight of me, she gasped, retreated into the bathroom, from which she asked "the gentleman" in a low voice to bring her clothes to her. "The gentleman" excused himself with great dignity and handed her the clothes through the open door.

As if to myself, I commented, "Oh! There's a woman!"

Riyad al-Kayyad laughed and asked, "Did you think I was gay, Wretch? Ha-ha!"

He shoved aside the laptop, brought two more glasses, and filled them. Then he topped up his glass. From the small fridge he brought a tray of ice cubes and placed it on the table too.

Clad in a red skirt and white blouse, the woman emerged from the bathroom. He introduced her to me, saying: "Fathiya Murshid." I rose. She extended her hand, and I shook it. Then he introduced me: "Mr. Mutahhar Fadl, your new boss, God willing."

Her smile grew wider as the look of admiration that twinkled in her eyes caused all the hair on my body to stand up. With a wink, he asked us to be seated and drop the formalities. Since curiosity was gnawing at my heart, I asked him: "What's up?"

Bringing his head toward me to indicate that he was disclosing a secret, he said, as the smell of whisky wafted from him: "We have orders to seize control of the newspaper *al-Nidal*.

I was so astonished I was speechless. He continued as all three of us moved our heads closer together: "The plan is for security forces to raid the paper's headquarters at ten p.m. and arrest everyone working there, from the doorman to the executive editor. Then the substitute team will be installed in their place. Naturally, tomorrow's edition will be released as if nothing had happened."

I whistled as I felt the world revolve around me. I asked, "Is this going down tonight?"

Riyad al-Kayyad's eyes bulged out as he replied: "Tonight! And you, Mutahhar, will become an executive editor." I swallowed, realizing that I was about to take a decisive step with incalculable future ramifications. Smiling, he placed his hand on Fathiya's back and said, "Our dear colleague Fathiya will work under your guidance."

As my eyes slipped unintentionally to her breasts, I asked, "Did you graduate from the Journalism School?"

Chuckling, she replied, "No, I earned a diploma in Computer Science. I can take charge of typesetting, layout, and production."

Scratching my chin, I commented, "Great! We'll need you more than anyone else."

Riyad al-Kayyad patted me on the shoulder and exclaimed: "Brilliant! This is the tone I like to hear from you: the tone of an executive editor!"

We were interrupted by a knock on the door. Then the waiter wheeled in the lunch cart. After distributing the plates and silverware on our table, he departed.

I began eating silently while I tried to think of some excuse to avoid taking part in this caper. I sensed I was in a swamp and that with every step I took I would become more embroiled in a lethal struggle between the ruling powers and the opposition. Meanwhile Riyad al-Kayyad chatted informally with Fathiya.

Suddenly, Riyad al-Kayyad interrupted his conversation with Fathiya and addressed me: "At six, the young men will arrive here. After half an hour while you get acquainted, you will all descend to the lobby. We have the next three hours to prepare the subjects for tomorrow's edition. After that, we will all drive to the paper's headquarters."

Fathiya rose to wash her hands. I leaned forward and whispered, "Speaking candidly, Mr. Riyad, I don't think I'm the right man for this job."

His mien changed, and anger was visible in his glare and in the swelling veins of his face. "Shut up! The entire plan is built on your participation in it. Be a man and leave this whimpering to the women. We are granting you the opportunity of a lifetime, spermatozoon."

He left me no space to defend my point of view, and I fell silent. He had a weird ability to dial up different emotions, and, suddenly, his frightening, frowning expression disappeared to be replaced by a jovial, smiley face. He said affectionately, "My son, your monthly salary will be five thousand dollars. This does not include incentives and bonuses."

I felt I was flying through the clouds. That sum was astronomical compared to my current salary of two hundred dollars a month. Staring straight into my eyes, he said, "My flight leaves at eight. I hope to hear good news from you, my son."

Fathiya rejoined us and competed with us in telling jokes and clinking glasses as our chests filled with happiness and delight flowed from our fingertips.

At five to six, Riyad al-Kayyad hid from sight the (now empty) whisky bottle and our glasses, and Fatihya drew a scarf around her hair.

In a few minutes, the young men began to arrive. I met Shareef, who would take the position of editorial director. He was a thin young man with hair as fluffy and curly as the wool on a sheep. His limp would hardly have been noticeable had he not carried a crutch. I did not feel entirely comfortable with him. Something about him was hard to digest. His glance kept flitting around, with sharp deviations of direction even as he stared at something. His face reflected his nervous personality. With Nur, though, by way of contrast, I hit it off. He wore a wide hat to ward off the sun's rays, and I guessed from the lineaments of his face that he had a gift for art or literature. He was slated to become the editorial secretary—in other words, most of the burden of our work would fall on his shoulders. The five other young men would work respectively as editors for local news, international news, investigative reporting, sports, and varieties. They were all approximately twenty-seven or twenty-eight. Except for Sharif, who had worked as a reporter for several local papers, the others were wannabes with no previous experience in journalism.

I contemplated the journalistic team I would be working with, including Fathiya, and quickly estimated their respective potential for intelligence-driven behavior. Some seemed fine people who would be easy to get along with. A few others appeared to be opportunists I would need to worry about and keep an eye on.

We waited out the time till it was a few minutes after seven p.m. Then, guffawing loudly, Riyad al-Kayyad evicted us from his room. The young men took the elevator to the ground floor while I stood at the door and said goodbye to my boss. I glanced at Fathiya, who was still standing inside. Then like a child asking permission the teacher's permission to leave a classroom, she said, "I'll catch up with all of you shortly." I shook hands with Riyad al-Kayyad and wished him a safe flight. As I turned toward the elevator, he seized my arm and whispered to my ear, "The older a man grows, the more he lusts for them!" I laughed and winked at him. Then I departed.

I fetched my laptop from the car and rushed to the lobby, which was a magnificent chamber big enough for a hundred and fifty people. The young men were sitting around a circular table that had been set up for us. On my vacant chair sat a black briefcase, and on the table in front of it were a notebook and a pen. I greeted them and examined my briefcase as I thought of Attorney Hammoud Shanta, whose grudge against me would only increase when he learned I had received a new bag, another *shanta*.

Sharif joked: "Never fear. None of us will mistake *your* bag for his!" He was the only person who laughed at his smarmy joke. I cast him a stern look. When he laughed, the muscles of his face tensed, making him look like a fox cub. Petit fours had been placed at the center of the table together with pineapple and orange juice. On a nearby table, the hotel's management had also provided a desktop computer connected to a printer.

We discussed the newspaper's header, division into sections, and production. We agreed to leave everything exactly the same so readers would not suspect any change in the editorial staff. Then I allotted tasks to them, and we set to work.

At a quarter to eight, Fathiya joined us, sauntering toward us with alluring feminine coquetry and flirtatiousness. She cast me the look that says: "Every molecule of my body desires you."

Three hours passed like a spritz of perfume without our accomplishing anything worth mentioning. Fathiya was typing the nonsense the young men wrote and printing it out to pass to me. Working with them was a nightmare. I estimated they would need a full year of training before they would be able to edit newspaper articles a reader could digest without suffering from mental diarrhea. The plan was for us to wait in the hotel until we received a call telling us to come and take control of the newspaper's offices, but I felt a gnawing curiosity to witness that hippie Ghalib Zubayta dragged away by his nose. After looking at my watch, I clapped to ask them to prepare to depart. We waited till Fathiiya had saved the material she had typed to a flash drive. Then we set off. Fatihiya sat with me in the front seat, the young men squeezed into the rear seat and the vehicle's trunk. We set off feeling pumped up. Sharif proceeded to make mocking comments about Ghalib Zubayta and his team, who would receive, he anticipated a "warm" welcome from the security forces.

We reached the street where the newspaper's office was located, and I parked fifty meters away. A Toyota Hilux belonging to the police was parked in front of the entrance to the building. Its rear section was enclosed and covered with heavy fabric. There were three other vehicles without license plates there, and a group of soldiers armed with automatic rifles formed a security cordon around the entrance.

I asked the young men to remain where they were and climbed out. Several local residents had gathered, trying figure out what was happening. I blended in with them and stood there watching. Then we heard shouting and a commotion. Soon soldiers appeared, dragging away four men, who were resisting arrest and cursing. One man, though, was weeping, asking for mercy, and begging them to release him. The soldiers placed their prisoners in the enclosed rear of the vehicle while brandishing their rifles to calm them and prevent them from disturbing the peace.

Finally, Ghalib Zubayta appeared, escorted by two soldiers, and trailed by an officer in civvies. I focused on his face, expecting to see it pale and distorted by fear, but it was as calm as a still pool. I envied him his self-control and nonchalance about imprisonment.

He climbed into the cargo section loftily, without waiting for a shove from anyone, and took a seat among his colleagues. Noticing me in the crowd, he parted his lips in a sarcastic smile. He was doubtless a man of iron will and possessed an unmatched ability to confront disasters. His bravery and composure in the face of calamity fascinated me. Then my feelings toward him flipped from one extreme to the other as I began to respect and admire him.

The squad car pulled away, leaving behind the other vehicles and several officers in civilian attire and revolvers concealed under the trench coats. Suddenly, someone emerged from the darkness and shook my hand warmly. He said, "Congratulations! The newspaper is yours, Sir."

I stared at him briefly until I remembered him. He was the head of the local branch of the intelligence services, in person.

Saturday

Chapter 25

We stayed at our headquarters till the first copies of the day's edition reached us. I received the new key to the offices, and the guards changed as we departed. Around seven a.m. I delegated Nur, the managing editor, to going to the courtroom in al-Jurum to cover the second session of Jalila's case. The group of young men invited me to eat breakfast with them in a nearby restaurant that served oven-cooked broad beans with *timis* stuffed flat bread. I excused myself and explained that I had ritually divorced myself from beans, renouncing them three times! All the guys laughed—except for Shareef, who commented sarcastically: "That fast? After only one night?" We all laughed. We were happy and would have laughed at anything.

I drove Fathiya home. She was tired and said that her day had been extremely long and packed with work! She lived in a very poor area, and the house her late father had left her was in a "vernacular" style. It had two rooms, a bathroom, and a kitchen. She was her father's first-born child and had supported her family since he died. I maneuvered the car so she could disembark directly at the stoop of her house, because the drains had overflowed, and the street had flooded, becoming a lake. I did not understand how she could enter and leave this house, for which one needed a rowboat! I waved goodbye to her as her young siblings poked their heads out to see the fancy car from which their sister had disembarked. A lengthy sigh escaped from my chest as I reflected on the psychological fissure affecting Fathiya. She had just spent hours in a luxury suite in a five-star hotel, tasted the bliss of an affluent life and was now returning to abject poverty.

What kind of person could stand this? I reflected that merry, gracious Fathiya, whose smile never left her lips, was a victim of a life spent in two contradictory worlds and that the sorrow inside must be too great for all the seas of the world to encompass.

I made a tour of the bookstands to make sure that copies of our newspaper, *al-Nidal*, had been distributed as usual. I found that people were buying our paper without any hesitation. According to the plan, the names on the masthead were those of the previous team of editors.

I returned to the apartment at nine a.m. and found Khatima asleep. I guessed that she had stayed up all night waiting for me to return. I stretched out quietly beside her, attempting as best I could to stifle the damn squeak that the bed-boards made. I was too tired to change out of my clothes. The last idea to pass through my mind before I fell asleep was that I had realized my dream of becoming the executive editor of a newspaper. But the realization of this dream was spoiled, and the pleasure associated with it was balanced by my inevitable self-hatred.

I woke at four p.m. and looked unsuccessfully for my phone. I called to Khatima, who brought it. She explained that she had removed it from me to keep it from disturbing my sleep. I found I had received dozens of missed calls. Khatima was right; obviously, it had kept ringing. I found messages from Riyad al-Kayyad, Attorney Hammoud Shanta, and my new colleague Sharif. And—what a surprise!—a message from my wife! I called her first. She answered and began cursing me without any preamble. She did not even say, "Hello." She mentioned that the satellite television stations had chastised me and that millions of people believed I was the living embodiment of Satan. Before hanging up, she demanded that I send her the children's living expenses! She left me crushed, with astonishment plastered across my face.

Then Khatima came to inquire if I was hungry. I asked her to fix me a bean sandwich and a cup of tea. I turned on my laptop and entered the web. This was an unparalleled scandal from beginning to end. The media had disclosed everything—as if they had been present with us all the past night. I had expected, as an experienced journalist who knew his way around the corridors of journalism, that such a discovery would take a certain amount of time. There was only one possible explanation: one of our crew must have leaked the information to correspondents for the news agencies, in return for a fee.

My reflections led me to Shareef, the man who was most likely to succeed me if my boats sank and I was forced to resign, but any of the other young men might have done it, motivated by ambition and a desire to advance rapidly. Or, perhaps, one of us still retained leftwing tendencies. I ruled out Fathiya because I was certain—and I'm never wrong about women—that she was almost leaping with joy at being chosen to work with me. It would not be to her advantage to torch my good name and spoil my reputation.

Shareef called while I was thinking about him. He was angry and spoke harshly. He bluntly accused Nur, the managing editor of leaking the news of the arrest of Ghalib Zubayta and his associates and our replacing them. I calmed him down and told him we would have a meeting at the newspaper's office in an hour. I requested that he respect the protocols of teamwork there, restrain his emotions, and forbear from making any further accusations.

I called Mr. Riyad al-Kayyad, who congratulated me on successfully pulling off the coup and downplayed the media frenzy. He said it was merely a tempest in a teacup and would blow over in a few days. He granted me permission to publish a new masthead with the names of our editorial team, saying there was no longer any need to dissemble.

I devoured the bean sandwich while I prepared to leave and donned new clothes. I gave Khatima a long goodbye kiss and told her, in what seemed like an apology, that I was really busy.

By the doorway of the building, I found several crumpled and shredded copies of the newspaper *al-Nidal*. This was a warning . . . but from whom? I did not know. There was definitely someone trailing me, someone who wanted to send me a specific message. I looked around but did not see any suspicious vehicles.

I phoned Fathiya and asked her to inform all the young men as quickly as possible to come to the newspaper's headquarters. On my way there, I bought qat, cigarettes, and the day's papers.

I found Nur was there before me. (The soldier had let him in.) He was leaning back and chewing qat in the newspaper's lounge. He handed me the reports he had written about the trials related to Jalila and Muhsina. In Jalila's case, the judge in the al-Jurum court had issued a ruling invalidating the medical examination conducted by the Russian physician Tatiana on grounds related to her criminal file and her consequent loss of competence. He had also issued a decision charging a Yemeni woman physician, selected by the hospital in al-Jurum, to re-examine young Jalila. In a third decision he authorized the hospital in al-Jurum to select a physician to perform a medical examination on Shaykh Bakri Hasan as well!

Interrogation of the rights activist Salam Mahdi had continued in the public prosecutor's office regarding the case lodged against her, and the deputy prosecutor had ordered a medical examination of young Muhsina, who according to the Organization for the Defense the Rights of Girls had died as a result of her husband's penile penetration of her.

Nur had also obtained an interview with Hadi Zuhayr, Jalila's grandfather. In it, he said that he refused to allow another physical examination to be performed on her, because more than a month and ten days had elapsed since the incident and because he stuck by the accuracy of the medical report by the Russian doctor, who had documented her condition at that time. He had also interviewed Attorney Shuʻayb al-ʻUjayl, who was defending the activist Salam Mahdi. This attorney had criticized the deputy prosecutor's decision to require another medical examination to establish Muhsina's virginity, since he considered that irrelevant to the case, because the question of the girl's virginity did not figure in the complaint. He demanded a careful investigation of the identity of the girl now impersonating Muhsina, who was deceased.

Except for a few errors in phrasing, Nur's effort was fine and presaged the advent of a gifted journalist. Governor Jabir Shanini called to inform me that he had issued a decree appointing Shaykh Bakri Hasan one of his advisers. I promised to publish this news on the front page of the next day's edition.

The arrival of Fathiya was announced by the fragrance of her perfume, which was one I was familiar with, since it was the perfume used by Nasama or Naseema, Riyad al-Kayyad's secretary. That womanizer must have a carton of it! Fathiya removed her high-heeled shoes and sat down at the edge of the group. She was opening up like a rose, and the goodness of the world sparkled from her eyes. I made a few slight corrections to Nur's stories and chose zinger titles for them. Then I handed them to Fathiya to begin typesetting them.

Shareef appeared suddenly in the doorway and cast glances at me and Nur that suggested more than he would say aloud. Even so, it was not hard to guess what was on his mind.

Riyad al-Kayyad called and suggested we publish an article criticizing the Adeni newspaper *al-Ayyam*. He wanted us to teach them a lesson. I immediately assigned Shareef, the managing editor, to write an article blasting *al-Ayyam* and describing it as lacking professionalism, violating the simplest rules of journalistic work, and demonstrating an over-zealousness to publish news of the death of the child Muhsina, who was later found and in good health.

Attorney Hammoud Shanta appeared with an announcement of all the charitable work conducted by Shaykh Bakri Hasan. We naturally had to publish this announcement free of charge. He made himself at home in our lounge, chewing qat with us, and that annoyed me. Had the Shaykh sent him to keep an eye on us and the paper?

By seven p.m. the entire crew was assembled, and we agreed to meet in my office. Hammoud Shanta stuck to me like a cat, even while we agreed to revise the distribution of work. I assigned each of them specific tasks. Once this meeting concluded, Hammoud Shanta handed me a poem he wanted published. I read it. It was a silly love poem like those adolescent boys write in secondary school, but I welcomed the idea of publishing it. I told myself that everything in the world was corrupt; what was wrong in corrupting the taste of our readers?

Nur asked my permission to leave early, saying that he hadn't slept since the night before last. I agreed and told him I would check his articles for him once they were typeset.

We finished our work around midnight, and Shareef took the

edition to the printers. I offered to drive Fathiya home, and she accepted. On the way there, she asked me where I lived and who lived with me. I did not tell her about Khatima. Instead, I told her I lived by myself in a furnished apartment. Her hint was clear and needed no further clarification. She was speaking to me and looking at me in ways that almost devoured me. For my part, I made a point of preventing my eyes from meeting hers and kept mine fixed on the road.

I boldly asked her, "Why haven't you married?"

"That's up to you. Find me a husband, and I'll marry him now before sunrise!"

"It's incredible that a girl as beautiful as you does not have a bridegroom knocking on her door. Have the men in my country gone blind?"

"All the men who presented themselves to me wanted me for a second wife."

"Are you opposed to polygamy?"

"I opposed it till I turned thirty and found a grey hair on my head."

"Does that mean that if a married man offers himself to you, you will accept?"

"Of course. What's important is for me to get married. You can't imagine what it's like to be a spinster in Yemen. If you did, you would take pity on me and marry me immediately. Ha-ha!"

"Ha-ha. What would you think about devoting a page in the paper to women? You would edit it."

"I agree on one condition."

"What is it?"

"That you show a little interest in the woman in the car with you!"

We laughed and I promised to look out for her.

Sunday

Chapter 24

I parked the car and began to walk around aimlessly. The afternoon sky was plastered with clouds, which would probably not shed their rain here but scale the mountains instead to drench Sana'a. People here are right to complain about Yemen's over-centralization!

I stopped at a bookstore. A stack of our newspaper, *al-Nidal* (*The Struggle*) languished there unpurchased. I noticed a tattered, dog-eared copy of a commemorative book about my father and felt conflicting emotions. Then I took the plunge and bought it.

I had never read it, even though it had been published ten years earlier, on the occasion of a celebration that opposition political parties organized to honor my father.

I remembered that I had not attended the celebration and had not said so much as "congrats" to my dad. I had arrogantly ignored the party and refused to read this book even when he gave me a copy. I was jealous of him and resented society's respect and veneration for him. I envied the extraordinary way people honored him. From that time on, our relationship deteriorated, and I started to avoid him and all the leftist dwarves who were captivated by him and bowed before him. I would not bow to him. His halo did not blind me. I neglected no opportunity to remind him of this.

My father had certainly discerned my loathing for him, and that hurt him. Someone may have told on me and informed him that I tore up my copy of the book and threw it in the trash.

If that wasn't bad enough, I turned my back on his leftist views and joined the ruling elite. With deliberate premeditation, I may have hastened his demise.

Monday

Chapter 23

I read the book about my father and learned something new about myself. I realized that my struggle had not been with the harsh circumstances of my life but with him. I had continued to wrestle with him even after he lay shrouded in his grave. Worst of all, I had sacrificed him for a rotten apple.

I fell in love with Houriya on our first day in the Communications Department, attracted by her forceful personality. Her conceited arrogance dashed the hopes of potential admirers, who fell around her like moths. For me, though, her sense of her own importance and her snobbery only increased my infatuation with her.

She humiliated me on numerous occasions, whether alone or with her girlfriends. I aroused her repulsion and aversion, perhaps because I was shabbily dressed, but did not give up. I absolutely did not despair. I struggled for two whole years till she relented and deigned to speak to me. I succeeded in changing her view of me—from contempt to infatuation. I think she read my essays and that changed her assessment of me. I later asked her about this, after we were married. She said then that she didn't know why she had fallen in love with me! I realize now that the professors' praise for my talents made me a center of attraction and even of affection for coed classmates. She may have felt jealous of them and fell in love with me for this reason!

By the time we finished our studies, we were already dreaming of the house we would share, the number of children we would have, and the countries we would visit during our holidays.

After graduation she asked me to visit her father, so he could meet me and decide our fate.

On the appointed day, I set out for his mansion. At the gate, guards stopped me and called inside. After searching me, they allowed me to enter. I walked through a garden that had a fountain at its center. A huge police dog barked at me, and I praised God that he was on a chain. I opened the aluminum screen door and entered a closed entryway, where I removed my trainers and placed them on the special shoe rack. Then I opened a wooden door so massive and heavy it could have been the entrance to a fortified castle. The moment I set foot on the luxurious carpet, a grating voice scolded me: "Wrong... close the door behind you." I did not dare look up to see who had issued this command. Instead, I turned and shut the door. After I thought I had corrected my error, I saw my future father-in-law, who stood, scowling, at the end of the hall. I shook his hand and introduced myself in a faltering voice. He did not bother to introduce himself. Instead, he said: "We close the doors to keep flies out." I nodded my head enthusiastically and smiled idiotically.

Casting me a steely look that would have splintered a rock, he asked, "Did you not understand what I said? You didn't close the screen door. Shut it!" I obeyed him shamefacedly, hurrying to the entry vestibule and then shutting the aluminum door. When I returned, he had vanished. After looking everywhere, I noticed a room to my right. It was illuminated by chandeliers and elegantly furnished. I decided to enter it and sat on the couch nearest the door. A pretty Filipino maid appeared and offered me mango juice. Then my mood quickly improved as I realized I was no longer inhaling the polluted air of the hoi polloi outside. I was instead breathing air scented with fine aloes-wood incense.

He returned, holding a puppy, and I stood up respectfully. He sat down in the center of the room and played for a time with the puppy. Then he turned toward me and asked, "Why are you standing there like a traffic sign? Come sit here." I obeyed him, overcome by a sense of belittlement and humiliation. I perched on the edge of the sofa, feeling disconcerted. I sat there for almost an hour and a half, until he excused me.

His master-of-the-universe presence reminded me of the inferiority complex I have suffered since childhood. I was embarrassed by my poverty, and my self-confidence evaporated. I began to fear I would act inappropriately. I stammered when I conversed with him, and my voice was so soft that my words scarcely emerged from my mouth. Sweat poured from my armpits and palms. I couldn't lift my head to look him straight in the eye.

He said he knew "everything" about me! He praised my family's authentic tribal heritage but spoke slightingly of my father. I did not object. In fact, I agreed with him. When he touched on this aspect of my life, he said something that would ring in my ears for a long time: "I want to marry my daughter to a government man. Are you prepared to become part of the establishment?"

I answered, "Yes." Then his expression relaxed a bit, and he dropped his haughty, hostile tone when addressing me. He warned me not to follow in the tracks of the scum who opposed the government. He mentioned that my father was a worthless vagabond who had destroyed himself and had harmed the nation more than helped it.

After this meeting, my situation stabilized, and money started to flow through my hands. I met Yemeni society's upper crust and felt that I had entered paradise.

Tuesday

Chapter 22

I did not like many of the essays about my father, but the book, taken as a whole, made a definite impression on me—one that was difficult to describe precisely.

In this country, you either bow to tyranny to eat your fill—or—pick up the pen and suffer the consequences. These are two incompatible paths; I chose the former, easier one. I discovered, however, that when a person opens his mouth to eat, he consumes not only tasty treats and delicacies but other items he had never imagined: shit, for example.

Meanwhile, back here in the Tihama, the Coastal Plain, Fathiya continued to pursue me with her love letters and calls suggesting we should go out for lunch or dinner. I evaded her politely, trying not to hurt her feelings. It was hard for me to explain what I was experiencing. Ever since we had embarked on the operation of wresting the newspaper *al-Nidal* from its proprietor, I had lost my interest in sex; I did not even approach Khatima! The reason may have been the intense pressure I was experiencing. Perhaps exhaustion and late nights had depleted my physical powers. I will mock myself to high heaven once I'm inducted to the Society of the Impotent! That's all I need!

The public prosecutor's office in al-Jurum received the result of the medical examination of the girl named Muhsina. It confirmed that she was still a virgin. I asked Nur to take a deposition from her husband attesting to his innocence. But Nur returned without it, because the husband had disappeared after false information was published about him. I asked Nur to return the next day and conduct an interview with Muhsina's father. We needed to show our readers and the inquisitive eyes of the world that he had stipulated to her spouse that their marriage would remain unconsummated till she came of age. Nur did not realize that this girl wasn't the real Muhsina, who had disappeared like holiday candy consumed by worms.

Wednesday

Chapter 21

I went to the office of the new Governor, Mr. Jabir Shanini, after receiving a call from him. There he handed me a check for ten million rials and asked me to go to the business office and sign a contract with them to distribute a thousand copies a day of the newspaper *al-Nidal* to all government offices in the governorate. This liberal financial support also was a face-saving ploy for us after the sharp decline in the newspaper's sales.

Nur returned from al-Jurum with the text of an interview with Ibrahim Belghith, the father of Muhsina, and a photo of the marriage contract. It contained a clause in which the girl's guardian stipulated that her husband not consummate his marriage with her until she came of age.

After we prepared this material for publication, managing editor Shareef added a sentence that had Belghith saying: "Since the girl grew up in our rural, conservative society, she would naturally come of age only at eighteen."

Nur objected to this addition, and we debated it with Shareef, but it would have been easier to conduct a debate with a billy goat than with him. So, we gave up and allowed his addition to pass.

Thursday

Chapter 20

The arrest of the previous editorial team attracted international attention. The situation is critical. Multiple major organizations of journalists have issued statements of condemnation. It seems we won't succeed. We now resemble a woman without panties: anyone, from the East or West can see her privates and even stretch his hand out to touch them!

The public prosecutor in al-Jurum is proceeding with the case against the human rights activist Salam Mahdi. We will learn next week the scheduled time for the first session. I believe her position is weak and that she will be convicted.

A day off today. We will not publish an issue tomorrow, because it is Friday. Fathiya suddenly appears this afternoon without an appointment. I don't know how she obtained the address. Khatima opens the door for her and shows her into the parlor. I find myself in an embarrassing situation. Khatima bares her fangs and does not leave us alone for a moment. Jealousy flares from her eyes like lethal rays, and she is ready to devour Fathiya alive! Fathiya is naturally conscious of the young girl's hostility and grasps that I am not the ascetic she had thought me. I ask Khatima to prepare tea for the guest, and she returns with it in less than a minute as if she were a jinni with seven hands! She does not grant us any opportunity to be alone and converse comfortably. Whenever Fathiya raises the glass to drink, Khatima coughs to make her feel disgusted. After two sips, Fathiya notices the girl's fingerprints inside the lip of glass and sets it aside, not hiding her revulsion. Khatima casts a victorious glance at her. Then Fathiya apologizes—I'm not sure to whom or for what—and excuses herself. I offer to drive her home, but she declines my offer abruptly and leaves without saying goodbye.

Half an hour later I receive a text message from her on my phone: "All you men are the same. All you like are young girls. Every one of you needs a shrink."

I give Khatima a hard time for her rude conduct with my work colleague and ask her to treat my guests graciously. She does not listen to what I say. Instead, she looks at my face while repeating something to herself. I can discern this from the movement of her lips and her eyes. I wish I were clairvoyant and could tell what's passing through her brain.

Friday

Chapter 19

I used the search engine Google to collect photos of my father, feeling a sudden yearning for this man I knew only through other people's eyes!

I think he died content with life and happy and satisfied with himself. As for me: not so much. I used to think that I was a profoundly happy person, that I had achieved success in life, and that I had vanquished hunger and poverty. But now I know I have never been victorious, successful, or happy. I'm a failure. My defeat has been real, even though I wasn't conscious of it. This is all the harder, *because* it never crossed my mind.

Saturday

Chapter 18

Despite the hostility that circumstances imposed on us, I have wept bitterly for him. I feel complicit in his murder, that my hand is soiled by his blood, which has been shed unjustly. They have discovered the corpse of my friend—who wasn't thought to be my friend—Sami Qasim, the local correspondent for the Adeni newspaper *al-Ayyam*, in a dense banana grove on the banks of Wadi al-Dud. They found him slaughtered like a goat, his eyes gouged out. They killed him in a hideous way, but his death was not devoid of heroism, because he died for his cause, and this is an appropriate death for brave men. Absolutely no one will think of shedding the worthless blood of fearful cowards who have never supported any cause. This is certainly a day that is heavy-laden with sorrow. I feel sorry for my journalistic colleague and for myself.

I am not embarrassed to say that I envy him his death. I need a legendary death like this if I am to raise my head high. I perceive that my desires are mutually conflicting and that my heart in not synchronized with my intellect. Perhaps—as Fathiya suggested—I need a shrink.

Sunday

Chapter 17

There was a hearing today for young Jalila's case, and results of the medical examination of the Shaykh were submitted. The girl's guardian, Hajj Hadi Zuhayr, also repeated his rejection of any further medical examination of his granddaughter. The judge proposed an amicable resolution of the case: namely that Jalila be married to Shaykh Bakri Hasan, there, in the courtroom and that he—the Shaykh—be required to pay the dowry customary in the region. Shaykh Bakri Hasan immediately expressed his acquiescence and announced that he was prepared to pay three times as much as the typical dowry for a virgin in the region. At that point, Hajj Hadi Zuhayr rose and announced his categorical rejection of this attempt at reconciliation.

I transmitted to my wife a modest sum—enough to purchase diapers and powdered milk. I did this only because I had to.

Khatima puts lots of fiery spices in my food and has me on a rich diet. I've gotten plump, gaining several kilos. I forgot to commend Khatima's abilities in the kitchen. She is a killer cook; I mean: a man can't keep himself from eating what she cooks, down to the last crumb, it is so tasty. I naturally grasp what she is up to; she is attempting to fortify my virility. She is mistaken; my problem hasn't been a lack of sex drive. It is my nervous fragility. My mood hasn't been conducive to cohabitation. In short, the thing dangling from my groin has been on strike. I don't know what its demands are. Nor have I, for my part, attempted to investigate the causes. Perhaps that son of a bitch believes the opposition propaganda and has gone on strike to express its solidarity with the demands of the United Nations, which has outlawed sex with minor girls. This cursed penis had become a human rights advocate without me even noticing!

Monday

Chapter 16

The authorities bowed to international pressure and this morning released Ghalib Zubayta and his gang. That tramp has become a national hero. There is strong elation on the opposition side.

We increased security at the newspaper's headquarters to prevent that foul creature from even thinking of approaching it.

I made peace with Fathiya and invited her to have dinner in an elegant restaurant. Without meaning to, I touched her leg under the table with mine. Then she thought I was being fresh. So she drew her leg away and commented with a frown: "My God, masturbating would be better for me than sex with you!" I did not fully understand what she meant, but I caught the gist of it: that she was ready to do anything rather than resort to me. I told myself: *She's cunning, by God: she's seems to have grasped my problem!* Nonetheless, my experience with women suggested that they do not always mean exactly what they say and that occasionally by merely considering a phrase from another angle we may discover that. But Fathiya did not seem to me to be the sort of person who pretends one thing and means the opposite. I felt she was a frank woman who expressed what she thought without beating around the bush.

We launched into a literary discussion, and I was surprised to find that she is an avid reader. She said she had read all the plays she could get hold of when she was an adolescent and that she had aspired to be a professional actress. We both laughed at this aspiration, which seemed unachievable in Yemen, a country that seemed closer to the Middle Ages than to a land that produced films and plays. When her eyes filled with tears, I wiped the sarcastic smirk off my face and remarked quite seriously: "I am sure that if allowed the opportunity, you will become a famous actress." She made no comment; her voice may have failed her. This had proved a difficult moment—one that was difficult for a person to experience without being shaken to his depths.

I contemplated her with a new eye. She was no longer some poor woman I could easily acquire. I saw her now as a human being who harbored deep inside her a talent that was a treasure, which no hand had reached for and which had not yet become visible. With any luck, this treasure would emerge, and she might become a star. Why not? She's beautiful, congenial, another Myriam Fares, and has grace and allure. Many women and men carry within them treasures but die poor because they were born in a poor, backward country that did not help them manifest the treasure buried beneath their skin.

Tuesday

Chapter 15

Shaykh Bakri Hasan has committed an atrocious error. Drunk and accompanied by armed supporters, he attacked the house of Hajj Hadi Zuhayr and threatened to kill him if he did not marry Shaykh Bakri to Hadi Zuhayr's granddaughter Jalila.

After the Shaykh and his group left, Jalila's grandfather went to the public prosecutor's office and submitted a complaint about the incident. He also contacted the human rights activist Salam Mahdi and recounted the affair to her in exquisite detail. In a matter of hours, the news was everywhere, and all of Yemen knew the Shaykh had not only become intoxicated and aggressive but was madly in love with Jalila!

Wednesday

Chapter 14

I lost my enthusiasm about working at the newspaper *al-Nidal*, but we had to continue providing fodder for our readers. The state needed to provide fodder for readers daily, without interruption. This fodder was just as necessary for citizens as fodder for livestock in their corrals. Without such fodder, the state would lose control of its herd. Newsprint and feed were both sourced from plants that grew in the earth, and this meant that the sop presented to people and animals came from the same source.

Thursday

Chapter 13

Unconfirmed reports say Ghalib Zubayta has been offered the position of editor for the newspaper *al-Sanabil al-Hamra'* ("Red Ears of Grain"). I remember that my late father published essays in that paper. May God be gracious to those bygone days when Yemen rocked from its north to its south—before the fall of the Soviet Union. Now it is merely a has-been paper with only a few pages and looks like some school publication. It is published irregularly with gaps of months at times. Occasionally it releases one or two issues a year. In view of the consequences, they should change its name to "Zubayta's Ears of Grain" in honor of the idiot who will run it.

Friday

Chapter 12

Khatima perfumed me with incense and said I had been bewitched by the evil eye! Then she asked me to accompany her to the public bath where she could wash me with water mixed with special additives that would decontaminate me. I played along with her, because I frankly was ashamed of myself, even though I did not share her superstitious beliefs.

The strange thing is that—and I have no explanation for it—I was cured by these ablutions and then had intercourse with her five times in a row in a normal manner. She said I had received the evil eye from Fathiya. She was certain of that, because, ever since Fathiya's visit, my "pestle" had stopped pounding! She cursed Fathiya rancorously and spewed out all the hatred and jealousy that had collected in her heart. I laughed at her frown and the way she blamed that poor woman for my tool's failure to pound.

Saturday

Chapter 11

I returned from the newspaper at 11 p.m. The lights in the apartment were off, and Khatima wasn't there; even her personal possessions and clothes were missing. I called her on the cellphone I had given her, but it was turned off. The first thing that occurred to me was that Shaykh Bakri Hasan had sent his chauffeur to retrieve her. I called the Shaykh and praised God when he answered. He said that he knew nothing about Khatima and that he had not sent anyone for her. I told him I would inform the police of her disappearance. He asked me to give him half an hour to contact his acquaintances in Dayr al-Dumu'. He would find out from them if she had returned to her family.

I endured a rough half-hour, feeling super-anxious as dark thoughts tormented my mind. Finally, the shaykh contacted me and told me that Khatima was not with her family. He said he would organize a search for her by men from the district on the morrow. When I thanked him, my voice was distorted by my sobs.

I was tormented by the thought that she might be in danger and that I was responsible. I don't know why, but this idea tortured me. I contacted the attorney Hammoud Shanta and told him what had happened. He asked me not to take it seriously and suggested that Khatima might have gone out and become lost on the way back. I was not pleased by his dismissive tone and told him that it was almost midnight and that her clothes were missing. She had left the apartment for some unknown place. He said he would contact the police stations in Hodeida to ask if they had received any reports about a missing girl. I told him I would wait to hear back from him.

I stayed up till all the roosters announced the arrival of the day, but he did not return my call.

Sunday

Chapter 10

I had no legal relationship that would allow me to report Khatima's absence to the police. So I called the attorney Hammoud Shanta again. He told me he had contacted the police stations, but that they had no information about her. He also said he had submitted a report in writing to the police, requesting they hunt and search for her.

I searched my phone for an appropriate photo of her and found one. I had decided to publish an announcement about her in our newspaper.

The court in al-Jurum held an initial hearing in the case brought against the rights activist Salam Mahdi on the charge of distributing fake news. Her position had become extremely difficult, because her key witness on her behalf and the source for her information was murdered.

Our correspondent reported that attorney Shu'ayb al-'Ajayl presented the court with a copy of the newspaper *al-Ayyam*, which had printed the information. Judge Miqdad al-'Addad, however, refused to accept this in evidence on the grounds that *al-Ayyam* is a private—not a government—newspaper. Therefore, what it prints does not count as evidence the court can admit.

Monday

Chapter 9

The Monday edition of my newspaper, *al-Nidal*, came out with an announcement about Khatima's disappearance, together with a photo. I placed my telephone number in the report and that of attorney Hammoud Shanta, for people to contact if they found her.

Fathiya altered her treatment of me and dropped her reserve. Once more she laughed and joked with me.

We received no tips about Khatima, and the police did not report they had found her. I felt anxious for her, fearing she had fallen into the clutches of a criminal gang that had raped and killed her. . . because we heard from time to time about girls who had met this bloody, violent fate. One suspicion that ran through my mind was that she had been the victim of a traffic accident and that her body was in the morgue of one of the hospitals.

After we left the offices of the newspaper, at approximately midnight, Fathiya climbed into my car with me so I could drive her home. We began talking about the Inebriates Restaurant, and she insisted that she wanted to dine there. I tried my hardest to dissuade her from this idea.

I drove to the restaurant, where we chose a table inside, far from prying eyes. This was a terrifying experiment but passed without any untoward events. It demonstrated that drunks are more polite and gracious than the typical man in the street.

Tuesday

Chapter 8

Today my final essay for my column in *al-Shaʻb* was published. In it, I bade farewell to the readers and apologized that I was currently consumed by writing a daily column for the Hodeida newspaper *al-Nidal*.

We finished work at the newspaper early—at nine-thirty. Fathiya jumped into my car and asked me to invite her once more to the Inebriates Restaurant. I apologized, pointing out that it did not open till after midnight. When she frowned in an alarming fashion, I suggested we get carry-out from a restaurant and eat at my apartment. When I mentioned that I keep a bottle of vodka in the fridge, she accepted happily.

We supped and boozed. In a whisper, she asked whether her spending the night with me would cause me a problem. I replied that her returning home to spend the night with her family was what would cause me a huge problem! She laughed wholeheartedly, fully understanding what I meant. We were on the same wavelength and in synch in an amazing way—as if each of us were the other's missing half.

Wednesday

Chapter 7

That puff pastry was kneaded from lust. We spent the whole day together in bed. I absolutely did not feel tired. I seemed to have a secret energy inside me. It must have been retained and held in reserve since my childhood for this woman and her body, which offered me a sincere feeling that it had been waiting for me since it formed in her mother's womb.

We dragged our feet to the newspaper with difficulty, not wanting to separate even for a moment. There we found a catastrophe awaiting us. The Human Rights Commission of the United Nations in Geneva had issued a decision criminalizing marriage to underage girls in Yemen and subjecting perpetrators of this crime to criminal penalties.

Riyad al-Kayyad contacted me and asked me to provide him with a folder of the Yemeni government's actions limiting underage marriage so he could to print it in *al-Sha'b*. He observed that the young reporters working for me must know how this was practiced on the Tihama littoral. All of us were to set aside other work and concentrate on this folder. He also ordered me to remain in the office till dawn—in case he needed me to edit any additional materials that might be requested. I announced a state of emergency at the newspaper, and we began squeezing our imaginations to invent these alleged achievements of the Yemeni government.

Judge Miqdad al-'Addad telephoned me and asked me jocularly

what international punishments were being threatened against Yemeni judges. I had difficulty restraining my laughter. Instead, I suggested that he should forget about marrying the Shaykh to Jalila—otherwise American drones would scour Yemen, meter by meter, to locate his house. The judge laughed and concluded by saying: "I wish to God that the Shaykh had never seen even her fingernail!" I asked him what he would do at the session scheduled for the coming Saturday. He replied that he had intended to issue a ruling that would have forced both sides to agree to a truce and complete the marriage—on the assumption that cohabitation had already occurred. Now, though, he did not know what he would do, especially since Jalila's case was still under the microscope of international journalism.

Fathiya grasped that tonight would not belong to her but to the United Nations, which she kept cursing and denigrating! At eleven, she asked my permission to leave, and I granted it. One of the young men took her place typesetting. She handed me a folded slip of paper before she departed. I opened it and found this message on it: "Call me when you return to your apartment, so I won't worry about you."

We struggled to do what we had to, and I sent the requested folder to Sana'a. We also created another, smaller supplement for our paper. It was a miracle, but we delivered the copy to the printers before daybreak.

We returned to our homes crawling on our bellies we were so exhausted, and I forgot to telephone Fathiya.

Thursday

Chapter 6

My mobile phone never stopped ringing. It rang incessantly as if an assassin were trying to slay it. I struggled to open my eyes and looked at my watch. It was almost 9:15 in the morning. I picked up the phone, cursing the caller. It was my wife's number. I felt alarmed and feared that one of my children had suffered some injury. When I answered, she swore at me bitterly. Without any preamble, she asked for a divorce. I was not capable of comprehending the live, low-minded, verbal ammunition she fired at me, because I was still half-asleep and drowsy from a lack of sleep. I promised her a divorce at the earliest opportunity and hung up. I really did not mean to insult her, but I wasn't fully conscious. When the phone started ringing again, I turned it off.

I dreamt I was walking down a road toward the sea, which I could see clearly before me. Then an intense sandstorm blew in, and I was unable to advance. Other people, traveling in automobiles, continued on and reached the sea without difficulty. I exerted exceptional effort to make my way to the seashore, which seemed to be sheltered from the sandstorm. A cookout and dance party was in full swing there, but I did not succeed in reaching it. I reversed direction and headed back, deciding that moving in any direction was better than lingering in the same place and leaving myself exposed to those grains of sand, which I felt were entering my nostrils on their way to my brain, transiting my mouth to my windpipe and lungs, blocking my ears, and making it impossible for me to hear, while also blinding my eyes.

Before I could finish this dream, loud pounding on the door of the apartment woke me. I pulled on my clothes and opened the door. It was Fathiya, and she threw herself into my embrace and began crying as soon as she saw me. Frankly, she was weeping so feverishly that I thought someone dear to her had died. When she mentioned that I seemed sleepy, I immediately woke up. She asked, "Do you know the news?"

Pulling my torso back, I asked, "What news?"

She opened her handbag and pulled out a tabloid paper she had folded multiple times till it was the size of a playing card. "Read what that wretched girl you sheltered has said about you!"

My body trembled, and my pulse rate surged as I gazed at the paper. My gaze focused first on its logo, which was composed of seven red ears of grain, and then on the bold headline: "Khatima, a child, tells the story of her flight from the apartment of a famous journalist who kept her as his sex slave." I felt that someone had struck my skull from the rear with a hammer. I turned to the tenth page, where a color photograph of Khatima occupied a quarter of the page. The caption read: "The Child Khatima Was a Victim of Sex-Trafficking of Minors in Yemen." They had published my picture on the opposite page with the caption: "The Human Monster, Mutahhar Fadl, the Journalist who Purchased the Girl Khatima, Enslaved Her, and Used Her as a Household Servant and a Tool for Forbidden Enjoyment."

I could not keep my balance, sat down on the floor, and rested my head in my hands. My right hand, which held the paper, was trembling, and I wasn't able to continue reading. So I let if fall to the ground.

Fathiya wanted to take the paper, but I prevented her and told her I would read the entire article, after I investigated the matter. Fathiya noticed that I was dumbfounded and paralyzed as I stared at the newspaper, incapable of moving. She lifted me from the ground and supported me till I reached the bed. She asked me to rest. I told her I would not rest till she left and took the paper with her. She said she would burn it. I told her, "I'm what deserves to be burned, alive."

Fathiya burst into tears. She was at a loss for how to console me. My marriage had collapsed. My reputation had been dragged through the mud. My wife had every right to ask for a divorce. I did not see how I could appear in public after this outrageous scandal or even look in the eyes any person who recognized me. The verdict against me had been pronounced, and I was finished. I no longer had any reputation or honor to claim. I had lost every right to be respected by other people. Death would be the best option for someone who, like me, found myself debased and besmirched in the eyes of my family, friends, and acquaintances. Everyone would shun him with the same detestation as if he had tested positive for the bubonic plague. My future had been smashed by a shattering blow from an axe. Even if I lived for ten thousand years, I would never be able to reclaim my renown, former status, or people's respect for my name and that of my time-honored family. What an unexpected ending for the hero!

Attorney Hammoud Shanta arrived and hugged me tight. He said: "We must present a solid front. Write an authorization for me to sue the rights activist Salam Mahdi and the newspaper *al-Sanabil al-Hamra*'."

I told him I would not sue anyone. "If anyone has wronged me—may God forgive him."

Fathiya volunteered that she was prepared to testify in court that the girl Khatima was living with me of her own free will, without constraint. I told her the matter would not go to court. The attorney protested incredulously, "You must not have read the entire article! The human rights activist Salam Mahdi says she will pursue charges against you in court that you enslaved a minor girl and took sexual advantage of her. She will establish in court that you sired the fetus in her belly."

I was stunned. The blood drained from my face, and I felt that a jackhammer was drilling between my ears. Fathiya and Hammoud continued talking, but I had no idea what they were saying. I just saw their lips move like froth on waves in the sea. I was far from them, plunging into blowing sand as the wind battered my face with indescribable violence from every direction. My two friends were beyond this storm. I was struggling alone with fate's wrath and might. The two of them were in another world, one that was settled and peaceful, and their feet were placed firmly on the ground. Their view was unobstructed. I was in a crumbling world encompassed by dangers and fears and shrouded by a dense fog.

Friday

Chapter 5

I am lying in bed, suffering from a fever, and tons of nightmares are pounding on the walls of my brain, almost exploding it.

Fathiya is caring for me.

Saturday

Chapter 4

Khatima stated that she fled from my apartment to the headquarters of the Organization for the Defense of Girls' Rights to seek protection from repeated rapes and the savage treatment to which she was subjected. She described me as a monster addicted to "fucking young girls". She said that the fate of another girl named Mona, who had been subjected to the same treatment sexual and physical liberties taken, was unknown.

I read and reread this account more than sixty times and thought for a long time about my future. Unfortunately, my enemies had left me no alternative. All I could do was return to my roots.

Sunday

Chapter 3

I decided to burn my university diploma when I returned to Sana'a, because it was of no use to me now.

I plotted meticulously how I would take my children, by force if necessary, and then travel to the countryside, to a region under my tribe's firm control.

I would invest all my savings to buy weapons and ammunition and rebuild my reputation there as a tribal man—a powerful, prestigious person, whose foes dread his awesome might.

I decided to lay claim to the tribal shaykhdom my father had renounced and retrieve it from the Hijam clan. I would recruit a strike force from my tribe: the most skillful marksmen and prepare ambushes for my enemies, eradicating them mercilessly one by one: Ghalib Zubayta, Salam Mahdi, and even Khatima, if I ever established that she was complicit and had not acted as she did under duress.

I will lead the courageous men of my tribe and launch raids against the offices of the newspaper *al-Sanabil al-Hamra'* and other papers and organizations that have besmirched my reputation. No one who has done me wrong will escape my vengeance. Not even a stone will be spared my punishment.

I will demonstrate my authentic mountaineer mettle and show them a face tempered by fire. I will impose my word on the land from east to west.

Monday

Chapter 2

The first day I left my apartment after the scandal, the sunlight hurt my eyes, and everything looked yellow to me. That morning I purchased a white outfit, black cloaks, a shawl, and a turban. That evening I perfected my presentation as a tribal dignitary by purchasing an expensive curved dagger, a Russian revolver, and agate prayer beads.

I used scissors to destroy my ID card and threw the scraps in the trash with no regrets.

Tuesday

Chapter 1

I wrote my letter of resignation from my position as editor-in-chief of *al-Nidal* newspaper and asked Fathiya to submit it for me to Shareef, who would replace me as the editor.

I packed my bags in preparation for a return to Sana'a and told Fathiya I felt an overwhelming desire to see my children and embrace them. After that, I would take care of a few matters and disappear from public view in my tribe's lands for several months, until people forgot about my case.

She did not believe me. Her hunch was that I was up to some mischief. Perhaps the look in my eye betrayed me.

I picked up my belongings and locked the apartment. Fathiya wept, and her voice was hoarse when she begged me to stay. I offered to drive her home one last time, but she rejected my offer. She said she would stay with me till the last moment.

I drove the car back to the lot from which I had rented it and turned in the keys. We took a taxi to the bus station. We sat in the taxi's back seat, where Fathiya clutched my arm. She leaned her head on my shoulder, and her tears dampened my shirt.

We took out my bags, and I left Fathiya—this loyal, sincere woman—to guard them. I went to the window to buy a ticket, but the agent told me all the seats for the day had been reserved and that I would need to travel the next day, if I wanted a seat. I thanked him and said I would sort things out myself. I could not bear to remain for even one more hour on the Tihama. I resembled a dying bird that seeks a place to bury itself.

We took a second taxi to a stand for Peugeot vans, and I quickly acquired a seat. I said goodbye to Fathiya with a handshake and only freed my hand from hers with difficulty. She remained on the curb, drying her eyes and nose, her face red from crying. She was unconscious of the sun's burning rays and the loitering men's leering looks. Once the requisite number of passengers had assembled, we all paid the driver, and drove off, just as the noon call to prayer resounded. I waved to Fathiya, who quickly disappeared from sight behind clusters of vehicles and people.

We reached the city of Bajil in an hour and stopped for lunch there. When I entered the restaurant, I was dizzy from hunger. I had consumed nothing but water since morning. I ordered a vegetable stew with half a roast chicken. I ate just enough to quiet my stomach and wrapped up the chicken, which I had not touched, and handed it to a poor woman, who sat in the dirt nursing her child.

Then I went to a nearby store and bought cigarettes and mineral water. I stood in a shady place waiting for the other passengers. I looked east toward the mountains, which were only a few kilometers ahead of us, and saw a flash of lightning; the sky was overcast with clouds.

After raising a cry and several tedious searches, the driver finally succeeded in assembling the passengers and shoving them inside the vehicle like a herd of sheep that moved only when directed by their shepherd's staff.

When we stopped at a petrol station to get gas, we began to

hear thunder clearly. Someone commented that we would soon see flooding streams and cataracts. An old woman came to beg from us, but no one gave her any money. Even I kept my hand away from my pocket, because she frightened me. She had the strangest eyes in the world. They were yellow and left you with the impression that they spiraled deep inside her. They were orbs capable of drawing anything deep inside them. Had someone told me something like this, I would not have believed him, but I experienced this myself, and it was definitely nothing like the phony fear we feel when watching a horror movie. This was a genuine fear that penetrated your heart and made you want to urinate. She suddenly poked her head toward the driver and told him: "Don't travel tonight."

The driver, who seemed calm, asked her, "What do you mean 'night', lady? It's still daytime."

"Haven't you heard of the old man's ghost that appears once a year? Tonight's his anniversary."

Swallowing hard, the driver replied, "I've heard."

Pointing to the east, she said, "He appears beyond Bab al-Naqa. Last year he caused numerous wrecks in which many people perished."

"He doesn't scare me," the driver said. "Even if he appears in front of me, I'll run over him and continue on my way." He laughed hysterically and handed her a hundred rials. Then he sped off, leaving her far behind.

All the passengers were terrified, and their limbs experienced chills. They wished privately that they could leave our van and return to their point of departure. I heard one man start reciting from the Qur'an. Another was muttering a prayer. I was the only passenger who was not afraid to die.

We passed through a military check point and then could see Bab al-Naqa, which was a pass between two mountains and separated the littoral plain from the mountains. To me, the pass looked like a woman lying on her back, her thighs open as if to push jinnis from her womb into life and light. I was overcome by the feeling that I was making the reverse passage: a return to my mother's womb. When I looked back, I could see the plain resplendent in sunshine and dazzling light. When I turned my head to look forward, I saw total darkness and sleet falling in torrents.

Once we transited the "Camel's Gate" pass, the day's light dimmed till it was resembled the flickering light of a candle burning low. An unusual whistling reverberated in our ears. Then drops of rain started to spot the van's windshield. The cold stung us, and we closed the windows. Those passengers whose teeth were chattering donned their jackets. The rain became more intense, and the driver was obliged to slow down. Then a pitch-black darkness enveloped us, as if night had fallen. The thunder of the torrents pouring from the mountains' veins became a black roar and inspired in the soul a fear of the forces of nature. The number of hairpin turns increased as the asphalt pavement twisted like a serpent. Lightning illuminated a human form standing in the roadway. One of us passengers shouted with alarm: "That's the Ghostly Old Man!" The driver turned on the vehicle's high beam. Then we could see this *shayba*'s facial features and thick red beard. He stared at us with glittering, deep-set eyes. The driver unconsciously slammed his foot down on the brake pedal. In a split second, the *shayba* crossed from our lane to the downhill one, and the driver removed his foot from the brake pedal, with a sigh of relief. From around the bend, though, came a heavily laden lorry at such high speed that it seemed to be flying from the mountain peak.

The lorry's driver swerved into our lane to avoid flattening the old man. By the time he noticed us directly in front of him, he did not have time to do anything. We collided with a mighty crash and found ourselves swimming through the air like birds.

Chapter 0

I found myself in a dimly lit, closed room with hundreds of lizards, snakes, and chameleons on its floor, walls, and ceiling. They surrounded me, threatening to harm me. Then a bugle blew, and those reptiles dried up and died. I crawled through the door's keyhole and escaped from the cramped space in which I found myself.

I crawled forward on my belly until a man came and lifted me to my feet. I tried to look at him but could not find where my head had gone. I asked him, "Where have I been?"

He replied, "This house is between your eyes.... Did you see what you're like inside!"

I said: "Scary... really frightening.... Is this me?"

He answered, "If you had not come out to meet me, people would certainly have been harmed by you."

***

I walked to Fathiya's dwelling. She had rented out her old home and leased a large four-room apartment located two streets away from the seashore.

I met her family—her mother, brothers, and sisters. They were all very affectionate to me and treated me as if I were special. Their eyes revealed that they knew how dear I was to their big sister, who was like a father to them.

Fathiya arrived to share breakfast with me. Smiling, she said, "Don't worry. Today we've stopped eating broad beans and have begun eating green beans, for your sake." She handed me a piece of paper with my wife's new telephone number but counseled me not to contact her. I asked her why not, and she said that my wife, Houriya, had remarried. She added that my children were living in their grandmother's house. I asked Fathiya if she knew who Houriya had married. She hesitated, but I insisted. Then, sighing, she said, "Ghalib Zubayta." I laughed and commented that he had married her to take vengeance on me. I had taken his newspaper away from him; so, he took my wife from me. Fathiya laughed and her expression relaxed. She was truly looking out for me and was worried about the effect this news might have on my feelings. She did not realize that hearing this news did not make me feel the least bit sad.

Holding a copy of the newspaper *al-Sha'b*, I asked, "What's become of Riyyad al-Kayyad?"

She said, "That gentleman has become a government minister."

I commented, "He was already virtually at that level."

She rose and closed the door. Then she sat back down and started to handfeed me, because she had noticed I had no appetite. "That gentleman's place was taken as chief editor by Qasim al-Tahhan. Do you remember him?"

I replied, "Yes, he was the editor of a yellow newspaper named *al-Masabih*."

As she continued to fill my mouth with food, she remarked, "You haven't asked me about our newspaper, *al-Nidal*."

I said, "I'm not interested in it anymore."

She continued nonetheless, "Big picture: your friend, Governor Jabir Shanini contrived a micro-conspiracy to oust that fool Shareef as editor-in-chief and appointed one of his own relatives to replace him."

I exhaled forcefully. "Yemen used to be called 'Arabia Felix'—Happy or Fertile Arabia. Now it deserved to be called the "Land of Sweetheart Deals."

I gestured with my hand to indicate that I had eaten enough. She remarked, "You were also the victim of a sweetheart deal."

Frowning, I asked, "How so?"

She picked up a paper napkin to wipe my mouth. "Do you remember the case against Shaykh Bakri Hasan?"

I replied, "Yes."

Her skirt had edged up above her knees, and she pulled it down to cover her legs. "The tale is long and involved. I'll give you a parable. Suppose there is a spot of green mold on this wall; what would we do?"

I answered, "We'd clean it off."

Squeezing her hands together, she said, "That's the right thing to do. But what has happened is, instead, that a picture of a famous boxer has been placed over the moldy spot. Even though the spot's edges are still visible, the eye does not notice it and, instead, focuses on the brightly colored picture of the famous young man. A small visual subterfuge suffices to hide mold that represents a danger to the residents of the house."

"You mean I'm the sucker whose image they've used to hide the shaykh's crime?"

She said, "Yes. They used you for this purpose. Once that interview with Khatima was published, the case against you dominated public discourse, while that against the shaykh vanished into the background and was totally forgotten. The newspaper *al-Sanabil al-Hamra'* published more scandalous reports about you and asserted that the authorities reported your death in a traffic accident to provide you cover and rescue you from the wrath of the public! Indeed, their conspiratorial imagination inspired in them the notion, which they printed, that you are now living under an assumed name in Cologne, Germany."

I laughed and commented sarcastically, "Those dogs know I love the beer brewed in that city!"

She said breathlessly, "They know everything about you. . . . Do you understand?"

I asked, "Like what?"

Lowering her gaze, she replied, "They learned about your relationships with Mona and Tatiana."

That did not upset me. I felt like some third party who wasn't involved in those scandals. "Do you still have those editions of the newspaper?"

She replied so emotionally that she had difficulty speaking coherently. "Yes, but I will not let you see them. You must leave that past behind you."

I smiled and told her, "You won't believe me when I tell you that I bear no grudge against anyone—not even Khatima or Ghalib Zubayta."

Fathiya's anxious expression left her face, and her eyes stopped bulging out.

I asked, "By the way . . . was Khatima really pregnant or was that another deception?"

Fathiya crossed her arms and licked her upper lip. "Khatima gave birth to a boy whom she named Qabel."

I won't pretend I wasn't upset by the name she had given a baby that sprang from my loins; it was the name of the Shaykh's family. I asked, "Where is she now?"

"The attorney (and poet) Hammoud Shanta married her. The boy lives with them."

I commented, "I had a feeling that he loved her. He loved her silently and did not dare tell me. Yes, he did, but I didn't notice. I remember I published a love poem by him. Now I get it! **She** was the beloved he was addressing!"

Looking cautiously at my face, she said, "I visited them two months ago to check on Qabel. The boy is the spitting image of you; he even has your eyebrows."

I thanked her for her concern for my son but realized that no word of thanks could express what she deserved. Resting her head on her hand, she admonished me, "I don't know what you intend to do in the future, but I warn you against Ghalib Zubayta."

I shrugged my shoulders nonchalantly and replied, "Even if he were lethal poison, I would not pay any attention to him or fear him; the fear inside me has died."

Leaning her torso and head toward me, she whispered, "What I am going to tell you now is top secret. I share it with you even though this endangers my life."

I said, "I promise on my honor—even though they haven't left me any—that I won't tell."

Wiping away her copious sweat and gasping for breath, she whispered, "Ghalib Zubayta is a government agent implanted in the Leftist Opposition."

Incredulously noting that I wasn't sweating, even though it was really hot, I commented, "That explains his role in the conspiracy they hatched against me."

Lowering her voice even more, she said, "Today he is a major Opposition leader. Rest assured that if this secret slips from your lips, they will kill you."

She was trembling, and I took her hand and kissed the knuckle of each of her ten fingers. "No one will ever learn this from me. Rest assured of that."

When I requested news from her of the human rights activist Salam Mahdi, Fathiya said she was still combatting child marriages and that her organization had expanded and now had branches in each of the governorates. I asked Fathiya about the charges brought against Salam of publishing fake news, and she replied that she had received a suspended sentence of three months in prison and the payment of a million rials in compensation. Fathiya said Salam was a very stubborn person who had never abandoned the case of young Muhsina; the latest development in the case was the discovery of the corpse of the real girl and revelation about the substitute girl.

My comment was: "No matter how the master criminals perfect their deception, the truth will emerge at the appointed time."

"Would you like to hear the latest news about the girl Jalila?"

With an apprehensive look in my eyes, I said, "Yes."

She said, "Jalila is currently in a nearby hospital, in critical condition."

Upset by this news, "I asked, "My God! What happened to her?"

Heading to the door, she replied, "Wait . . . I have something to show you."

She returned with a copy of the newspaper *al-Sha'b*. She said, "Shortly after your traffic accident, the court in al-Jurum delivered a verdict that was not subject to appeal. It aroused no commotion, and no one paid any attention to it, because everyone was obsessed by the charges against you."

I took the newspaper and began to read the text of the judgement: "With reference to the charges brought by the guardian of the juvenile Jalila Muhammad Hadi Zuhayr that the accused Shaykh Bakri Hasan Muqbil sexually assaulted the aforementioned child, it was established by the court, based on the medical report found credible by the public prosecutor, that the minor Jalila Muhammad Hadi Zuhayr was the one who sexually assaulted Shaykh Bakri Hasan Qabil. The medical report attested to by four physicians mentioned that the penis of Shaykh Bakri Hasan Muqbil had scars and abrasions resulting from bleeding that were evidence of the violence of her sexual assault. Therefore, the court in al-Jurum rules as follows: 1. Shaykh Bakri Hasan Muqbil is found innocent of the charges against him. 2. the minor Jalila Muhammad Hadi Zuhayr is convicted of the charge of sexual assault. We therefore order her imprisoned for three years in reform school with immediate effect. This judgement cannot be annulled or appealed."

The next thing I knew I was ripping up that newspaper. Even I was surprised that I reacted this way. I felt sorry for Fathiya and admitted that I should not have done this to something that didn't belong to me. She began to tear the paper into even smaller pieces, which she tossed out the window. She said, "You did the right thing. That was nothing I needed to keep."

Still stunned by the hideous verdict, I asked her, "Was Jalila locked up?"

Placing her hand on her chin, she said, "Yes.... A week later they released her, and the Shaykh asked to marry her. She rejected him. The next day he dispatched a group of ruffians to attack her. They found her playing with her six-year-old cousin Fa'iza and her four-year-old cousin Halima in the alley in front of her house. All three girls were beaten with cudgels and sharp instruments. They were then transported to hospital in critical condition."

My Adam's apple shook as though it would fall. I said, "I would like to visit them. I won't rest till I apologize to Jalila and ask her to forgive me."

Collecting the breakfast dishes, Fathiya said, "I'll go to the bank first to request some time off, and then I'll return, and we can do whatever you wish."

I washed from the neck down and shaved my groin. I found that Fathiya had provided me with underwear, trousers, and a shirt—all of them new.

Her mother offered me a cold drink. She was a lady whose expression revealed her goodness and dignity.

Fathiya called me on her mother's phone and asked if I still smoked. I replied that I didn't know. The topic had not occurred to me! She told me she had left a pack and a lighter on the TV. I found that she had even remembered my favorite brand of cigarettes. I turned the pack over in my hand and sniffed it. Then I realized that I *had* given up smoking.

There was a strong coffee smell wafting through the whole house; Fathiya's mother roasted coffee beans and ground them.

Fathiya returned with a garland of jasmine blossoms and put it around my neck. Then we set off for the hospital. On the way there, she showed me a picture of my son Qabel on her mobile phone. He looked just like my son Habel. Fathiya laughed and commented: "If your genes were for sale in supermarkets, women would rush to buy them!"

Still gazing at my son's picture, I asked, "How does Hammoud treat him?"

She replied, "Your friend Hammoud loves him very much and showers him with everything. Apparently, Hammoud is sterile. He did not father any children with his first wife nor now with Khatima, his second wife. If you want, we can go to al-Jurum to see your son. You have every right to that."

That thought made me uncomfortable. "No . . . no," I said and handed her cellphone back to her.

"I need to tell you that Hammoud married Khatima when she was in her eighth month and that when her son was born, Hammoud was entered on the birth certificate as the father."

I sighed and commented, "He did the right thing. Hammoud deserves him more than I do."

We reached the hospital and entered the ward where the three girls lay encompassed by lethal silence, sorrow, and tears. We saw Jalila, who had turned eleven, lying dead on a bed, and I was overwhelmed by an enormous grief, because I had not been afforded an opportunity to ask her forgiveness. My pain was indescribable, but my eyes could not shed any tears. I took the jasmine garland from my chest, lifted her head, and placed around her neck.

Her angelic face shone with a look of purity and sacrifice. I sensed that she was one of God's *wali*s, one of his saintly friends, and that she had sacrificed her spirit to atone for the sins of us all. During the few years of her life, she had endured what no human being could. She had been raped, convicted, and imprisoned. Once she was freed from prison, she had been beaten to death.

The physician entered and asked if we were members of her family. He said her grandfather had gone to his village to borrow money to pay for a shroud, for the corpse washer, and for the other funeral expenses.

We visited the other two girls: Fa'iza and Halima, whom the doctor said were feeling better and recuperating. This physician suddenly pulled out a clear, plastic bottle and suggested we donate money to the poor. There were some bills of different denominations inside the bottle.

I asked him angrily, "Why didn't you give Jalila's grandfather money from your flask?" He stammered and then responded that if he opened the container he would be forced to appear before the benevolent committee that received the flasks, and stripped of this role, etc. I don't know why, but his face reminded me of the Shaykh's companions who had attacked Jalila and pummeled her repeatedly and then stabbed her with their daggers. So, I grabbed the bottle from the doctor and tossed it out the window onto the street below. The doctor cursed me in the local dialect, saying he would f... my mother. Then he ran to the window, where he saw that speeding automobiles had run over his collection jar and that bills were flying into the air. This sight naturally broke his heart, and we were tossed out of the hospital.

On our way to Fathiya's house, Fathiya stopped at a newsstand and purchased a newspaper. She said, "I know you're heavily addicted to reading newspapers." I took the paper from her and placed it on the car's dashboard ledge without looking at it.

I said, "I'm no longer interested in newspapers."

"Wow!" she said. "You've changed totally, Mutahhar. Should I understand from your words that you will quit working as a journalist?"

I replied without any hesitation: "Yes."

She asked, "Have you thought of another profession?"

I pursed my lips thoughtfully and then said, "I don't know what I'll do. I sense I'm a new man who hasn't yet discovered his predilections in life." I asked Fathiya shyly, "Do you have any news of Mona?"

She said, "No . . . no one knows anything about her. . . . Even your friend Hammoud Shanta told me once that her fate is clouded with obscurity."

I commented, "The Shaykh may have sold her to an Arab millionaire who took her back to his country."

She asked me, "Did you know she was a slave?"

I sighed and admitted, "Yes."

"Is it true that you were in love with her?"

I bowed my head, remembering my days with her, and said, "Yes, I was in love with her, and 'love' doesn't come anywhere near to describing what I felt. She was a tormented spirit, and I was a desperate one. Our two spirits united to share the pain. We were drawn to each other the way heavenly bodies attract each other."

Fathiya screamed as she twisted in her seat: "I beg you: don't make me jealous!"

I turned on the car radio and heard the voice of Minister Riyad al-Kayyad, speaking on some program. Suddenly I addressed him as if he stood before me: "Why did you conspire against me?"

He immediately answered: "My son, we conspired against you to make you happy! Ha-ha, ha-ha, ha-ha, ha-ha, ha-ha, ha-ha." He continued laughing till his giggles deafened me and I turned off the radio.

I asked Fathiya if we could go to the sea and swim. She had no objection and phoned her mother not to expect us for supper. We had a wonderful time and enjoyed swimming in the warm water, which caresses the body like silk and provides a healing balm for the spirit.

A black and white Sacred Ibis approached us. I got goose bumps when I realized that it was my father. I longed for him so much that I chatted with him about the essays written dedicated to him in the book: *A Man Whom Struggle Created*. He listened to me calmly. When I had my say, he pecked me between the eyes and flew away.

I wailed and shared my torment with Fathiya: "My son Qabel will kill his brother Habel, and my sins will be inherited by the next four generations of my descendants."[4]

Fathiya sadly watched the sunset and then dove into the water. For my part, I floated like a cloud resting in the palm of a hand, and the winds lifted me high into the air.

***

The Peugeot van stopped rolling over and over and came to rest on its back at the bottom of the wadi. The water flooding the wadi rocked us affectionately, like amniotic fluid in a mother's womb, intoning a gentle lullaby to lull us into a calm sleep.

---

4. Abdullah Yusuf Ali, *The Holy Qur-an: Text, Translation and Commentary* (McGregor & Werner, 1946) Sura 5 (al-Ma'ida, The Table) verses 30-34, note 731, page 250: "The two sons of Adam were Habil . . . and Qabil. . . ." Cain and Abel are mentioned but not named in the Qur'an.

Afterword

I last saw Mutahhar Fadl in al-Jurum's police station, where I assumed he had come to interview an officer I also wished to question—especially after I saw them enter the station together. Because I had helped unmask him, I was surprised when Mutahhar lurched away from that officer to greet me. As he stretched his hand out toward mine, I opened my fist, which I had unconsciously clenched, expecting him to apologize and shake hands. Instead, he dropped onto my palm a thumb-drive—on which I later found the manuscript of this memoir. I realized he had been arrested when the officer jerked him back by the cuff on Mutahhar's other hand. I immediately left the police station, before anyone wondered what had just transpired or tried to search me.

I was not surprised to learn the next day that Mutahhar had died. That his death occurred near Bab al-Naqa—in the manner predicted in his memoir—did give me pause. Unless Mutahhar was clairvoyant, whoever was responsible for his death must have staged it to mimic his memoir after reading it on his laptop, which the police no doubt salvaged from the wrecked van.

I have agonized over my decision to release this memoir to a publisher in Beirut for many reasons. One was its portrayal of me as complicit in the very child-trafficking I fight against! In the end, though, I decided that this apology for one man's life deserves to be made public. I wanted to call this book: "Complicit!" or "Confessions of a Cad," but finally decided to retain the title chosen by its late author, Mutahhar Fadl, *honi soit qui mal y pense*.

Salam Mahdi
Human Rights Activist
Hodeida, Yemen

Translator's Note

This novel skewers Yemen's ruling elite and its journalists in a relatively calm period between the country's civil wars and before Covid-19. Since it was written, conditions in Yemen have deteriorated disastrously with another civil war, invasions by foreign countries, and the pandemic. Most characters in this novel are depicted as complicit, including in the sex-trafficking of minors, and no character is mocked more dramatically than the narrator Mutahhar, who may appear to be sexist, racist, and self-centered but who is, all the same, a sympathetic character. *The Economist*, in an article entitled "The Arab Spring at Ten: No Cause for Celebration," stated bluntly: "Corruption makes everyone complicit." In the same article, on a scale from one to ten (ten being the most democratic) Yemen was awarded a score of 1.95.[5]

Mutahhar is arguably a tragic hero. Aristotle in the *Poetics* wrote: "Tragedy is a representation of a serious, complete action by people acting . . . [and] accomplishing by means of pity and terror the catharsis of such emotions." Check. This novel describes a person's self-incrimination and terrifying death. Further: "Tragedy has six parts. These are plot, characters, diction, reasoning, spectacle, and song." Check, except no songs. "Character" is exhibited through the reader's grasp of the hero's motives. Since Mutahhar is the narrator, we eavesdrop on his heartaches and hear his justifications for his actions, many of which seem ill-advised. Aristotle also decreed: "Reversal

---

5. "The Economist," p. 78, December 19, 2020, "The Arab Spring at Ten: No Cause for Celebration."

and recognition are two parts of plot." Check. "A third is suffering: a destructive or painful action." Check. Finally, for Aristotle: "A recognition is a change from ignorance to knowledge, and so to either friendship or enmity, among people defined in relation to good fortune or misfortune."[6] Check. By the conclusion of this novel, Mutahhar, whose name means "Purified," has experienced, in addition to suffering, an Aristotelian recognition and change of fortune.

Toward the end of the novel, a reader learns of Mutahhar's fraught relationship with his late father, who was a prominent leftwing journalist. It is not a total accident that the executive editor of the pro-government newspaper for which Mutahhar works, refers to him, on good days, as "my son," emphasizing the Oedipal motif. This editor is not only Mutahhar's boss but his supreme handler.

Mutahhar Fadl, who is as fond of qat as the next Yemeni and a gourmand if not a gourmet, explains his "pragmatism" this way: "Society has matured, and notions of heroism evolve from one age to the next. I count as a hero in this age." Arguably, his honorable wish to save beautiful, young Mona from the plight of sex-trafficking is partly responsible for his own fall from grace. Because he is a "pleaser," Mutahhar agrees to play the antihero, without suspecting that he has also thereby become a patsy, fall guy, fool, and scapegoat. How could he realize that he is any of those when he considers himself a sophisticated urbanite surrounded by provincial buffoons on Yemen's Red Sea Coast?

---

6. Aristotle, *Poetics I*, vi-vii, x-xii, 3.1, 3.1.1, 3.4.3, & 3.4.2. Adapted from Aristotle, *Poetics I*, trans. By Richard Janko (Indianapolis & Cambridge: Hackett Publishing Company, 1987) pp. 7-8, 14-15.

Wajdi Al-Ahdal

Author

Wajdi Muhammad Abduh al-Ahdal is a Yemeni novelist, the author of short stories, a screenwriter, and a dramatist. Born in 1973, he received a degree in literature from Sana'a University. He won the Afif prize for the short story in 1997, a gold medal for a dramatic text in the Festival for Arab Youth in Alexandria, Egypt, in 1998, and the youth prize of the President of the Republic of Yemen for the short story in 1999.

His short story collections include: *Zahrat al-Abir* ("The Passerby's Flower," Sana'a, 1997), *Surat al-Battal* ("Portrait of an Unemployed Man," Amman, 1998), *Ratanat al-Zaman al-Miqmaq* ("Gibberish in a Time of Ventriloquism," Sana'a, 1998), *Harb lam Ya'alam bi-Wuqu'iha Ahad* ("A War No One Knew About," Sana'a, 2001), and *Wadi al-Dajuj*. His novels are: *Qawarib Jabaliya* ("Mountain Boats," Beirut, 2002), *Himar Bayna al-Aghani* ("A Donkey in the Choir," Beirut 2004), *Faylasuf al-Kurantina* ("Quarantine Philosopher," Sana'a, 2007), and *Bilad bila Sama'* ("A Land Without Sama'[or a Sky]," Sana'a, 2008), which was published in English as *A Land Without Jasmine* and was co-winner of the 2013 Saif Ghobash Banipal Prize for Translated Arabic literature. A bilingual dramatization of the work was produced in London at the Battersea Arts Centre, April 4-6, 2019. See: https://thearabweekly.com/land-without-jasmine-puts-stage-plight-yemeni-women. His screenplay *al-Ughniya al-Mashhura* ("The Enchanted Song" was published in Sana'a in 2006, and his play *al-Suqut min Shurfat al-'Alam* ("Falling off the Balcony of the World") was published there in 2007. Al-Ahdal traveled to the United States for a residency at the Vitosha Cultural Center in Ann Arbor, Michigan in the summer of 2012.

William M. Hutchins

Translator

William Maynard Hutchins has translated numerous works of Arabic literature into English including Return of the Spirit by Tawfiq al-Hakim, *The Cairo Trilogy* by Nobel Laureate Naguib Mahfouz, and *The Fetishists* by Ibrahim al-Koni. His translation of *New Waw* by al-Koni, won the ALTA National Prose Translation Award for 2015. He received National Endowment for the Arts grants for literary translation in 2006, 2012, and 2020. He was co-winner of the Saif Ghobash/Banipal Prize for Translation from the Arabic for *A Land without Jasmine* by Wajdi al-Ahdal, 2014, London, UK. His translation of *Ibn Arabi's Small Death* by Mohammed Hasan Alwan took second place in the 2023 Sheikh Hamad Awards for Translation from Arabic to English. (First place was withheld.) Hutchins earned degrees at Yale University and the University of Chicago and has taught at the Gerard School, Sidon, Lebanon, the University of Ghana, the American University in Cairo, and Appalachian State University (Boone, North Carolina), where he is currently a professor emeritus.